SHADOWS OF THE PUPPET

was printed in an edition limited to 500 copies,

of which this is copy number: ___335___

Santa Barbara Review Publications
Santa Barbara, California 93108-2508

ISBN 0-9655497-0-4

Printed in the United States of America.

If you wish to know more about Santa Barbara Review Publications
write to:
James T. Aeby
Santa Barbara Review Publications
P.O. Box 808
Summerland, California 93067
e-mail: jtaeby@west.net

For
my parents
my sisters
and all our children

For Jill
though there may
be shadows — there
is always light.
Om + Peace.

Medha

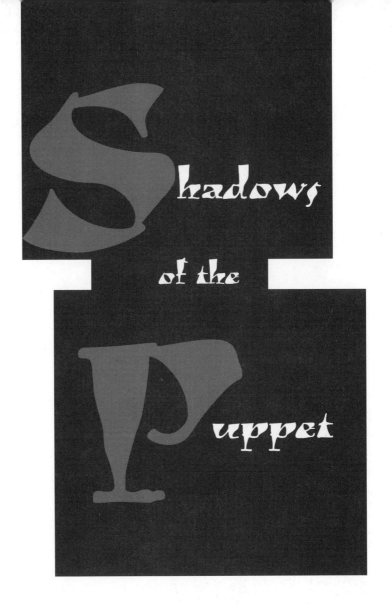

Shadows of the Puppet

by **M**ediha **F. S**aliba

SANTA **B**ARBARA **R**EVIEW **P**UBLICATIONS
California

Acknowledment

No book gets into print without the guidance of loyal friends and teachers. Shelly Lowenkopf at the Santa Barbara Writer's Conference gave me the hope that I had written an honest story. Leonard Tourney, the mystery writer, taught me to look for life's inner spirit. Patricia Stockton Leddy, publisher and editor of the *Santa Barbara Review*, gave me strength and inspiration to continue through many rewrites. Without the love and support of my husband Gil, I would never have completed this fictional memoir.

To those who come after
so that they may better understand
those who came before.

Some names of people have been changed,
but the dates and names of places are true to history.

Prologue

Gray water buffalo plow muddy fields
Green rice paddies turn gold and plump
Native women, their long black hair tied up with cloth
    their sarongs hitched up to their knees
    and some with their brown breasts
    drinking in the wet sun
work the fields beside men—
                  planting
                      bending
                         reaping

Vast fields of rice stalks dance in the breeze
    sing to the coconut palms bordering their paddies
    pay homage to the mighty volcanoes in the distance.
Who made the fertile soil that gave the Dutch
East Indies their richness?
        gave Java its beauty?
            gave the people their mystic charm?

1881 Batavia

In the *kampungs,* away from the colonial homes of the Dutch elite, the natives lived their quiet life. Outside bamboo huts women, nursing naked infants, cooked in earthen pots; the fragrances of cloves, turmeric, ginger, and hot peppers wafting through the narrow streets. Theirs was a life content with what they had, accepting what was to be. They believed *Semar,* a spirit guide, watched over their Java, and they would not question his actions.

These were the sights, and smells, and people that Pierre-Jacques van Gils, a Belgian adventurer—signed on with the Dutch Colonial Army—fell in love with. He often walked through a *kampung*, his tall lean body a giant compared to the natives, and his platinum blond hair and blue eyes a contrast to their brown skin and black curious eyes. He nodded his head to those who smiled at him, and on occasion tasted food offered by some shy girl or a daring man.

On such an excursion Pierre-Jacques encountered Saitem, a young Javanese girl. She was not so different from others of her kind. She had the same smooth brown skin, black eyes, raven-colored hair that floated down her back like water. She had the same petite yet sturdy frame, but something charmed him instantly. A mysteriousness clung to her; and her kindness, coupled with her gentle understanding of his European ways, enticed him.

Uncertain at first, Pierre-Jacques began to seek her out regularly. She was always there to quench his thirst, offer a bowl of rice covered with mildly spiced *nanka*, corn, and river-farmed greens. "You are not my kind, yet I feel you know me," he told her one evening when the full moon cast shadows through the coconut trees. "As a shadow knows its master," she answered, "different but the same and forever connected."

Soon, a friendship born of loneliness and fascination bloomed into a love affair.

As his concubine, Saitem bore Pierre-Jacques nine children, four boys and five girls. Although this was unsanctioned by the Catholic Church, he freely gave the children his name, a gift that entitled them to the privileges of the colonial Europeans. A gift, that made his children eligible to attend Dutch schools. They would receive an education denied Indonesian natives, except those of high rank.

Not until Maria, their oldest daughter, elected to become a nun in the Franciscan order in Mendut, East Java, did Pierre-Jacques and Saitem exchange formal marriage vows. The

Catholic Church decreed and Pierre-Jacques obeyed, as did Saitem.

To Saitem it was just a matter of formality. A custom of the *Belanda-toto*, the white gods who ruled their island. She accepted her new rosary beads and put them in her room along with her Islamic *Tasbih* beads and her bowl of incense for the spirits. She accepted her daughter's decision to enter the Church. Later, she accepted Pierre-Jacques' decision that the boys be sent to the motherland to receive their colonial appointments. Pierre-Jacques knew best as to how their children would survive in the world of the *Belanda-toto*, but she would leave her native imprint on their souls, and her children, and her children's children would feel the spirits of her world and understand the shadows: the shadows that were there hidden in the myths of the *Wayang*, the shadow puppets, and would be felt under the shadows of World War II when the Japanese would overrun the Dutch East Indies and change life forever.

Henriette at age nine
with her grandmother Saitem, holding younger cousin.

ONE

WAYANG

May 1940

Not looking up at us, Father sat back in his chair, the dark cane of the rattan creaking from his weight. A cut glass wall-lamp cast a shadow over his bent head so that he reminded me of a *wayang*—shadow puppet. Without moving into the light he stretched his long muscular arm to the table, idly pushing the silver spoon and fork back and forth on his delft blue dinner plate. His military reserve status required he report to Bandoeng, he announced.

"But you're retired," Mother said, folding her napkin and laying it on the table. She ironed the fine crocheted edges with her hands, watching her own slow deliberate motions. "You're forty-eight." She looked up, searching my father's face. She picked up the napkin and dabbed at the corners of her mouth, then folded it back into her lap.

Angelica, my younger sister, and I exchanged nervous looks.

"Why do you have to go?" I asked. "What can the East Indies do against Hitler? And the Netherlands has already fallen."

Father looked up, his large jaw tight, accentuating the squareness of his face. "It's not Hitler. It's the Japanese. They've taken Chinese Manchuria, and are threatening French Indo-China." He sat forward, leaning his arms on the table. "The sad thing is that the Dutch could have found themselves in a better situation if they had given the *Inlanders* the opportunity to participate in the government and share in the defense of the country. Remember? I said we should arm them."

"For goodness sake!" Mother blurted. "Those natives might go crazy if they were allowed to carry sophisticated weapons."

"Not if they're fighting for their own country," Father answered. "The Dutch were just afraid of losing control."

"Well, the government does need to be careful," Mother said. "And the government didn't know then that the Japanese would be such a problem."

Angelica's eyes grew large and her gaze quickly darted from Father's face to Mother's, no doubt seeking comfort, but not finding any.

"Don't frighten the children," Mother said, giving my father that look meaning they'd talk later.

"They're not children." He looked at both of us.

I openly met his gaze, proud that he didn't think of me as a child, but afraid of what he had to say. I was just short of seventeen and Angelica had recently turned fourteen. We weren't children, but I wasn't in a hurry to become an adult.

Father looked back to Mother. "If Indo-China falls, only Malaya and Singapore will lie between us and the Japanese."

My thoughts wandered and my father's voice faded. I felt for my bracelet, stroking its finely-carved gold surface with my thumb. Bandoeng. Why couldn't we all go back? Why couldn't we have the life we had before? We'd moved here to Oengaran nearly a year ago, as a retirement haven for my father, but still I thought of Bandoeng as home. It was the city where the stories of the *Ramayana* and *Mahabharata* were made real to me. A place where my grandfather, Pierre-Jacques, spoke of mysterious choices, and my grandmother, Saitem, filled me with the legends of her people—native people, whose spirits I imagined moving through the shadows. . . .

"*Oma?*" I called, running through the large house on Bandoeng's main square. "*Oma* Saitem, are you here?" They had bought the house in the early 1900s, after my grandfather retired from the Dutch army. By the time I was old enough to remember, tiny shops selling dry goods, meat, and vegetables had sprung up around them. The city was growing—but their house stood in a stretch of property shaded by red flamboyant trees, coconut palms, a small grove of banana trees, and various fruit trees—papaya, *rambutan*, even *durian*, in season, all nestled and safe from harm. It was my favorite stopping place on my way home from school.

"*Oma*, where are you?" I called in my grandmother's native Javanese. The smell of incense permeated the heavy carved mahogany furniture; leather *wayangs* stared at me from the wall, their red eyes watching every move I made.

Sometimes the house was quiet, except for the steady whir of the over-head fan. Soft puffs of warm air blew, as I stood watching the shadows twirling on the wall. I glanced around. *Oma* often talked of spirits. "They are here, you know. Watching over us," she'd tell me. And I'd look, never seeing them, but sometimes I thought I felt them. Like that day when I rushed out the back door glancing over my shoulder. Nothing followed; no shadows, no puffs of air, no sounds, only an essence that clung to my skin.

"*Oma* Saitem," I called. A parrot flew across the courtyard, raucous and screeching. I jumped, startled, and momentarily frightened.

"She's in the kitchen," came a booming voice from off to my side. In a rocking chair, shaded from the afternoon sun by banana trees, my grandfather sat, dressed formally, as usual, in white dress slacks and a long-sleeved white cotton shirt. He smoked a cigar and sipped a glass of golden liquid—whiskey.

I breathed a little easier, stepped to the rain-water barrel to wash the perspiration from my face and snipped a piece of jasmine to put in my hair, before greeting my grandfather.

Most of my cousins were afraid of *Opa* Pierre-Jacques because he always looked so serious, never joked, and insisted on impeccable manners; but *Oma* Saitem had told me the stories, stories of when they were young and when he first came to the Dutch East Indies. An army officer, he fought the fierce natives in Ajai, Borneo, and Sumatra. He crossed Java from Surabaya to Bandoeng in an ox cart, with only native guards carrying fire torches to keep away the tigers. His gray hair, platinum blond then, and his sharp, clear, blue eyes made him stand out above all others—a variable god to Saitem.

"The Dutch aren't really worried about the Japanese, are they?" Mother's husky voice intruded into my thoughts.

I blinked to refocus my surroundings. Mother had stopped playing with her napkin and sat slightly back from the table, one leg crossed over the other and her arms folded over her ample chest. Her face, round and full from the sweets she loved, was raised in that superior pose she so often took when making a point.

"I heard the Japanese have just been lucky. Up until now they've only had to fight Orientals. Fighting Europeans is a different story. With us, they haven't got a chance."

"That's foolish thinking." My father pushed his chair back roughly, and stood up. "Our islands will have trouble." He paced back and forth beside the table, his hands thrust deep in his pockets.

"Does this mean you have to fight?" I whispered, not able to keep the quiver out of my voice.

He stopped in front of me, the amber color of his eyes almost completely hidden by his dilated pupils. "No, they'll need me to oversee some things at the railway. I know the place and can relieve the young men who are needed for the military."

"Is there going to be fighting here?" Angelica asked. Her eyes were wide. Her hands made tight fists in her lap.

Father hesitated.

Oengaran was a small mountain town. It didn't seem a likely place for enemy interests. There were some ruins of an old Portuguese fort, lovely hillsides of tangerine and tobacco plantations, a small central square surrounded by a few shops, a church, and a lower school. I had to take the bus to Semarang— a half-hour ride— to attend the high school on Oei Tjong Bing Street. There was nothing an enemy would want here.

"I don't know," Father answered. "We don't know what is going to happen. It's in the hands of God."

My father's voice remained calm, but I could see the shadows of concern spread across his face, just as the shadows had dulled the eyes of *Opa* Pierre-Jacques that day. "Choices," he had told me that afternoon. I would have to make choices.

"Good afternoon, Henriette," *Opa* said formally. "And does your mother know you are here again?"

I looked directly into my *Opa's* eyes. Age had not made them less blue. "No." I didn't tell him that Mother only objected because of *Oma* Saitem's influence. Mother loved my paternal grandfather. I could still see her stabbing the air with her index finger, shouting, "It's Pierre-Jacques' blood that gives your father the position he holds at the railway company. It's Pierre-Jacques' blood that offers your Uncle Kees his job and your Aunt Teresa the position of Mother Superior. Pierre-Jacques, Pierre-Jacques, Dutch, Dutch, white, white."

She never considered our native side, her own native side—a mixture of Bornean and East European. In fact, most Indo-Europeans made a point of hiding their roots. Not many were like my father, proud of who he was—native and Dutch.

"You must not make your mother angry," *Opa* said.

"But she doesn't understand!"

"She understands more then you know." A rattle in the banana leaves made him turn.

I looked too.

The parrot that had frightened me earlier sat on a ripening stalk of bananas, watched us, then flew away, his blue and red wings brightening in the sun.

"I'm a big girl now, *Opa*. I should be allowed to do some things for myself."

Opa looked back at me. "You are young and much like me when I was a youth."

I liked that. It made me feel strong and daring. I straightened my shoulders and lifted my chin. "What's wrong with that?"

He didn't smile. "Life is always changing, Henriette." He swirled the golden liquid in his glass. "You cannot imagine the choices you will have to make." He took a big sip, then leaned his head back, staring at the clouds drifting over head. "Yes, a lot of difficult choices."

"What do you mean, *Opa* ?"

Slowly he refocused on me.

"What choices?" I repeated.

He didn't answer right away. "Nothing." He waved his free hand, as if clearing cobwebs from his mind. "Nothing. I'm just an old man talking."

But a deep furrow wrinkled his forehead, and a shadow dimmed the blue of his eyes. I shivered and the sudden fear of something I could not put into words made me always remember that moment.

How did my grandfather know what was to come? Did *Oma* Saitem's spirits talk to him too?

"When do you have to leave?" Mother asked, her lips pulled tight, as they always were when she wanted to pretend control.

"I want to go with you," I said, wondering what I had missed in my lapse. "Why can't we all go with you?"

Father shook his head. "There's no need to move. I'll be at the base in Bandoeng only a few days each month. I can take the train back and forth. You won't even miss me."

I stood up and hugged his waist. "I'll miss you, Papa."

He patted my back and kissed the top of my head.

A week later we stood at the train station waving good-bye to my father. Kromo, our driver, stood behind us poised with an umbrella, to protect us from the soon-to-fall rain. The station was no more crowded than usual. I looked around wondering if other families were saying good-bye to their fathers. I could-n't detect anyone.

When the train had chugged away, Kromo drove us back up the mountain, where, as my father had predicted, life went on as usual. And as he had promised he was back in just a few days.

The next month went equally well, as did the following months, but with each trip he returned with more bad news of Allied setbacks in the war against Germany and the growing strength of the Japanese.

"The world is realizing that the Japanese are no joke," Father reported, as we sat together on the veranda watching the sky turn papaya-pink before plunging us into darkness.

"But why doesn't somebody do something?" Angelica asked, swatting angrily at a moth attracted to the porch light. "The Dutch, the British, somebody."

Mother patted her hand and stroked her cheek. "Our government will protect us. The Spice Islands are important. The government probably knows something we don't. They won't let the Japanese walk in and take over."

"You're right." Father's voice sounded bitter. "They do know something we don't. Rumor has it that the *Prince of Wales* and the *Repulse*, a brand-new British battleship and a battle cruiser, are on their way here. If they weren't afraid of something happening, those ships would not be coming."

It was true then. The *wayang* were real. Life imitated the shadow puppets. Once, when my father and I had escaped on our own to see a *wayang* show, I wanted to watch the *dalang* unpack his many puppets from their special carrying case. My father absolutely forbade it. "You can't see them," he said. "That's part of the magic. People like us, the masses, may only see the *wayang* as a shadow. Others, like the Sultan and high officials, watch from the other side. To them life is less of a shadow, less of a mystery. They see the costumes the puppet wears, allowing them to know if he is dressed for battle or peace, if he is smiling or grimacing, if he holds a hidden *kris*. The masses never know."

Clearly, this was our situation now. We would only see the shadows of what the governments were doing.

"They won't get by the French," Mother insisted. "They'll go crawling back home." She gave her head a firm nod. "Now let's not talk of it anymore. Enna," she called. "Bring the coffee and cake."

As the months dragged into a year, I hoped that the mere passing of time would restore the easy carefree life of the thirties, but eavesdropping on my parents one evening, I knew all my dreams were lost.

French Indo-China had fallen and the Japanese were continuing their march. I leaned on the wall for support, silently listening with my ear to the cool paster.

"Perhaps the presence of the Americans in the Philippines will make them keep their distance," Father's voice whispered.

"But the United States isn't in the war." There was a long pause. "What's the matter?" My mother's whisper become even softer. "I can tell something is wrong."

Tears formed in my eyes. Without hearing or seeing I knew my father would be gone longer and more often.

I tip-toed back to my room and cried. I was afraid.

Reaching under my bed, I pulled out my old *jepara*-wood box, and slid open the lid. I lifted out a small book of Javanese *pantuns*, given to me on my sixteenth birthday by my dear friend, Tjeng. That was the day we left Bandoeng for Oengaran. I had only read a few pages, then given up, the language being easier for me to speak than to read, but I loved the little book with its flowery Javanese words. I set it aside and took out the square milky-white candle I had made for my grandfather from dozens of candle stubs discarded from horse-drawn carriages. How he loved my candles. I smoothed the white, never-used wick.

I pulled out Saitem's batik. The *lereng* print, dyed a rich brown through which the natural yellowing of cotton peeked, felt cool on my skin. I wrapped it around my shoulders, rocking back and forth, recalling how I had helped her make that very batik. Tears rolled down my face. "Saitem. Saitem, can you hear me?" I closed my eyes.

"*Selamat sore,* Henriette," *Oma* Saitem greeted me in Javanese. She sat on a low table, her pots and pans surrounding her. Frequently, she busied herself sorting blooms, roots, and stems. She wore a loose-fitting batik sarong and her tailored white blouse. The blouse was a source of great pride to her. It indicated her status as wife of a *Belanda Toto*—pure Dutch. A status not many natives could claim.

"Good afternoon, *Oma*. What are you doing?" I asked, peeking into the pots, from which a combination of fragrances drifted.

"I'm preparing offerings for the spirits." She looked up at me, her wrinkle-free face framed by thick gray hair pulled in a bun at the nape of her neck. Her thick lips parted into a smile. "But I haven't forgotten something for you." There was always something good waiting for me to eat. Nene, the servant doing the wash in a sink just outside the door shuffled her aging body into the kitchen, drying her hands on an old rag she kept slung over her shoulder. With a near-toothless smile, she handed me my treat, along with a delicate silver spoon.

"I also have a *seketip* for you," Saitem said, producing the small coin from its special hiding place in her ear. "You can buy yourself popsicles for a week now. Here is a *seketip* for Angelica, too. You give it to your sister. She never has time to come see me."

At first I wanted to return the second coin, tell her that Angelica preferred to think of herself as Dutch and not wanting anything to do with her native grandmother; but then, feeling it would serve no purpose, I dropped both coins into my dress pocket.

"Can I help you with anything?" I asked, heaping the creamy coconut and brown sugar pudding onto the tiny silver spoon.

"When you're finished eating, we can work on a batik."

I spooned quicker. *Oma* told the best stories while we worked on batik.

"Slowly, slowly," Saitem laughed. She was never in a hurry.

I smiled, but the pudding was gone in no time, the rich, creamy taste lingering on my tongue. I could easily have eaten a second one, but I didn't bother to ask. My grandmother believed a treat was a treat, not a meal.

Saitem stepped off the table and slipped her flat brown feet into rubber sandals. She walked outside, automatically scanning the sky. "It will rain soon, so we will work inside today."

We crossed the flowered courtyard, entering a small room through wood-shuttered doors. The room filled with the fragrance of the potted jasmine outside, and a shaft of sunlight fell on her small Catholic altar. The statue of Mary and Jesus stood glowing amidst fresh flowers and a string of prayer beads. In the corner, neatly rolled up on the floor, lay Saitem's Islamic prayer rug. And in the center of the room stood a stand made of bamboo poles, over which draped Saitem's unfinished batik.

No sooner did we seat ourselves on the palm-leaf mats, when the afternoon rain began its gentle music, softly, almost inaudible, then crescendoing. Small birds flew for cover and chirped under the overhang as if complaining to *Oma* and me.

Over a small charcoal fire, Saitem heated wax to the proper temperature in an earthen pot. Then she filled a special spouted spoon with the hot wax, allowing me to blow on it before she painted it onto the material. With steady hands, Saitem applied the wax to spaces that would later block the dye. Her face took on a trance-like expression. "Never cut a batik," she whispered. "It is like cutting a prayer. This art comes from your ancestors and with each batik I work on, I can feel their spirits with me."

I looked around. Was the sun trying to come through the clouds, or had a spirit's shadow crossed the open door? I inched closer to Saitem.

"The batik a native girl wears when she first becomes a *woman*," Saitem continued, "is never washed or worn again. Forever after, that batik carries special powers. Later, when the girl becomes a mother, that batik will have healing powers for her children."

"But, *Oma,*" I sighed, looking at my pastel-plaid dress with the crisp white collar, the likes of which I had always worn. "I didn't wear a batik, then."

Saitem's hand stopped. She looked at me, then filled the spoon with more wax. "Then you will have a different talisman. Do not worry, child, the spirits will always help those who ask."

"But who do I ask? How will I find my talisman?"

Saitem smiled, but didn't break the rhythm of her strokes. "It will find you. Wait. The time is not right."

She had me blow on another spoonful of wax, and so the afternoon went; painting batik and telling stories, until *Opa* came in and reminded us of the time.

He shot me a knowing look and I hurried to my bicycle.

How I missed both of them. I wiped the tears from my cheek, then unfolded the batik completely and pulled it over my entire body. Like a shield, I wanted it to protect me from what lay ahead. I wanted it to have healing powers.

TWO

WAR

Father traveled back and forth to Bandoeng, his time at home becoming increasingly less. I joined my mother listening to the news on the radio and reading whatever information newspapers offered. I was afraid to know, and at the same time afraid not to know.

On the 8th of December, the radio broadcaster, in a voice steeped with doom, announced the Japanese had bombed Pearl Harbor the previous day.

Mother and I knew that if the American naval base had sustained devastating losses, the Japanese would be free to move southward.

I looked away from the radio, a numbness coming over me. Tiny dust particles dancing on a shaft of light streaming through the window caught my eye and I allowed myself to be mesmerized by them. When I turned to my mother, she had tears in her eyes, and I knew she was thinking the same as I.

"What about Papa?"

Mother didn't answer. She grew steadily more pale and I knew that the horrors I had read about in books could soon become a reality. The approaching war was no longer a rumor.

I tried to shake off the horrible images that war conjured, but the images only loomed larger and uglier. Even the word was ugly. War.

Enna brought hot tea, while we listened to more details. How many casualties were yet unknown. Four of the eight American battleships were sunk, one was beached, and all others badly damaged.

"This is it," Mother said in a monotone, her eyes not blinking. "The Americans will surely enter the war now. Maybe with them we still have a chance."

News of the bold Japanese victory at Pearl Harbor brought the Dutch East Indies state railways to a halt. The trains were immediately commandeered for military personal only. Every available able-bodied Dutchman was drafted. The reserves were put on full-time duty, and I became painfully aware that my father was not coming home.

The market place hummed with rumors that American planes would arrive to help turn the tide, but in the days that followed I only heard more bad news. The Japanese had landed in Burma and Malaysia, and had sunk the two British war ships, the *Prince of Wales* and the *Repulse.* On December 25 the Japanese captured Hong Kong, further dampening holiday spirits, and like so many others, I spent Christmas and New Year in quiet worship, dreaming about what once was and praying for a better tomorrow.

Christmas and New Year were *Opa* Pierre-Jacques' favorite. The whole family would come from all over the island to spend the holidays together. Like me, *Opa* loved the Christmas bread, baked fresh with lots of raisins and sprinkled with sugar. And best of all, he enjoyed ordering the fireworks late on December 31st. "Time to frighten away the lingering evil spirits?" he'd ask Saitem, with a half-smile. And when she assured him that she had taken all the other necessary precautions: scrubbed the house from top to bottom, brought in new palm mats, decorated with cut flowers, burned incense in every room, and made offerings of small puddings which lay in every corner of the house, he ordered the fireworks to begin. Christmas would never be like that again.

THREE

IKLAS

Angelica and I were busy sorting bis-
cuits, canned food, and drinks as emergency
supplies for our make-shift air-raid shelter,
when we noticed Mother climbing in behind
the wheel of our car. At first we just
watched with curiosity, but when Kromo
began cranking the engine, we dropped
what we were doing and hurried over.

"You two stay out of the way," Mother
shouted, as we approached. "Kromo is
going to teach me how to drive."

"Why?" Angelica asked. "Women don't
drive and we have two drivers."

"Women *do* drive!" Mother said.

I'd never seen such a look on my mother's face. Her small
black eyes were wide and determined. Her lips were pulled
into a firm line, her cheeks flushed.

"We need to be prepared," she said.

"For what, Mama?" Angelica clutched the car door at the
open window.

"Oh, Angelica, don't ask so many questions. Go sit on the
veranda. Henriette, you too." Mother gripped the steering
wheel of the humming car. "What do I do, Kromo?"

Kromo looked uneasy as he began explaining.

Angelica and I retreated, watching from a safe distance. We could see Kromo pointing, leaning close to Mother, nodding his head. The car rolled forward slowly, jolted, stopped, then jolted forward again.

By mid-morning Mother had the hang of it, although not before she ran the car off the road and into a small papaya tree that generously donated its life to stop her. Once we knew she was all right, we laughed and called Solani, the gardener and alternate driver, to help Kromo push the car up out of the gulch and back onto the dirt pathway.

After a week, Mother's confidence allowed her to drive on the difficult mountain roads. She drove slowly but seemed in control and soon was able to run errands in Semarang.

Sometimes, I stayed after school in Semarang as well, visiting with my friend Hellie, and listening to the news. Hellie was my closest friend. At home, her family called her Liem Swan—her Chinese name, the name she never used in school. Hellie was tall and stately like her Dutch mother, but her dark eyes and rich olive skin told of her Chinese father. "You know how they can be," she told me when I first learned her Chinese name. And I did know. Being mixed left us in a strange place. Some natives admired us because we were part white, other natives disliked us for the same reason. It made me wonder who I was. Me, with my dark wavy hair, dark eyes, and skin that turned brown if I wasn't careful. Was there a central person I could be? Many *Indos* compared notes to see who had more white blood, but the *Belanda-totos* always felt superior to any of the mixes, and they often found ways of making snide remarks to remind us of our inferiority.

It had been no different in Bandoeng. There, we mixes stuck together as well. Wilhamena—Willie as she liked to be called—Anneka, Alynne. We grew up understanding our place: less than the *Belanda-toto*, better than the native. Willie and Hellie would like each other.

In the quiet sculptured gardens of Hellie's home, she and I often prayed to their Buddha. We touched his elbows, whispering "Please. Please help us." We prayed for the American planes, for someone to stop the war, for peace.

But the situation became more desperate by the day. The Japanese captured Manila early in January, and soon after landed on Borneo and Celebes.

Students had already been notified that school could be closed at any time. Our school was a small one, because even though it was a state high school, its high tuition fees and scholastic requirements prevented many from attending. The *Belanda-totos,* were mostly children of plantation owners; a few were *Indo,* like me; even rarer were children of high Indonesian officials; and the rest were Chinese or Chinese mixes like Hellie.

The upper grades, such as mine, were nearly empty, due to the enlistment of the eighteen-year-old boys, and many of the young girls stayed home out of fear. So it was only a matter of time before the school would close.

I did my studies close to the radio, to hear any breaking news. Occasionally I glanced up at the grandfather clock, solemnly ticking on the wall opposite me. Five-forty-five, and Mother hadn't come home yet. It would be dark soon. Angelica was probably already out back, talking to the geese, getting ready to let them out of their pen to do their nightly watch. She had a way with them.

I read a few more pages. From my seat, I could see the front yard through a large window. and was relieved when my mother finally drove up the dirt drive. The car came slow and steady, tired-sounding, as if it too wanted the happy days to return, days of picnics and weekend outings.

I walked out to greet her. "You're so late." I said, opening the car door. "I was getting worried."

Mother's clothes were rumpled and her damp hair was pushed back off her dirt-streaked face.

"Are you all right?"

"I've been in Semarang all day." She looked on the verge of tears.

My heart lubbed a few erratic beats. I touched her shoulder. "What's wrong?" I was sure she was going to tell me the Japanese had landed.

She took a deep breath. "I've been delivering medical supplies to troops. Singapore will fall any day. If it hasn't fallen already. There's nothing between them and us but the sea. British and Australian troops are retreating. They're coming through here, through Java. Their hope is to reach Tjilatjap and sail from there to Australia."

I breathed a little easier. The Japanese weren't here yet. Maybe there was a chance they wouldn't come, they'd be stopped.

My mother seemed to read my mind. She looked me full in the eyes. "They're going to land here soon. They need our oil. They'll come. I never thought it would happen, but now I'm sure they'll come. God only knows what they'll do."

We walked into the house together. I longed for my father. He would know what to do—where to go, but we had not heard from him in weeks. Communications were minimal. All we knew was that he was in Bandoeng.

At night, as I lay in bed, I thought of Saitem. "You have no control over your life," she'd told me. "Your life is already written. Do not fight it." And then I remembered *Opa* telling me I would have many choices. If my life was already written, why did I have to make choices? Or was life a lesson of making the right choices?

I fell into a restless sleep, dreaming of Saitem, of *Opa,* of shadows and choices. The priest began to chant the mass, the smell of incense filled the church. Wisps of smoke drifted upward carrying my grandfather's spirit. Images of Sundays when the whole family would go to church together floated before me.

Saitem walked next to *Opa,* wearing her tailored white blouse with her formal batik *Kain,* the delicate fan pleats in front bouncing partially open as she kept up with *Opa's* long strides. *Opa* looked grand in his formal tails and high hat, but he never stepped over a discarded candle stub. Those he saved in his pocket for me. My father and mother walked behind them, and Angelica and I followed.

Once Saitem had taken her Islamic *Tasbih* beads to church instead of her rosary. *Opa* was not concerned. He simply said

God would not mind if she prayed with those in church that day. He was understanding and tolerant of such things.

The day of *Opa's* funeral, Saitem held tight to her rosary beads. Her mouth made words I could not decipher, and so I listened to the monotone of the priest, as the incense continued to swirl. My eyes clung to the spiraling smoke, my mind conjured *Opa* Pierre-Jacques' face. He smiled, not wearing the stern look needed to maintain the image of the Dutch Colonials.

"Nothing is black or white," the image said.

I jerked awake, looking around the dark room, listening to the gentle babble of the stream out back and the muted honking of the geese guarding our property. I slid out from under the mosquito netting and looked out the window. Coconut palms and banana trees stood silhouetted in the moonlight. They were still and peaceful. The shadows hid the ugly reality that daylight brought.

I went back to bed and tried to go to sleep, but the memories that awakened me would not end. After the church service I clung to Saitem, as my father, his brothers, and four military pall bearers carried my grandfather's flower-laden coffin to its final resting place in the burial ground reserved for the Dutch elite. The priest murmured his final prayers, and a Dutch honor guard fired a salute.

Back at my grandparent's home, Saitem and I sat together on the floor in our special room, the wood statue of Mary holding Jesus looking back at us. Saitem removed her gold serpent bracelet from her wrist and placed it on mine.

"I will not be here for very long," she said in a low, wispy voice. "This will bring you good luck. It will bring you courage and strength."

"Where are you going, *Oma?*" I asked, but she didn't answered. She was praying.

Less than a month later, *Oma* Saitem followed Pierre-Jacques.

"Why? Why did she die?" I cried, burying my face in my father's shoulder.

He stroked my head. "Dry your tears, Henny," he said in a hoarse whisper that told me he hurt too. "The Javanese don't cry. It will make it difficult for *Oma* Saitem's spirit to leave this house, this world."

I looked into his eyes. The eyes that were so much like Saitem's. They were sad, but shed no tears, just as Saitem had shed no tears for *Opa*.

Inhaling deeply, I wiped the tears from my eyes with the back of my hand.

Father kissed my forehead. "That's my girl. Now come." He led the way to where Saitem's body, specially washed according to Islamic law, lay wrapped in a plain white sheet on the bier. Family and close friends, who had come to pray, gathered in preparation to go to the cemetery.

My father took my hand and Angelica's, guiding us back and forth under Saitem's bier three times.

"Now we are *iklas*," he said. "We have quieted our emotions to show that we can detach from *Oma*. Now she knows she can pass into the next world."

I didn't feel any less detached, but I concentrated, forcing myself to dissociate from the ache in my chest, willing myself to release my grandmother. Slowly, we joined the others behind the bier for the procession. Our family, in a line of three cars, drove behind her horse-drawn carriage, while others rode in carriages, or on bicycles. It was a silent procession devoid of music or loud crying.

At the graveside, I stood between my mother and father, holding Angelica's hand. My lower lip trembled, my dry throat ached, and my eyes burned, but I wouldn't cry. I refused to stand in the way of Saitem's departing spirit.

"Saitem," I sighed, rolling over in my bed. Brushing the tears from my eyes, I glanced back out the window. The shadows of night were lifting and the sky was touched with red.

FOUR

BHAGAVAD-GITA

In school the following day, it was announced that authorities would distribute "emergency diplomas" to seniors. There were no hours of testing. No week of waiting with anticipation to see grades. No announcement in the paper of scholastic victories. There was nothing but a scrap of paper.

"Congratulations," I said to myself. "You've graduated." For a fleeting moment I visualized myself at the university in the Netherlands, but the image quickly disappeared. Maybe when the war was over.

"Mama," I shouted, "Singapore has fallen!"

Mother rushed into the room where I sat beside the radio. Angelica followed close behind. They stood listening to the broadcast, Mother's eyes growing darker, and Angelica clutching Mother's hand.

"They've underestimated the Japanese." Mother slumped into a chair. "I've underestimated them."

Angelica kneeled beside the chair. "What's going to happen? Are they coming here now? Will they kill us?"

"No, of course they won't kill us." Mother snapped, but I'm sure she wondered, as did we.

"Then what will they do?" Angelica persisted. Her eyes looked wild. Frightened. Mirrors of my feelings.

"I don't know." Resting her face in her hands, Mother massaged her forehead and temples. "I don't know," she whispered, once, twice.

I thought she looked suddenly older, harder. She was not the same woman who planned luncheons and laughed with the Dutch elite. Her dress hung in rumples, strands of graying hair escaped the knot at the nape of her neck, and her fingernails carried traces of working in the vegetable garden.

Abruptly, Mother stood up. "Pack some things. There is a British convoy coming through here today, and we're going to join it. We'll be safer in Wonosobo."

"Safe from what, Mama?" Angelica whined.

Mother took her hand and squeezed it. "Just safer."

"Come on, I'll help you." Taking my sister's hand, I headed for her bedroom as Mother hurried to pack for herself and give orders to the servants.

"Why is it going to be safer in Wonosobo? What's going to happen here?"

"I don't know. The Japanese are coming. No one knows what that means. Let's just do as Mama says." I threw some clothes into a bag, then the two of us went to my room to do the same.

"I wish Papa was here." Angelica's lower lip trembled.

I stopped what I was doing and looked at her. "Me too." Sitting on the bed beside her, I put my arms around her and for a moment we consoled each other.

"Do you think Papa's all right?" Angelica asked through her sobs.

"Of course he's all right! He's strong. He can handle anything," I answered with such conviction, I almost believed it myself. But I worried. I prayed daily to God and all the spirits.

"Come on. Mama's waiting," I grabbed up our bag of clothes and gently pushed my sister along.

Quickly we loaded our belongings and food into the car, while we listened for the sounds of the expected convoy. Enna and Solani waited patiently to accompany us. Kokie and

Kromo would stay behind and manage the house. I was not afraid for them. If anything happened they could go to the *kampung* and be absorbed into the shadows of their people.

Just as the sound of the approaching convoy could be heard, Uncle William drove up with his secretary, Marianne.

"Jeanne, please, can Marianne stay with you?" He asked my mother.

"But we're going to Wonosobo," Mother answered, staring at the young woman.

"Please, Jeanne. She's pregnant and needs someone to be with her."

Marianne was a petite thing, with milk-white skin and ebony hair. Her swollen abdomen made her condition obvious, and she was more than well along.

"You know what it's like there! Where's her husband?" Mother whispered, as Marianne returned to my uncle's car for her handbag.

"She's not married," my uncle whispered back. "Please, take her with you."

Mother looked suspiciously at Uncle William, but it was Marianne's pathetic face that must have convinced her.

No sooner had we packed Marianne's things when the convoy approached in a swirling cloud of dust.

I shared the back seat with Enna and Marianne, while Mother sat in front with Angelica. Solani pulled the old car in line with the convoy.

We found ourselves staring into the canvas-covered trucks. Men, mostly Australians, I guessed, who had battled the Japanese in Malaya and Singapore, sat with bloody bandages, their eyes dull with pain. Some lay on the truck floors with heads bandaged or bloody stumps where once a leg or arm had been. No one talked. They just swayed with the truck on the bumpy road.

Solani caravanned behind the retreating convoy until the junction to Wonosobo. There he turned off the main road, and headed up the mountain. The small cottage, where once we had shared such happy weekends, loomed before us as a welcome hideaway. The thick pine trees, that previously had shaded us, were now like silent sentries who would guard us by night.

Unlike the happy days of the past, when the hours sped by too fast, the days now dragged. Hour upon hour we sat, waited, listened. For what, we did not know. Each broadcast on the battery-operated radio made us more somber, filled us with more anxiety.

"The Dutch must hold them off," Mother murmured, almost as if in a prayer. The others nodded. After the first week, I gave up listening to the radio and sat a short distance off, losing myself in the past.

We used to come up and sleep to an orchestra of insects accompanied by the rustle of wind through the pine trees and the rush of water from the nearby river. Now those sounds seemed swallowed by fear, but I forced myself to hear them.

Mornings we'd breakfast on the sweet rolls we had bought in Ambarawa and an array of pink and sweet papaya, finger-size bananas, and tangy guavas.

Sometimes after breakfast, we'd drive up to the Dieng Plateau.

The narrow unpaved road to the Plateau permitted one-way traffic only. Morning travelers made their way up the mountain. In the afternoon, traffic would be reversed. The road wound past two sleeping volcanoes, Soendoro and Soembing. There the foliage was large acacia trees, bright green, the pollen of their yellow flowers dusting the road, and slender casuarinas, their dark green leaves dropping like wet feathers. We passed hillsides of tall corn, pale green mounds of cabbages, and endless rows of tobacco. Men and women with conical hats worked the fields, carrying their harvested crops in large baskets on their backs. The road climbed higher and higher until it flattened out at the Dieng Plateau.

"Just look at this view," Father would always say as if seeing it for the first time. "Look! Look at those mountains. To the east stands Merbabu, a silent giant, and next to it you can see the smoke rising from the cone of Merapi."

Angelica always worried about it erupting, and the plume that snaked its way into the sky had me worried as well, but my father seemed more concerned that Mother had remembered the food. His appetite grew in high altitudes. His happy mood was infectious.

The first time we came to the Dieng Plateau Angelica and I were eager to look around on our own, but Father stopped us.

"I will find a guide and then we can go."

"Oh, Papa, we don't need a guide just to look over there," Angelica pouted.

"I said, wait. You have no idea of the dangers." He turned and walked toward the group of guides, who eagerly surrounded him.

Angelica and I waited, while Father negotiated. When he returned, he was followed by a barefoot little man. Sumo, although old and slightly hunched, with only a sprig of white hair left on his head, walked with a bounce in his step. His T-shirt was a dirty gray and his sarong came just below his knees. Veined legs and calloused feet protruded from under the sarong, yet his eyes were clear and his smile genuine.

Sumo marched purposefully three meters ahead of us, carrying a bamboo cage containing a yellow chirping bird.

"These old stones are parts of buildings that have been here for a very long time," Sumo began in Malay. "They are not part of an ancient city, but remains of shrines and temples. This was a place of pilgrimage."

Angelica and I walked slowly through the pale green grass, curiously examining the black stones illuminated in the bright sunlight. I listened carefully to the guide, but Angelica grew more interested in the little bird.

"Why do you carry this bird?" Angelica finally asked, offering a blade of grass through the wooden slits.

"Oh, he is the most important member of our tour," the guide answered. "You see, this area is very dangerous. Maybe the gods still live here. Sometimes, perhaps when the gods get angry, the earth rumbles. Small cracks open in the ground. We cannot see them, but poison gas leaks out. The bird is a warning. When he falls over, we know that we must quickly leave the area."

"Dead? The bird may fall over dead?" Angelica's eyes grew large at the insensitivity of the guide.

"Sometimes. But it is a good warning, *noni*. That way no harm will come to us."

"How awful for the bird."

He patted Angelica's head with the soft fondness of an uncle.

She recoiled, with an icy stare.

"Do not be sad, little *noni*. He gives his life for a good cause. Besides, sometimes the bird lives. Come now. I have much to show you. See, here is Bima, Arjuna's brother." He spoke excitedly as he showed us the great treasures. "Do you know Bima and Arjuna?"

Angelica gave him a blank look.

"They are from the *Bhagavad Gita*," I answered.

The guide looked impressed. "That is correct, *noni*. Come, let us continue." He took his job seriously and insisted that we stay behind him as we strolled along, taking time to look at flowers and stones along the way.

"Come, now I will show you the waters," the guide pointed proudly beyond the ruins.

We walked past three small varied-colored lakes. The guide explained that the lakes were volcanic craters. The different colors were a result of water mixing with minerals. Copper gave a reddish color, while sulphur gave a more yellow color.

"And the green color?" Angelica asked.

"I think that is just natural beauty," the guide laughed.

"What about that mud color?" Angelica made a face, backing away from the stinking steam.

"That is sulphur too. Those are still active craters. The minerals have not yet settled."

"Must they always stink?" Angelica held her nose, as we passed the bubbling, mud-gray lake.

I glanced nervously into the bird cage. The bird chirped happily from its perch as if encouraging us onward.

At the end of our tour, we rested in the cool of an acacia tree, and Mother unpacked our picnic. The sticky rice, wrapped and baked in banana leaves, tasted especially wonderful.

"The gods must be happy with you," Sumo said, as he graciously accepted one of the tasty *lempers* my father offered him. "They did not send any bad gases, and our little bird friend still lives."

Angelica fed the bird rice crumbs on her finger until the guide excused himself, leaving to find a new customer.

We continued to rest and picnic in the shade until we felt the afternoon chill creeping in. Then we climbed back into the car and slowly made our way down the narrow mountain road. Clouds were beginning to wrap the Dieng Plateau in an eerie mist.

"You know," Father said, "they say when the clouds embrace the mountain like they're doing now, it means the gods have returned to demand the temples for themselves."

Staring out the back window, my imagination shaped clouds into Arjuna arriving in his horse-drawn carriage.

"I think the end is near," Mother's voice broke the spell. They were all still huddled around the radio.

"Come on," I called to my sister. "Let's take a walk."

Angelica hesitated.

"I don't want to listen to any bad news."

Reluctantly, Angelica came along.

We walked up to the old secluded Catholic convent. There, an aging priest and a group of nuns still occupied and cared for the grounds. Outside the convent natives peddled their wares of fresh produce. Pyramids of bright green cabbages stood next to white corn. Mounds of potatoes, baskets of brown—not the best quality—rice, local fruits, and spices became a cacophony of colors and smells.

The pungent aroma of fresh cloves, cardamom, and cumin reminded me of Saitem. I looked down at my bracelet, feeling my grandmother's nearness and wondering what really happened to souls after the bodies were buried. Did they go to a special world, a heaven, or were they able to be near family, see us, help us? Catholicism said, heaven, hell, or purgatory, but then who were the spirits? What were the shadows that Saitem spoke of?

"Let's go back, Henny," Angelica tapped my shoulder. "It's getting dark."

I nodded and turned back down the dirt road. Angelica was not comfortable in the dark. She walked fast, almost ran, down the road toward our cabin.

When we returned, Enna was preparing a dinner of rice and vegetables over an open fire. On the small veranda, a Petromax lantern hung from a bamboo stick, casting a light on the coconut matting where we would eat sitting on the floor like natives, but not without plates and silverware. Mother would never allow that. Eating with our hands would be descending far too much into our native roots. Father and I enjoyed such behavior on occasions, but never Mother or Angelica.

Stepping onto the veranda, I made myself comfortable in the far corner where Father and I usually sat across from each other, telling stories, discussing school work. A breeze whispered through the light green leaves of the betel nut vine that climbed up the bamboo latticed porch. Tiny bright green bug-eyed frogs made croaking sounds from within the vine. They were the music for our evening and I hoped they would sing loud.

"Rumor has it the Dutch and their Allies are heading for Tjilatjap," Mother said. Her face sagged and her lips pulled downward.

I looked at my own shadow cast on the matting. "They want to escape to Australia too."

"Who's going to protect us then?" Angelica wanted to know.

No one answered.

It wasn't long before we heard Surabaya had been attacked from the air and the Japanese had landed there, as well as in Batavia and Bandoeng. There was no doubt that the island was now crawling with the enemy.

FIVE

WONOSOBO

A week later, we were still in Wonosobo. Afraid to go anywhere, I had taken to sketching scenes from memory; water buffalo plowing wet rice paddies, native huts, birds, and flowers, anything that reminded me of good times.

"Listen, it's the Japanese talking," Marianne said. We crowded around the radio and listened to the static-filled voice. It spoke Malay, but with accents on the wrong words, and pauses in the wrong places.

"No harm will come to anyone," the voice said. "But all must register with the Japanese authorities. Trains will operate as normal. All stores are encouraged to stay open for business."

"Do you believe them, Mama?" Angelica asked.

"Do we have a choice?

"We could pretend we don't know anything, not register, stay here," Marianne said. "We could live here until the war is over. There's nothing here they want."

"But if all they want is for us to register with them, we might as well." Mother looked at each of us. "We could go home where we can be more comfortable."

"What about Papa?" I asked. "Do you think he'll be able to come home?"

"Maybe." Mother brightened. "Maybe. Solani, Enna, we're going back to Oengaran tomorrow. Be ready to go first thing in the morning."

Enna and Solani nodded, and I thought I caught a meaningful look pass between them. I suddenly wondered how the native people felt about the Japanese. Did they secretly want the Japanese to succeed? Did they consider the Japanese victories as an indication that they were not inferior, as the Dutch had made them believe?

I listened for the sound of a *beduk*. My father said the village drum had many uses; the call to prayer for the Muslims, an alert to fire, volcano eruptions, or celebrations. I wondered if there was a drum beat for war or the enemy. I heard nothing but the wind through the trees and the sound of my own heart.

"I'd like to stay," Marianne said, her sweet face gray with dark sunken eyes that lacked luster. "It's peaceful here, and the sisters at the convent can help me when the baby comes. It won't be too much longer."

"Are you sure, Marianne?" Mother asked. "We have room in our house. You can stay with us, even after the baby is born."

"Thank you. I'll be fine. Marto and Kamsie have offered to help me."

Mother considered the offer. Marto and Kamsie were a native couple in the village who had come to know our family over the years. They were friendly with Enna and Solani as well as respectful of us.

"I want to stay," Marianne said.

The drive back to Oengaran felt endless. The road appeared the same. Nothing was different. There were no Japanese. Maybe it was all a bad dream, but when we arrived after noon, Kokie came running towards us even before we stopped the car. Her lips moved with words we could not yet hear.

Kromo followed, also with a quick step and a frown on his face.

"The Japanese," Kokie breathed excitedly, when we stepped from the car. "They come here almost every day to look for the owners of the house."

"What do they want?" I heard the quiver in my mother's voice.

"They never say. I told them you went to Wonosobo." Kokie shot a look at Kromo.

"I told her not to say anything," he answered.

"I was afraid. They look so mighty. I am sorry. I had to tell them," Kokie buried her head in the dirty cloth she used for an apron. Her body heaved with silent sobs.

"There's nothing to do but cooperate," Mother said. She patted Kokie on the shoulder, then turned to Angelica and me. "Bring me your valuables: jewelry, silver, extra money." Mother glanced at my wrist. "And Henriette, take that bracelet off too."

"But I've never taken it off."

"Don't argue!"

Inside the house, Angelica and I brought what we had. Silver combs and brushes, various gold earrings and bracelets, and a few Dutch guilders. Mother placed them on the tattered cloth that lay spread out on the floor.

"Henriette, where's your bracelet ?"

"Pinned in my pocket. I want to keep it with me. *Oma* said it would bring me good luck."

Mother frowned. "Such nonsense." She folded the cloth with quick jerky movements, then tucked it away beneath a loose tile. "Don't blame me when it's gone."

The next morning, Angelica and I were finishing our breakfast on the veranda, when we noticed a stranger approaching. His tailored khaki uniform and shiny black boots looked uncomfortable in the steamy heat. The boots squeaked unpleasantly as he marched up the drive, followed by a young native dressed in the customary sarong and T-shirt.

Angelica screamed, running inside, "Mama, Mama."

I froze, standing beside the table.

Mother already stood at the door when the stranger stomped up the wooden stairs.

The soldier spoke in Japanese.

I stared openly at him. He was my height, with black,

piercing, emotionless eyes, and thin lips that sneered, as he continued to speak in the gibberish that meant nothing to me.

"What does he want?" I asked my mother. A sudden impulse made me ask the question in Malay.

"I don't know," Mother whispered, also using the island language.

The native, who had accompanied the Japanese soldier, translated. "He wishes to know if that is your car?" He pointed to our black Chevrolet sitting in the garage.

Mother nodded.

The soldier and the native exchanged words.

"He says, all motorized vehicles are for official use of the Japanese only. He wants the car keys."

"What? He wants to take my car?" The question sprang from my mother's lips, but she quickly fell silent again. A hint of anger, mixed with fear, flitted across her eyes.

"Can he do that?" I whispered.

A smile curled the soldier's lips, as his dark narrow eyes turned toward me. Slowly he looked me up and down. The smile lingered.

On my neck the sweat turned cold and I could feel tiny hairs bristle, like a frightened dogs.

"You young and healthy," he said in broken Malay. "Walk."

I felt the hopelessness of the situation, and the iciness of his stare.

With a nod of her head, Mother motioned for me to get the car keys.

With deliberate calm, I walked into the house. I didn't want him to know how much he frightened me.

"The car is yours," Mother said when I returned and handed her the keys.

The soldier's brown sweating hand closed around the key and my mother's fingers. He squeezed her hand, grinned, then slowly released her, and abruptly turned, marching down the steps. We stood watching until he was gone from view.

Mother, letting out a long sigh, closed the door and locked it.

Two weeks later the same Japanese soldier returned to take my bicycle, and later to take Angelica's. There was nothing we could do. There was no reason to go anywhere anyway. We were afraid to go to far from home. We busied ourselves with planting our garden, growing yams, potatoes, and vegetables. We gathered fruit from the dozens of fruit trees on our property. Natives from the *kampung* helped us fill baskets with coconuts, papaya, mango, and more. We took one basket of each for ourselves. The rest Mother let the natives take with them.

"It's been over four months since we heard from your father," Mother told me, as she and I walked to the Chinese broker. "Your father's Dutch guilders are almost gone."

"What are you going to pawn?"

"A pendant. The gold one with the diamond."

"But Papa gave that to you on your birthday."

"We'll buy it back once this is all over," she said, as we entered the cluttered little shop.

I knew it wasn't true, but said nothing. I was learning to keep my mouth shut when arguing made no difference.

Mother placed the pendant on the dusty counter, the dim light making the gold and diamond sparkle that much more. The shop owner made no secret of his delight, as he fingered the pendant with greedy pleasure. Smiling and bowing, he counted out Niponese *rupiahs*. The new occupation money was printed on poor-quality paper and looked like play money. Mother collected it up, recounting carefully to make sure the Chinese wasn't cheating her, then she placed the money in her purse.

When we arrived home, I walked to the quiet stream beyond our house. There, the war had not changed anything. Water, rolling gently over the rocks, babbled innocently. The coconut palms reached for the sky of crystal blue, lush vines embraced trees and brought forth a sweet smell of honey suckle, and wild parrots screeched at each other.

I stretched out in the shade feeling soothed by the beauty. A red and blue parrot eyed me from the branches above and I wondered if it might be the same one that had visited *Oma* and *Opa's* home so many years ago. Reaching into my pocket, I felt for my bracelet.

"Saitem, oh, Saitem, send the spirits to watch over us—especially to watch over Papa."

Nearly a month after we left Wonosobo, Marto arrived; tired, hungry, and looking nervous.

"Henriette, get him something to eat and drink," Mother ordered, sitting Marto down in one of the cushioned out-door rattan chairs.

I rushed to Kokie in the kitchen, and returned with some weak tea, a small bowl of lukewarm brown rice, and sliced papaya.

"It's Marianne," Marto was saying, as I handed him the tea and placed the bowl of rice on the table beside him. "The baby has come."

Angelica smiled. "A boy or a girl?"

"The baby is a fine boy, but Marianne—"

"What? What about Marianne?" Mother asked impatiently.

"Marianne—she—" He took a sip of tea. His hands shook as he brought the cup to his mouth. "She was not well."

"Is she sick?" Mother asked.

"No, no. Marianne, sweet kind lady. She is not sick anymore." He stopped. Looked at his hands.

There was a long silence. We all knew what must have happened but we needed Marto to say the word, tell us she had died. When he finally managed to explain that the baby was being cared for by the priest and sisters, we all had tears in her eyes.

"I shouldn't have left her behind. I should have made her come with us." Mother wiped her eyes and blew her nose. "I'm going to get the baby, bring him here. He'll have a home with us."

"But Mama, how will you get to Wonosobo? We have no car," Angelica said.

"The baby needs a home. I can't just leave him there."

SIX

INDO

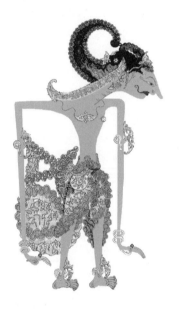

Early the next morning Solani arrived with a *tjikar* and driver. The cart's wooden wheels were in good condition and the few holes in the bamboo roof wouldn't prevent it from offering sufficient protection from sun and rain. Straw had been placed at the bottom of the cart to offer some comfort, but I couldn't imagine myself sitting there for the long trip, much less my mother.

The two well-fed oxen, attached to the cart with an elaborate wooden yoke, stood patiently chewing their cud. The barechested young driver, an acquaintance of Solani, wore only a faded sarong and a black Javanese cap on his head. He greeted Mother cordially, his brown-stained teeth protruding as he parted his lips into a smile.

"Solani has told you how far I need to go?" Mother asked the driver.

He nodded, "yes, *njonja*."

"You think your animals can go such a distance and back?"

"They are very fine animals, *njonja*. Notice that one is white, and the other black. You will be traveling in harmony."

Even though Mother paid little attention to native superstition, the comment put me at ease. It was something Saitem would have said and I believed the spirits would be with Mother, protecting her from danger.

She held up some Niponese *rupiahs.* "You get the rest when we get back."

The driver held up his hand. "No *rupiahs.*" He pointed to her ring.

Apparently Mother had anticipated this problem. She fumbled in her pocket and pulled out a silver earring—one of mine. "You'll get the other one when we're back."

The driver examined the small hoop, then smiled his approval.

"I put some old clothes in the *tjikar,*" Kokie said. "You can tear them up for diapers. There is food and water as well."

Mother nodded, then climbed into the cart.

Marto climbed up beside the driver. He hadn't quite recovered from his long journey, but was eager to get back to Wonosobo, and delighted that he would get a ride.

"Henriette, you watch your sister and stay out of the way of those Japanese."

"How long will you be gone?" Angelica asked.

"I don't know. Maybe a week."

"A week? Why so long?"

"Because a *tjikar* is slow." Mother gave a sign to the driver, and the cart moved down the road.

Angelica and I watched until the cart was out of sight and we could no longer hear the clip-clop of the oxen. Then she turned to me.

"Do you think Mama will be all right?"

"Yes. She's tougher then I thought. Besides, she looks like a native. She won't draw attention to herself."

Angelica raised her chin. "But we're still *Belandas.*"

"Well, you better shut up and not be too proud of it right now. And consider yourself lucky that our registration cards don't say *Belanda,* but *Indo.*"

"Why? It's just a piece of paper that says who you are."

"There's always a reason for making a distinction." I went inside and found a book to read.

We began watching for our mother after the fifth day. We ate breakfast, played cards, did puzzles, took afternoon tea, all on the veranda in hopes of her return. When night came, I stayed up reading long after Angelica had gone to sleep. I started with the local newspaper, but soon gave up, tired of reading about the Japanese victories, and not sure if it was all true. Ultimately I turned to my favorite author, Voltaire. His writing gave me strength and inspiration. And like his *"Candide"*, I could only live one moment at a time, not knowing what the next day would bring.

"What if something's happened?" Angelica asked, as we waited the next morning.

"Nothing's happened. She'll be here."

"Are you sure?"

"You can't ever be sure of anything."

"But what if she doesn't come back?"

"Then I'll take care of you. Now stop it. You're almost fifteen. Grow up." I put my hand in my pocket and rubbed my bracelet for good luck. I would not allow myself to think of Mother not returning. I would not allow such negative thoughts to enter my mind. Saitem had said, "negative thoughts bring negative actions."

By the seventh day, we were pretty much living on the veranda. Many times we heard the unmistakable clip-clop of a *tjikar,* but to our disappointment, it was filled with bamboo, fruits, or other such things.

Late in the afternoon, when we had given up hope that Mother would return that day, a *tjikar* pulled onto our property. We stared, at first not sure, but then Mother stepped down from the back, and with a deep sigh, I let go of my own fear.

"Mama's home! Mama's home!" Angelica dropped her cards and ran. I followed.

In our mother's arms lay a tiny bundle. The infant was small and pale, hairless, but with bright brown eyes. He didn't cry or fuss. I wondered if he understood the desperate star under which he had been born. I felt sorry for the new little baby and was suddenly very proud of my mother.

Angelica hugged Mother's waist, as she peeked at the new-born in his clean but shabby clothes.

"He's so small!" Angelica said, touching his toes.

"You were once this small too," Mother laughed.

"Does he have a name yet?" I wanted to know.

Mother tapped his button nose. "I thought we'd call him William, after your uncle."

Enna joined us and Mother handed little William over to her. "There's an extra bottle of food for him," Mother said, pointing to the back of the cart. "Feed him and put him down for a nap. I'm sure he's tired." We started for the house, "Oh, and tell Kokie she better see if we have mung beans to cook up for more baby food. I'm sure there's no milk to be found."

Enna nodded and disappeared into the house, cooing and clucking at the baby, as she must have done for us many years ago.

Mother lowered herself into the rattan rocking chair. "Ahhh, it feels good to sit in something comfortable."

"Do you want this extra pillow for your back?" I offered.

"That's nice." Mother nestled into the soft cushion. "So, did you two have any problems while I was gone?"

"No, but we were worried and missed you," Angelica said, taking the chair beside her.

Mother smiled, leaning her head back, closing her eyes, and rocking gently. She took in a deep breath and let it out slowly. "You know, I had a lot of time to think while I was on the road." She opened her eyes and stared at the distant coconut palms. "Now that we have our registration cards, we can travel. If there is room on the train I want to go to Bandoeng to get your *Oma* Van Zeel. It would be better if she lived here with us. She's old and I'm sure life is easier here in the country."

"Maybe we can find Papa!" Night after night I prayed for him. I dreamed of the war ending and us being reunited. I needed to see him. "I'm going with you to Bandoeng."

"Me too," Angelica said.

Mother stopped rocking. "We can't all go."

"I'm going!" My fists were clenched and I met Mother's stern gaze with one of my own.

"If she goes, I go!" Angelica pounded her fist on the arm rest.

"Shhh!" Mother hissed.

"If you don't take me with you, I'll go on my own. I'm eighteen." Prepared to fight, I took advantage of Mother's tiredness. Perhaps too tired to argue.

Mother began slowly rocking again. "Angelica, I need you here to help take care of little William. He's your brother now, you know."

"Oh, Mama, why can't I come?"

"Because you can't. It's settled. You stay here with Enna and the baby. Henriette will come with me. We won't be gone for more than a few days."

Luck was with us. Although it was crowded, we were able to find seats on the train, and the wait for departure was not long.

The train had a rhythm of its own and plodded along the mountain tracks at an unbearably slow pace. We passed over the Tjimanuh River, where native women washed their clothes, and young children, naked, and as yet unthreatened by the enemy, splashed in the water, happy in their play. We passed fields of greens and golds, the countryside slipping by, as I rocked back and forth, listening to the chug-chug and the clank of metal on metal. Strange how situations change perceptions of the same thing. I couldn't enjoy nature's beauty. All I wanted was to get to Bandoeng. Fast. But the train moved along slowly, and the colors blurred in misty thoughts.

"*Selamat pagi, noni,*" Samsu, the friendly ticket man, greeted and bowed to my father and me.

"*Selamat pagi,*" I returned, as I brought my palms together, bringing them to my face in the customary greeting bow.

Samsu smiled, obviously delighted at my greeting him in his native fashion.

My father and I boarded the train, seating ourselves in the comfortable second-class compartment near the windows, where we could view the scenery and enjoy the fresh air.

The train departed on time, starting its peaceful chug-chug into the green countryside. We passed by the Tjikapudung River, where native women washed their clothes, young men bathed their water buffalo, and children laughed. We passed rice, corn, and cassava fields, separated from one another by coconut palms and giant swaying bamboo. Flamboyant trees with their red blooms dotted the green country side, and heavy *nanka* fruit hung ripe for picking. The mighty volcanos looked purple, majestic, their peaks stretching to the heavens like giant obelisks.

At the various stops, my father and I left the train to see the station managers. We were greeted with friendly smiles and *selamat* bows before being escorted on an inspection tour. At the last station, the manager invited us to stay for lunch. My father accepted. "It would be unkind to disappoint the loyal manager," he explained to me.

The manager's home was little better than a hut, but had the distinction of a cement floor and two rooms. His wife bowed eagerly from her outdoor kitchen, then gestured that we enter.

"Please, come in. Sit down," the station manager said, indicating the fresh coconut palm mats on the floor.

Stepping onto the palm leaves, I watched cockroaches make a run to hiding places in the wall of the hut. I caught my father's eye, ignored the frightened black creatures, and sat down on the mat, hoping they all escaped in time.

"You know, you have a very special father," the man commented as he and my father joined me on the mat.

I smiled.

The man's wife entered, handing each of us a bowl of rice, topped with a sorry-looking fish, boiled river-farmed vegetables, and a teaspoon of hot peppers.

Sitting on the ground, our legs folded under us, we held our bowls in our hands.

"I'm sorry, we have no silverware," the manager apologized.

I smiled and cupped my fingers to grasp the sticky rice. It went easily into my mouth.

The manager's face brightened. He looked at my father, then ate in silence.

As the train made its lazy trip back around fields and tiny villages, afternoon rain clouds began to gather. I had forgotten my umbrella, but my father didn't seem concerned.

He looked up at the sky. "We'll make it home in time." He reminded me of *Oma* Saitem. Both of them could read the weather. I took a deep breath to smell the thickness in the air, felt the heaviness. I watched the clouds move, hide the sun, make long shadows. I listened to the birds. I wanted to read the weather too.

The rain waited to wash away the sticky heat until we made it home. Then the clouds let loose with such urgency that the streets instantly flooded, and vendors ran for shelter under trees and on open verandas.

Mother laughed at our good luck. She and Angelica had been watching for us.

"Let's take tea here on the veranda. It's pleasant now that the rain has cooled the air." Mother called into the house, and Enna soon arrived with tea and cakes.

I took a cup and sat down beside my sister.

"That ugly Tjeng came to see you today," Angelica grinned. "I think he likes you."

"Don't be ridiculous, Angelica!" Mother snapped. "That boy doesn't have the nerve to like a Dutch girl. He's Chinese. What are you thinking?" But she shifted her glance to me.

"We're friends," I answered her look.

"He scares me," Angelica lowered her voice, "and I wouldn't want to be seen with him. Think what people will say. Mama says you're judged by your friends."

I rolled my eyes and pulled my lips into a thin line. I didn't want to get my mother into another bad mood. I ignored my sister's comment and stared out at the rain. The downpour had changed to a gentle drizzle and the vendors were back on the street peddling their vegetables, coconut drinks, *saté*.

"Come now," Father said, as he enjoyed a second cup of tea, "let me hear you practice your piano. Play something nice for your mother and me."

Angelica made a face.

I stuck my tongue out at her, then got up and went into the house. I opened the black mahogany lid, warmed up my fingers with a few scales, then lost myself in the slow romantic strains of Chopin.

Chopin still played in my head as our train pulled into Bandoeng's station, but I awakened from my reverie quickly. I breathed in home. I looked around, half expecting to see my father. But there was no one we recognized. We took a *betjak* to *Oma* Van Zeel's.

"Since when do they have these bicycle-powered carts?" I asked the man who stood on the pedals straining forward, to get the *betjak* in motion.

"Since the Japanese requisitioned all motorized vehicles," the man said. "We natives know how to survive. You see, we have invented a whole new way of transport."

"And what if they take your bicycles?" I asked.

The man looked over his shoulder. "Then we will pull the cart ourselves." He turned his attention forward, pedaling the cart into traffic.

I sat back and looked around at my Bandoeng. Two years had passed since we left. It looked the same. We wove in and around horse-drawn carts, over fly-attracting droppings, whose stale odor mingled with the sweet smell of cooking noodles from the Chinese *warung* nearby. We rode along the murky Tjikapoendoeng River, where barefoot natives carried baskets of mangosteen, papaya, and *rambutan,* balanced from bamboo sticks across their shoulders. The streets, the shops, the people all seemed unchanged, but now armed Japanese stood on nearly every corner.

Our *betjak* wove through the streets, the man's callused feet straining on the peddles, sweat streaking the back of his shirt.

"Jeanne! Jeanne!" *Oma* Van Zeel shrieked, when we arrived. "You are all right!" My grandmother fell weeping into my mother's arms. "It's so good to see you. They've taken them all, Jeanne. They've taken all the boys," *Oma* wept.

Mother looked at her sister-in-law, Anne. "What does she mean?"

"The Japanese have interned your brothers." Aunt Anne's eyes clouded over and a tear made its way down her cheek before she wiped it away with her finger.

My mother's lip quivered slightly. I knew what she was thinking, but was afraid to ask. "And my father?" I asked for us. "Where is my father?" I felt a nausea growing in my stomach and took a deep breath to clear the black speckles that dotted my vision.

"He's in Tjimahie with my Piet. It's a prisoner-of-war camp, thirteen kilometers from here. Mostly *Belanda-totos*."

"But Papa is half Javanese," I shouted. "They can't do that to him."

"*Indos* who can prove they are half native are exempt, but for your father and uncles it doesn't matter," Aunt Anne sighed. "The Japanese interned anyone in uniform."

She tried to reach out and take my hand, but I backed away.

"Come sit down, Henriette. Let me get you something to drink."

I remained motionless, as my mother followed my aunt and grandmother into the living room. Mother slumped into the couch beside *Oma* Van Zeel.

"There's more," Aunt Anne continued.

I remained by the door, a statue of numbness, listening, wondering what more there could be.

"The Japanese have given us three days to get out of this house," *Oma* Van Zeel sobbed.

"Why? How can they do that? Anne?" Mother's voice rose, as it used to when she wanted to scold me, but her rage hung in the air without a victim.

"It's true," Aunt Anne answered. "It's happening more and more. They take the nicer houses to use as homes for themselves. And many other people have been displaced because whole streets are being fenced off to be used as camps."

"But where will you go? Where do these displaced people go?"

"We're lucky. My sister, Florence, is alone and happy to have us, but others are less fortunate. Some are forced to rent a room, a garage, anything, it doesn't matter."

"But their belongings. What do they do with their belongings?"

I could see my mother taking silent inventory.

"We can only take what we can carry. The rest we must leave behind." Aunt Anne looked around. "Maybe after the war it will still be here."

"My God, it's worse then I thought," Mother said. "Anne, I came to take mother back to Oengaran with us, but of course you are welcome also."

"I don't want Florence to be alone. She needs me now, but I'm glad you're taking Mama. We'll be all right. We have *Indo* on our registration card. We are safe."

"Isn't it ironic," I blurted from where I stood. "Native blood has saved us. All those *Belandas,* who previously hid their native blood, are now desperately scrambling around for proof of their ancestry. It makes me laugh."

"Stop it, Henriette. It won't always be like this," Mother said.

"'Asia for the Asians', they're shouting. I don't think there's a Dutchman left in a place of power. Eight days. That's all it took, before the mighty Dutch surrendered."

"That's enough, Henriette."

"Come sit down," Aunt Anne said softly. "You're upset. It's been a shock to find out about your father."

I backed to the door.

"Sit down," my mother said sternly, as if I were still a little child.

I turned and ran from the house before anyone could stop me. I made my way along the familiar streets, avoiding the Japanese guards. I didn't want to look at them. I didn't want them to look at me. I remembered walking these same streets holding my father's hand. Now, everything had changed, all my dreams shattered. I felt for Saitem's bracelet still pinned in my pocket. Saitem had promised it would bring me good luck. But in times like these, what did good luck mean? Just being alive? Having food? Finding my father?

I walked in a daze. I had no idea where my feet carried me. I let the spirits be my guide. I came upon a group of Dutch prisoners sweeping the street. Fierce-looking Japanese soldiers shouted harsh orders, pointed guns, and shoved the prisoners along. I scrutinized each of the captives, some younger than myself, but my father was not among them.

I found myself passing buildings near my old neighborhood, the neighborhood then reserved for the Dutch civil service employees. Not nearly as luxurious as those of the wealthy Dutch elite, it far surpassed the humble *kampungs* of the natives. Gardens boasted orange and red hibiscus, purple bougainvillaea, white cannas, but all this loveliness belonged to another time and now hung in the shadows of khaki-colored uniforms and polished black boots.

The next thing I knew I was at Tjeng's door step. His slanted eyes, disheveled thick black hair and uneven teeth were a welcome sight.

"Henriette!" Tjeng burst out, bowing to me in an excited greeting. "Come in, come in. Mother, come see who is here."

Tjeng's mother hurried in from another room. "Hello, hello," she bowed.

"Mother, you remember Henriette, don't you?"

"Of course. She went to temple with us, once or twice. Come in. Let me get you something. Life is more humble now, but we still have a few good things. The Japanese have not gotten everything yet."

Before I could refuse her hospitality, Tjeng's mother had shuffled off.

"Tjeng, I need your help," I whispered. "Can I borrow a bicycle? My father—" I choked. "He's in Tjimahie. I want to go there."

My friend's eyes widened. "That is very dangerous!"

"Please, help me. I must know if he's alive, if he's all right." Tears began to stream down my face. "I must know. I must know."

"What is it, child?" Tjeng's mother asked, returning with tea and rice cakes. "Why are you crying?"

Tjeng explained and his mother quietly took her handkerchief and dried my tears. "The Japanese are not sympathetic to their prisoners or their families."

"But I have to go. I have to try." The tears came fresh. "I'll never forgive myself if I don't try to see him." My lips quivered uncontrollably. I pressed her handkerchief against them, and pleaded with my eyes.

"If you're that determined—" Tjeng's mother patted my hands— "there is a way, but you can't go by yourself. I have friends who have successfully tried this."

"What? Oh, how? Please tell me!" I wiped my eyes and blew my nose.

"You must listen carefully to what I say and do exactly as I tell you. Tjeng will go with you." She looked at her son.

He nodded his acceptance.

"Now, while I explain, you eat. Do you remember these cakes?"

I smiled through my tear-blurred eyes. The days of excitement and pleasure over tea cakes had vanished. I tasted one, but delicious as it was, I could hardly swallow. I listened carefully to every word my friend's mother said.

"When can we go?" I asked.

"Leave early tomorrow. It is too late to go today. Tjeng will have a bicycle waiting for you when you get here. Now, sit and drink your tea and eat another rice cake. Nothing will change in the next twenty-four hours."

SEVEN

TJIMAHIE

Tjeng was ready when I arrived early the next morning. The bicycles were old, but usable. I didn't care. I would have walked the distance to Tjimahie if I had to.

"Slow down. We have to get off our bikes at the corner," Tjeng cautioned me.

I gave him a quizzical look.

He nodded toward the Japanese guard. "We have to bow."

"I won't."

"Yes, you will," Tjeng said sternly. "That's what they want, and that's what you'll do. What do you hope to gain by defying them?" He slowed his bicycle to a stop, got off, and bowed to the soldier.

Obediently, I followed Tjeng's example. Behind my gesture, I tasted the bitter disgust of the occupied and dominated.

We passed through crowded streets, stopped, bowed whenever we passed a Japanese sentry, but finally we left the city behind, bicycling on open country roads. It almost seemed like 1938 instead of 1942, but I couldn't allow myself the luxury of daydreams.

When the gates of the old Dutch army base finally came into view, armed Japanese soldiers with tense, unhappy faces stood in clusters around the entrance. Their dark slit eyes were like burning coals as they watched Tjeng and me approach.

"Don't look at them!" Tjeng whispered. "Remember what my mother said. Just bicycle and talk as if you don't care about the camp."

Through the bamboo slates of the compound I could see moving shadows. Just shadows. My heart pounded in my temples. I wondered if one of them could be my father.

"Don't stare at the fence!" Tjeng ordered. "Just talk. So Henriette, it's nice to see you back in Bandoeng. How's your family?"

"My family is fine." I shouted, then paused, waiting for someone from beyond the bamboo prison to interrupt. Nothing happened. No voices. I continued. "We're here for a visit. We're taking *Ibu* back with us to Oengaran." We purposely used the native term for mother instead of the Dutch *Oma*.

"That's nice. It will be better for her there," Tjeng answered. We circled the grounds twice, repeating our conversation, but no prisoners interrupted.

Other people arrived, circling the camp in the same way. Some on bicycles, others on foot. They all spoke loudly to each other and occasionally, I heard a voice from beyond the bamboo utter a loud "Yes" or "No" or "I'm fine."

Still hopeful, Tjeng and I began a third trip around the compound.

"So, Henriette, you're back in Bandoeng. It's good to see you," Tjeng shouted.

"Yes, my family is all fine. We're here from Oengaran to pick up my *Ibu*." From the corner of my eye I continued to search the shadows that moved within the compound.

"Will you be staying long?" Tjeng continued.

"I don't know yet. I—" I stopped short, as I thought I recognized a voice from within! I listened.

"Yes, I'm feeling well today, Piet. How are you?" The raspy, but familiar, voice said.

"My clothes are dirty, but I've had enough to eat," the other voice answered.

I threw my bicycle down and ran to the fence. Skipping over the shallow gutter that surrounded the compound, I tore violently with my fingers at a small hole in the bamboo.

Tjeng tried to stop me, but he was too late.

"Papa, Papa, are you there? It's me, Henriette. Are you all right?" Through the hole in the bamboo I could see the pale, sunken-eyed, bristly face of my father.

"I'm fine, fine," Father whispered. "But, go away. It's not safe to come here." He put his lips to the fence, and I forced my cheek close, to receive his kiss. At once I heard retreating footsteps and he was gone.

Out of nowhere a guard appeared at my elbow. He grabbed me roughly by the arm. "What are you doing?" He demanded in broken Malay.

"Nothing. Really. Please let me go," I pleaded as I tried to twist myself loose from the steel fingers that held me.

The Japanese soldier stared at me with cold, hard eyes. "Who are you looking for? Your boy friend?"

"No. No—my father." I admitted, burying my face in my free hand and breaking into loud sobs. "I just wanted to see my father."

"We are leaving," Tjeng said, taking me by the shoulder. "We do not want to make any trouble. Please, sir," he said bowing lower than usual to the soldier. "She is just a young girl wanting to see her father. Just like a daughter you might have."

I stole a look at the soldier. His eyes softened momentarily, and his vise-like grip released me. I fell like a lump of jelly to the ground.

"Go home," he said. "Do not come back. Do you know what we do to prisoners whose family become a problem?"

I shook my head. I looked back down at the ground. He took a step toward me. I could see his black dusty boots just inches away. I held my breath, bracing for the worst, expecting him to strike, kick.

"They are beaten, pushed up against the barbed wire fence and left in the sun to bake for hours. Or they are made to kneel on small pebbles until their knees bleed and the stones grow into their skin."

A cold sweat poured over me. I trembled without being able to stop myself.

"Do you want that for your father?"

My head moved slightly back and forth, but it no longer felt connected to my body. Black patches danced before my eyes, and the sound of the soldier voice began to fade.

"Do you?" The guard called, from what seemed like far away. Then steel fingers dug like claws into my cheeks. He forced me to look up at him. I could feel his stale breath on my face, and the bitter taste of bile crawled into my throat.

"Do you want that for your father?"

"No," I whispered, my faintness driven away by the pain his digging finger inflicted on my cheek.

"Then go home, and never come back." He strode off, leaving Tjeng and me to catch our breath.

"Come on, Henriette, let's get out of here."

"At least I know Papa is alive," I murmured, willing the strength back into me. My hands still shaking, I wiped my face with the hem of my dress. I massaged my cheeks. All I would allow myself to feel was the gentle brush of my father's kiss.

Slowly I pulled my bicycle up off the dusty ground and we started back to the city. I pushed hard on the bicycle pedals, the pressure helping to drive away the weakness in my legs.

We rode in silence, while I savored the bitter-sweetness of having seen my father. I would never forget the touch of his warm dry lips.

"Life will never be like it was," I said to Tjeng finally. "I have to stop thinking it will."

"Of that, I too am sure."

"I'm going to stay here and look for a job."

"In Bandoeng?"

"Yes, there's no work in Oengaran."

"But where will you stay? We have taken in as many homeless as we can."

"I'll find a place."

"What will your mother say?"

"I don't know. I don't care."

We pedaled for a while longer, making our way once more through the crowded city streets. The city looked suddenly different. Now, I viewed shops as possible jobs. I considered neighborhoods and houses for a potential home.

"Thank you, Tjeng. Thank you for coming with me. I didn't know what I was asking of you."

When I returned to my grandmother's house, my mother, Aunt Anne, and *Oma* Van Zeel were in the living room. They sipped cold drinks, while huddled over an old picture album.

"Henriette! Where have you been all day?" Mother asked. She wore her stern, European, controlling look.

"To Tjimahie," I said, and watched her face change to shock.

"No, child, you didn't! That's far too dangerous." Aunt Anne said.

"I did. And I saw Papa!"

Mother dropped her glass. It shattered at her feet, the pink liquid making a sanguineous puddle on the tan colored tile.

"How? When?" Mother's eyes became pools of hope. Her back straightened and she made an effort to get up off the couch, then fell back. "Is he—is he all right?"

"I couldn't see much. Just his face." I sat down in the chair opposite her. "He looked pale. We couldn't talk. A Japanese guard came and Papa ran away before the guard knew who I was talking to."

"At least we know he's alive. Your father is strong. He's a survivor."

"Uncle Piet is all right also," I said, turning to my aunt. "At first I didn't recognize his voice, but I remember Papa saying his name."

Anne hid her face in her hands. "They'll be all right," she whispered. "They've got to be all right."

"Mama," I started, before I lost my nerve. "I'm going to stay in Bandoeng."

"What are you talking about?"

"I want to stay here and get a job."

"You can't. I have to go back to Oengaran."

"I know. I'm staying here by myself."

"That's ridiculous!" Mother's voice was cutting. "You just come home with me. I need you to help look after Angelica and the baby."

"No. Angelica doesn't need looking after, and Enna and Kokie are both there to help you with William. I'm staying."

"Where would you stay? How would you live?"

"I'll find a way."

EIGHT

BHAGAVAD-GITA

May 1942 Bandoeng

I threw myself into a cushioned chair, my dusty shoes sliding off my feet. "I can't find a job, *Tante* Anne."

She glanced up from the table-cloth she was mending. "It's only been a week or so. You'll find something." She took a few stitches, examined her work, then stitched on. "Have you tried the Staats Spoor? I heard they were hiring women."

"You mean the Rikuyu Sokyoku Railway Company?" I spat out. "You want me to work for the Japanese?" I poured a cup of tea from the pot sitting on the table, took a sip, then sat silently watching my aunt embroider delicate red flowers over a tear in the yellowed cloth. She worked slowly and methodically, examining both sides of the cloth after each series of stitches.

"Henriette, you don't know how long the Japanese will be here," Aunt Anne said, laying her work in her lap. "At this moment we are an occupied people. We have no choices."

"You think the Japanese will be here forever?"

"I don't know. I'm sure the natives didn't think the Dutch would be here for over three hundred years either. I'm just saying you have to look out for what is now."

"But Papa," I whispered, "and *Oom* Piet."

"I know," she blinked her eyes several times and I could see her throat swallow hard. "But there is nothing we can do for them. Now we must look after ourselves."

A clatter in the street and voices nearby made both of us hurry to the front door. I peeked out the window, careful not to be seen. A young woman, petite, with bronze skin and almost blond hair, stood on the veranda.

Aunt Anne peeked from behind me. "It's Teena," she said. "A sweet girl. She lives a few blocks from here."

"I'm so afraid," Teena cried, when Aunt Anne opened the door and bade her come in. In the street, two native boys with a dilapidated cart stood with a mattress, a rocking chair, a few pots and pans, and two suitcases. "I'm afraid of being alone," she sobbed. "They've taken my husband, and now they take my home, everything. What will become of us?" Her hand fell to her stomach and the small motherly bulge.

"There there," my aunt consoled. "We have room for you." She waved at the boys to start unloading the cart, as she guided Teena to the living room.

I followed, sympathetic. "Here, take some tea. It'll make you feel better."

Teena took it with shaking hands. "How can I live if I don't know where my Freddie is?" New tears flooded her cheeks. She put the cup down without taking a sip. "Rumor is that Tjimahie is empty. My Freddie is gone. Gone, and I don't know where."

My aunt and I stared at each other, my fear reflected in her face.

"We'll take care of you," Aunt Anne soothed. "We'll all take care of each other." Aunt Anne clung as much to Teena for support as the young woman clung to her. "Come, let's take your things to your room. You can rest. Henriette, we'll put her in the room next to yours. Will you—"

The front door slammed behind me, as I rushed down the steps to the bicycle Tjeng had given me.

"Tjimahie." The name echoed in my head. "Tjimahie". Cold sweat formed on my forehead, neck, and upper lip. Was Teena's information correct? Did they move the prisoners? Where, where would they move them? Perhaps the Japanese realized their mistake and set Papa free. My legs felt weak, almost powerless on the bicycle pedals. I pumped harder, faster, until the hot breeze dried my cold sweat and the blood began to circulate in my body again.

The memory of my previous experience haunted me, but I pushed the ugly images away. I had to go. I had to see for myself.

The ride to the camp was endless. Planted rice paddies flashed by in a blur. Horse carts and other bicyclists disappeared in a confused whirl. My eyes were riveted to the road. All I saw was the path that led to my father.

As the entrance to the camp came into view I pedaled faster, holding my breath. Then my feet fell from the pedals and the bicycle rolled to a halt. I clung to the handle bars for support, nausea creeping up from my stomach, to my chest, where it sat heavy on my heart. The camp gates stood wide open. Nothing moved inside. Not one shadow passed the bamboo fence. There were no visible prisoners. No guards. I stared, desperately trying to comprehend what I saw. Where was everyone? Where was my father?

"What do you want?" A rough voice startled me.

"I— I—nothing, I don't want anything," I responded, in a whisper. I found myself staring into the cold eyes of the same officer who had held me so tightly when Tjeng and I had first visited the camp.

The muscles in his jaw relaxed slightly. He sighed, a glimmer of sadness jetting across his narrow black eyes. "They are gone."

"But my father. He is half Javanese. Maybe they released him."

"We released no one. They are all gone. Shipped off."

"To where? Please, where have they gone?"

The guard lifted his chin, his jaw twitched, the muscles tightened. "Go home," he whispered through clenched teeth, then turned and walked away with slumped shoulders.

I looked at the bamboo fencing, and touched my cheek where I could still feel my father's kiss. I closed my eyes and tilted my face toward the heavens, silently begging for an answer. The tears I could no longer control streamed down my face. "Why? Why is this happening to me?"

The gathering rain clouds made no answer. Banana leaves swayed in the breeze and birds chattered. Nature had no response for my agony.

A *sri-gunting* bird, with its long scissor-like tail and wings spread wide, flew over head. The shadow made me think of *Garuda*, the mythical bird of the Hindu god, *Vishnu*. I wanted the giant creature to sweep down and save my father and me from this nightmare. Stories of the *Ramayana* and the *Mahabharata* crashed forward from the misty past.

The *gamelan* orchestra's hollow percussion sounds coupled with the rhythmic deep gong, filled the night air, signaling the beginning of the performance. I cuddled closer to my father, and he put his arm around me.

A drum announced the entrance of the first shadow. The plain white sheet came magically alive.

"That's Bima," my father said.

I recognized his shadow too and knew that the story would be from the *Bhagavad Gita*.

The *dalang* began his story telling. "Bima, wanting to win the war against the *Sujudana* was in search of the special waters in which he should bathe to give him strength."

"I don't know this story," I whispered.

"Shhh," my father held a finger to his mouth. "This is a good one."

"I will ask the guru where I can find the waters," Bima said, and the sound of the *gamelan* turned eerily deep and slow.

I knew Bima was doing the wrong thing. "No," I whispered to myself, but couldn't give him any advice.

The guru instructed Bima to go to the highest mountain. There he would find the waters he searched for, and as Bima's shadow climbed high, the guru laughed to himself. "Stupid Bima, now for sure the *Korawas* will be rid of you. The two giants meditating on the mountain will kill you for disturbing them."

"Don't go," someone behind me said, and I squeezed my father's hand. Others in the audience hissed and booed at the guru. My father joined them.

The *gamelan* music crescendoed. The giants appeared, striking Bima. One, two, three blows. Bima staggered, nearly falling, then grabbed their heads and crashed them together.

I clapped wildly with the rest of the audience. We cheered. And then to my amazement, the giants turned into gods.

"How is that possible?" I asked my father. "Evil giants become gods?"

"If you believe too strongly in one idea, you can become a slave to it," my father whispered back. "The very thing you thought so good, can swallow you up." Then Bima shouted, angry that there was no special waters on the mountain. He returned to the guru.

"It was just a test," the guru said. "Just a test to see if you were worthy."

"Don't listen to him," I said.

"The magic waters are actually in the middle of the sea. There is where you must go."

"He's lying, he's lying," I said, along with those around me, but I had no idea where the special waters would be.

Bima headed for the sea, and the guru chortled under his breath. "The monsters of the sea will surely kill him."

As Bima stood on the shore, contemplating the water, a tiny figure in his own image appeared. The creature slid across the sheet and bowed to Bima.

"If you want to see the magic, enter me," the tiny god said, pointing to his mouth.

Astonished but obedient, Bima entered the tiny mouth. "I can see the whole world in here," Bima shouted.

Everyone around me nodded in agreement. "Ahh, yes," they all murmured.

"Papa, I don't understand."

My father leaned close. "The power is within Bima. You must look within yourself for strength."

I felt my heart grow, as Bima emerged the wiser.

The *gamelan* music crescendoed, dipped, then drifted into eerie silence. The hypnotic night came to an end, as the puppet-master fell silent. The sheet returned to its blank nothingness, and the *gamelan* music evaporated into the misty darkness.

The audience applauded wildly. Then, taking with us the inspiration of Bima's journey, we departed with the others.

"So, did you enjoy the performance?" My father asked, as we each pulled out flashlights to avoid the pot holes and the deep rain gutters.

"Oh, yes."

"We have incredible strength within us, Henny. Always remember that."

Did my father know how true those stories were? I brushed away my tears. I would dig deep into myself, find my strength.

Slowly I turned my bicycle around and pedaled home. "Home," I muttered, "where is home?" I rode back toward the city, blinded by recurring tears. I had never felt so lost, so uncertain, so abandoned. I didn't know whether I felt more anger, fear, or hate. Emotions consumed my insides, with no hope for release.

Rain fell, gently washing the salty tears from my face. The smell of wet dirt mingled with the sweet fragrance of moist grasses and wild foliage. My cotton dress clung to my body. The rain soothed away the afternoon humidity, taking with it my naivete.

Like the shadow puppets locked safely in their carrying case—away from human sight—I locked away my pain. The gold serpent bracelet, pinned in my pocket, tapped gently on my right thigh with each up-stroke of my leg. It reminded me of Saitem and it gave me courage. Aunt Anne was right. There is no sense in worrying about yesterday or tomorrow. There is only today, now.

NINE

RIKUYU SOKYOKU

Parking my bicycle with the many others, I nervously entered the main building of the Rikuyu Sokyoku Railway Company. The familiar halls were devoid of Dutchmen and humming with Japanese, but otherwise appeared the same. I looked from one corridor down another, not sure which way to go.

"Nona?" Someone called.

I turned to find Samsu, my father's friend, standing beside me.

He bowed his warm greeting.

I returned the gesture. "Samsu." I smiled. "It's good to see you."

"You have grown into a lovely young lady. I almost did not recognize you. What are you doing here?"

"I'm looking for a job. Papa is a prisoner, somewhere—we don't know when he'll be home."

Samsu's smile faded. "Yes, I could have guessed."

"Can you help me find a job?"

He hesitated, pulling thoughtfully at his hairless chin. "Perhaps. Come, we will see what I can do. I will take you to see Mr. Yamacura. He is in charge."

I followed Samsu to an office I had visited with my father years ago; although nothing had changed physically, it appeared grayer, colder, sterile.

A young Eurasian girl sat at a desk, smiling behind sad eyes. At Samsu's request, she disappeared momentarily through a door at the far end of the room. Upon her return, she motioned us to enter.

Mr. Yamacura stood beside a neat desk, looking out the window. He was not tall and wore the same khaki-colored military uniform as the other Japanese soldiers. Large sweat stains made dark circles under his arms and in the small of his back. His black boots were spotless, and when he turned around his eyes were calculating.

Samsu and I bowed. My heart pounded in my chest and I couldn't think of what to say or do next. Thankfully Samsu spoke for me.

"My niece is looking for a job," he said.

Mr. Yamacura looked me up and down, making sucking sounds on his teeth. He walked slowly around the desk, approaching me from behind.

I stood motionless, too afraid to look at him, but smelling his approach.

"Do you speak Japanese?" He asked in broken Malay, his face suddenly in front of me, staring into my eyes, his voice surprisingly gentle.

A whisper of a 'no' blew from my lips.

"Do you type?"

I shook my head.

"I believe the ticket office at the bus division needs help," Samsu suggested.

Mr. Yamacura looked from Samsu back to me. "Yes, I believe you are right. They do need help." His thin lips curled into a smile. He walked to his desk. "Are you good with numbers? The job requires some bookkeeping."

"Yes, I can do that. I was the top in my class."

He contemplated me a moment longer, then bent over his desk, and scribbling on a scrap of paper. He handed the note, written in Japanese, to me. "You begin tomorrow."

"Thank you," I bowed, feeling stiff and awkward, afraid and a traitor.

I arrived at work just before 7:00 a.m. Mr Yamacura made it clear that punctuality was imperative. I joined co-workers, a mixture of natives and Eurasians, waiting in the street.

Promptly at seven o'clock a Japanese official led everyone in the Japanese national anthem. I moved my lips, but even if I had known the words, I wouldn't have sung them. And when I was obliged to bow in the direction of Japan and its imperial ruler, I did so with hate in my heart. After this display of respect to Japan, I followed the example of the others and performed *taiso,* a form of Japanese calisthenics. Armed soldiers watched making sure we complied.

When the crowd dispersed, I hurried to the central office of the railway station and presented Mr. Yamacura's note. A native co-worker showed me to my office, a small but airy room, on the second floor overlooking the main street.

"Starting tomorrow," the man said in Malay, "you will go three mornings a week to Japanese language classes." He paused, seemingly to enjoy my shock. "There are no exceptions," he answered my stare. "Your superiors must be addressed in Japanese, and be careful not to speak any Dutch. It is not permitted. It is as if the Dutch were never here." He spat out the word, "Dutch", making me keenly aware of his resentment to the past colonialism. "Do you understand?"

I detected the condescension in his voice, but nodded. The man, probably with no more than an elementary school education, now enjoyed a new-found power. He, like many other natives, had been given a sense of self-esteem by the Japanese. For a moment I wanted to run away, but there was no place to run, and no one to console me.

I bit my lip. "Thank you. I will do as you say."

A few weeks later, Samsu poked his head into my office. "Is everything all right?"

I looked up, happy to see a friend. "Yes, I didn't realize I would be digging bomb shelters and learning Japanese, but I'm fine. The work keeps my mind busy. It prevents me from thinking too much about what I have no control over."

Samsu smiled. "You have grown in many ways. You are no longer a child."

"No," I agreed. I had lost that cherubic childish look. I looked down at my shrunken waist, and thinning arms. "No, and I'm not the Dutch girl I used to be. Just look how brown I've become."

Samsu laughed. "Now you are willowy and graceful, like a young *Sita.*"

I could feel a blush creep into my cheeks. *Sita* was my heroine from the *Ramayana*. She was a princess, loving and gentle, and her *Rama* loved her beyond all else. To be compared to her was the highest compliment. "I hope I have her wisdom."

"Your father took care of that." He said, smiling with fatherly eyes. "Let me know if there is anything I can do for you."

"Thank you. I'm happy just knowing you're near."

Samsu nodded, then closed the door quietly behind him.

I stared after him. "Papa," I cried softly, the lock-box of pain momentarily opening.

TEN

BUDDHA

As the weeks slid by, life took on a routine: work, waiting in ration lines for rice, talking of old times in whispered corners, staying indoors after dark, and praying that the Japanese wouldn't take our home. Another young mother with two children joined us, and Teena had to share a room with me. It was a livable arrangement, but in a chance meeting with my Aunt Nora at the open market, I eagerly accepted an invitation to live with them. The family had relocated from Djokjakarta to Bandoeng just before the Japanese invasion. Their hope was that Bandoeng's landscape would keep the Japanese out.

"Yes, many thought that," Aunt Florence agreed when I told her of my leaving.

"But your mother was happy knowing you were with us," Aunt Anne said.

"It's for the best," I answered. "Teena's baby is due any day now and she will need the space."

That night, at the home of my Aunt Nora and Uncle Kees, I slept securely beside my cousin Marie, as we had done when we were children. It seemed like only yesterday when we played at the Borobudor.

"The jungle seems intent on swallowing up this temple," Uncle Kees said, pulling bushes aside, as we made our way on foot from the clearing where our cars were parked. Marie, Angelica, Jantje, and I hurried along the dirt path to the steps of the decaying temple.

"Look how big it is!" I gasped, as we stood looking up at the moss-covered stones. From a distance it had not looked so large, a mere speck. But now, before me loomed a tremendous structure of nine superimposed terraces. It formed a pyramid, with steps ascending as if to the heavens.

"Do people still pray here?" I asked my Uncle Kees, when the adults had caught up with us.

"Not any more."

"They say it is haunted," Marie whispered, opening her black eyes wide.

"Spirits? Humph, I don't believe in spirits," Angelica said, with a smug look.

"I do," Jantje said, his eleven-year-old eyes large with excitement. "Let's go up and see if we can find one."

"Can we climb to the top now, Papa?" Marie asked. "I'll show Henriette the interesting points," she quickly added.

"Yes, yes, of course, but be careful. These steps are very old, slippery, and uneven."

Laughing and chatting, we started up the terraces. Angelica and Jantje immediately raced for the top. Marie and I felt ourselves too mature for such childish games. We were sixteen. Systematically we walked the temple, one terrace at a time. Marie explained that I should look at the terraces in threes, because each set of three symbolized one distinct spiritual phase.

Circling the three lowest spheres, we saw examples of good and bad deeds, in the earthly life of human beings. The remnants of intricate stone carvings depicted Buddha in his worldly princely state, enjoying himself in an island scenery filled with tigers, elephants and monkeys.

Marie and I scrutinized the carvings and tried to decipher their meanings, but we couldn't stifle our giggles over Buddha's more earthly temptations—exotic, big-busted women, mounds of food, palaces. On the second sphere we enjoyed examining the variety of carvings depicting later events in Buddha's life, and finally his renunciation of all human desires.

We continued our ascent, until we reached the highest terrace. I was not prepared for the view or the feeling that overcame me. Coming out of a dark passageway, I suddenly came into the light. From this height I could see three hundred and sixty degrees around. The bright blue of the sky contrasted with the deep green of the encroaching forest. Pale-green rice paddies glimmered in the distance. And beyond the paddies the landscape turned purple as Mount Merapie with its pale plume stood beside Mount Merbabu, its mate, both appearing as descended gods. I thought surely this was the closest I would get to a Hindu Nirvana.

I stood in the center of the entire temple, next to a solid bell-shaped *stupa* of about thirty meters, looking down from where I had come. There were seventy-two smaller bell-shaped *stupas* encircling me. Marie explained they were repetitions of the symbol of the Holy Mount Meru and each *stupa* housed a Warjrasattva Buddha, a symbolic Buddha who has attained enlightenment and returned to earth to help others find the way.

"Come look," Marie said. "You can see the Buddhas."

I followed my cousin. Inside the stone lattice-work of the *stupa* was a life-size statue of Buddha, its eyes closed expressing a look of peace, and its hands pressed together in prayer.

"They say, if you can touch the Buddha it will bring you good luck," Marie said. She put her arm through the square hole and tried to touch the statue.

"Can you touch it?" I asked, watching her twist and contort her body in the hopes of making her arm longer.

"No, I can't feel a thing. You try."

I thrust my right arm through the hole. I twisted and turned, but without success.

"Wait, let me try the other arm," I said. I tried the left arm, my cheek flattened against the warm stone. I twisted and turned my arm, the gold serpent bracelet dancing with each move. "I can touch it! I can touch the elbow. Just barely, but I can feel it! Marie, try with your other hand."

Marie tried her left hand. "I can't. I can't feel a thing. I guess you will have better luck than me," she sighed, only half serious.

"It's just a silly superstition."

"Of course."

Marie and I rested in the shade of a *stupa,* talking about school and friends and laughing about boys, until we were joined by the rest of the family.

"Ah, here you girls are," Uncle Kees said, sitting beside us. "So, has Marie told you all about the Borobudur?"

"Yes, she has. She's a good teacher."

"Good," he smiled.

We all breathed in the Nirvanic air, while resting and chatting of old times and how we all were grown.

Soon a breeze began to blow and large billowy clouds drifted overhead. The afternoon sun lined the clouds with silver, then they turned dark, and in the distance we heard the rumble of thunder.

"We'd better start back to the car," Aunt Nora said.

"Oh, can we stay a little longer?" Marie pleaded. "Please. Just a little longer?"

"We'll meet you at the car," Uncle Kees answered. "Not too long, now."

Our parents started down the steps, quickly absorbed in their own discussion.

"At dusk, when the shadows cover the temple, is when the spirits come out," Marie whispered.

"Have you ever actually seen one?"

"No, but I believe in them." Marie looked slowly over her shoulder.

"Me, too, " I admitted. "*Oma* Saitem believed in spirits."

The clouds formed black shapes above us, and as the

shadows grew yet darker, the four of us stopped talking. We sneaked about the terraces searching for our own private spirit. Suddenly Angelica screamed. The shrieks came from the fifth terrace. Marie, Jantje, and I raced toward her.

"I saw a spirit! I saw one!" Angelica gasped.

"Where? Where?" Marie and I shouted.

"Back there in the corner!"

Marie and I moved in the direction Angelica's finger dictated. Slowly we turned the corner. We both screamed, jumped back, and ran toward Angelica and Jantje.

"What did you see? What did you see?" Jantje demanded.

"Something was there! I don't know what, but something was there," I panted.

"Come on," Jantje took charge. "We have to look again."

The four of us walked on tiptoe. Not one of us spoke. Jantje and I took the lead. As we came to the corner, Jantje took my hand, and stepped bravely around.

"Just like girls!" He accused. "Nothing! Look! There's nothing!" He threw up his hands in disgust. "Nothing!"

"But we saw it! It was really there," Marie insisted.

"It was," Angelica said. "And I didn't believe in spirits." She paused for a moment, looking at me. "Maybe *Oma* Saitem was right."

Rain began to fall. At first the tiny drops merely bathed us gently, but soon large drops formed into a downpour, as if the spirits intended to drive us away and have the temple for themselves. On the smooth, slippery steps we hurried cautiously down from the Hindu Nirvana, and raced for shelter with our parents.

For the first time in months I relaxed and felt the protection of family. My aunt and uncle lay in a room down the hall, asleep. Jantje breathed quietly in a bed across from us. I listened. The sound of his and Marie's even breathing sang me to sleep.

The days passed slowly and although my white armband with its single red orb was a constant reminder that I worked for the enemy, life went on. I found new security in knowing that my aunt and uncle and cousins had sworn to stay together, and that I now was also a part of that pledge. The closeness of the family and the togetherness of the community made life endurable.

Late one afternoon the radio announced that individuals living in the area which included ours, whose identification card read *Belanda,* were to report to a "protection site" within the following week.

"I'm not letting you go alone," Uncle Kees said to Aunt Nora, as we sat discussing her card. "I'm going with you."

"I'm going too," said Jantje.

"Me too," Marie said. "We promised to stay together."

"You're all going into the camp?" I asked.

"It's not a camp." Aunt Nora told me, patting my cheek. "It's for my own protection. My papers say I'm Dutch."

"But *Oom* Kees, Marie, Jantje, me, our paper don't say *Belanda.* What will they do with us?"

"We will be protected as long as we are together," Aunt Nora assured me. "They will give us food. If we go early in the week, we can get one of the better houses in the "protection site". Jantje, tomorrow morning, you get a *dokkar* to help us move."

I listened quietly. I knew my aunt had no choice, and I understood the desire of the family to stay together. I too didn't want the family to separate, but the image of Tjimahie was too vivid. The shadows of the prisoners moving behind the bamboo enclosure were like *wayang.* They could not move without their *dalang,* and I would not let the Japanese control me.

"Henriette, you shouldn't come with us," my aunt said, as if reading my thoughts. "Your mother may need you."

"But Mama, she can't stay alone in the house." Marie squeezed my hand.

The following day I waved good-bye to my aunt, uncle and two cousins. I watched as the *dokkar,* piled high with their belongings, clip-clopped away to the "protection site". I felt confused and wanted to run after them, to stay with them, to feel taken care of, but something told me 'no' and that inner voice was strong. Instead, I strapped my small suitcase on the back of my bicycle and went in search of a new place to live.

Mrs. Troel was a odd lady, short and square, with a round dark face, framed with a mass of tight graying curls. Her nose was typically wide, but her eyes were unusually large, black, and piercing. She was generally quiet and kept to herself, but now and then she spoke to me about *goona goona*, a form of voodoo on her home island of Ambon. She suspected many people of using *goona goona* against her, but I often heard strange mutterings emanating from Mrs. Troel's bedroom, and wondered if she practiced the mysterious art against the Japanese.

Though curious, I ignored Mrs. Troel's strange behavior. Saitem had taught me that patience and tolerance were often better teachers than accusations made from ignorance. And after all, Mrs. Troel seemed harmless enough; and her room was cheap, and close to work.

"Those disgraceful women!" Mrs. Troel growled as she came out onto the veranda where I sat reading by myself.

I looked up to see where my landlady directed her anger. It was at the large, bamboo-fenced house across the way. From within the fencing we could hear peals of laughter, giggling, and men and women talking. Through the bamboo slats, if I concentrated, I could see Japanese men playing badminton in their underwear. And "those women" were with them.

"Whores!" Mrs. Troel waved her hand. "Dirty whores!" She turned to me. "I bet they are not going to starve. The Japanese are plotting to starve us all, you know." She made her eyes wide, so that her pupils danced in a pond of white. She looked like a native mask used in ceremonial dances. "Do you see it too? Do you?" She brought her face close to mine. "There is less and less food. Less rice, less vegetables, less everything. Do you see it? Not just for us, but the natives as well. Those who do not have land to grow their food will starve. Starve, I tell you."

I noticed it too. It was not only rice and vegetables that were scarce. Milk, yeast to make bread, eggs, spices, tooth paste, toothbrushes, and soap were impossible to find. For weeks now, I brushed my teeth with the bristles of a crushed palm nut, sprinkled with salt. I could not yet bring myself to use the powdered charcoal that many were forced to use as toothpaste.

I watched with Mrs. Troel as two trucks pulled up in front of the house across the street. Laughing Eurasian women, aided by several Japanese, climbed into the dusty flatbeds.

"Humph," Mrs. Troel snorted. "It is probably time for their check-up. Any sick or diseased ones will be thrown aside, like bad hens."

The trucks roared away. "The good ones they will keep for whores or send off to be 'comfort women'." Mrs. Troel spat over the veranda then went back into the house, mumbling and chattering to herself.

I closed my book and brushed a stubborn lock of hair from my face. It felt greasy. It needed a good washing, but I had very little soap left. I hoped that Mustapha would soon send word that he had a new batch of soap ready and I could luxuriate in washing my hair.

I considered myself lucky to have located Mustapha, a toothless native, who made the precious commodity in a steamy shop not far from where I worked. The soap had a sour disinfectant smell, but it was better than nothing, and Mustapha always let me know when it would be ready. Once word got out, it disappeared fast.

"Mustapha has soap for you," the messenger boy at work told me a few days later.

On my break, I hurried to the workshop, only to find that Mustapa had not sent for me and there was no soap ready.

Puzzled I returned to my office and sent for Hassan.

"Why did you tell me the soap was ready if it wasn't? I went to see Mustapha—"

"Oh—oh—not Mustapha. Mustapha. That man outside—there." Hassan walked to the window and pointed down to a street-side shop across the way. Seated on a stool outside was a man.

"I don't know him!" I said, scrutinizing the figure. He looked young.

"He seems like a nice fellow," Hassan said, with a devilish smile. "He said to tell you he has nice-smelling soap for you."

"Nice-smelling soap?" I looked back down at the stranger in the street. "He has nice-smelling soap?" I squinted, trying to get a better image.

Hassan smiled. "Would you like me to take him a message?"

I took time to think, staring at the figure below, then looking back at Hassan. "How did he know where I worked?"

"He pulled me aside and pointed you out to me this morning. I told him where you worked. I hope I have not offended you."

I looked back down at the young man. "No, you haven't offended me. Tell him I get off work at four o'clock, and I will stop by then."

Hassan bowed, leaving the room with a smile still on his lips.

I watched from the window as he lazily crossed the street. A foreign feeling of excitement stirred within me. My cheeks felt hot.

The hours before closing crept by, but when at last four o'clock arrived, I hurried down the stairs like an excited school girl. I made an attempt to fluff my wavy hair that now hung limp with need for washing. I pinched my cheeks for color, and smoothed my faded floral-print dress over my shrunken waist and bony hips.

Casually, but with my heart dancing like a butterfly, I walked across the street, dodging the onslaught of bicycles, *betjaks,* and *dokkars.*

The young man stood up as I approached. He was taller then I imagined, and very good looking.

"*Selamat sore,*" he bowed. "I'm Mustapha."

"*Selamat sore,*" I returned shyly. "My name is Henriette. Nice to meet you." He was not European. And definitely not native. He had olive skin, hazel eyes, and a distinguished nose, unlike the short flat noses of the natives. He was tall and lean with strong hairy legs that protruded from his khaki shorts. His sun-darkened arms were lean but muscular and his long fingers were smooth, expressive as he talked.

We made polite small talk, both of us observing the native custom of not coming to the point right away.

"The messenger said you have nice-smelling soap," I finally stammered.

"I do. Come in, come in."

I followed Mustapha into the dimly-lit store where rows and rows of shelves were stacked high with colorful batiks, sandals, candles, glassware, and rugs.

Behind the counter stood an elderly man, tall and lean like Mustapha, with a thick, well-groomed, graying beard.

"*Salam Aleikum,*" he greeted, in a language I did not understand, but recognized as Arabic.

I bowed to greet him.

"Welcome to my store," he continued in Malay.

"This is my father, Mr. Banawei," Mustapha introduced.

I smiled. "Good afternoon."

From the back of the store another young man approached.

"And this is my brother, Darsan."

Darsan bowed silently.

I tried not to show my bewilderment at the difference between the two brothers, Darsan, short and dark, with brown, almost black eyes.

"Let me show you the soap," Mustapha offered. From a cupboard tucked behind the counter, he pulled out a small package.

Through the coarse wrapping paper I inhaled deeply. I couldn't stifle the gasp that sprang from my lips. "Oh!—What a wonderful smell!" I took another deep breath, then saddened at the thought of how expensive the soap must be. "How much is it?" I asked, enclosing the bar in both my hands as if to capture its delicious fragrance.

"We have a special price today," Mustapha said, as he handed me two more bars of the sweet-smelling soap. "Three for ten cents."

I couldn't believe it. I wanted to ask how that was possible, but feared he might change his mind. I paid the ten cents quickly. "Thank you."

"Thank you."

"Look what I have, Tante," I announced my good fortune to Mrs. Troel. I addressed her as Tante, because it was the custom of the Ambonese to call everyone either uncle or aunt, and I didn't want to offend the strange woman.

"Let me see," the old woman crooned. Her big eyes narrowed and a furrow of wrinkles formed on her forehead.

"Smell it. It smells wonderful." I handed her a bar of the soap.

Mrs. Troel put the soap to her large wide nose and inhaled with a snort. "You can't use this!"

"Why not?"

"Where did you get this?" She took a step backwards, clutching the soap to her chest.

"I bought it from a man."

"Ah—this man. He may be trying to do *goona goona* to you." She hid the soap behind her back, away from my reach.

"No, no, he's a very nice young man," I protested. "Give the soap back, please."

"Humph," Mrs. Troel snorted again. She threw back her head, her nostrils flaring like an unhappy water buffalo. "I will try it first and see if anything happens." Without another word, she disappeared with the bar of soap.

Silently I scolded myself for confiding in the suspicious woman, but it had taught me a lesson. From now on I would keep my affairs to myself.

The next morning, I purposely rode my bicycle slowly past Mustapha's shop, but there was no sign of him outside. Throughout the day, I looked for him from my office window, but to no avail. In the afternoon, when I left work, I looked again. Still no sign of Mustapha, and I was not so bold as to walk in and look for him.

For the next three days, I kept a watchful eye over Mustapha's shop, but he never appeared. I tried not to admit my disappointment, dismissing the soap incident as merely that, and nothing more. I forced the handsome young man out of my mind, remembering that Saitem never dwelled on anything she could not control.

Henriette and Mustapha as a young couple.

ELEVEN

MUSTAPHA

Aunt Menny was a tall, big-boned woman like the Dutch farmers, but with dark hair and an olive complexion. Accidentally coming across my name in the registration office, she said she hurried right over. "Family should be together," she said. "Come live with me? It's better than living with strangers."

What a blessing. I hadn't known Aunt Menny very well growing up, but here she was ready to help me. I longed for friendly companionship and family. I was tired of eating breakfast and dinner by myself. Without hesitation, I accepted my aunt's invitation. Leaving the world of the *goona goona* would not be a hardship, but to my disappointment, I soon discovered that life with Aunt Menny was not what I had hoped for. In the small room we shared, I felt more a slave than a companion. Dirty dishes were left for me to wash, and Aunt Menny somehow never found time to scrub down the dusty floor, or stand in the long rice-ration lines. I never knew what she did with her day. She didn't confide in me.

It didn't take me long to realize I had made a grave mistake, but now I found myself trapped. Housing was increasingly difficult to find, and horror stories of young women disappearing, their whereabouts completely unknown, frightened me. I determined it best to stay with Aunt Menny.

Hello, Henriette." A voice surprised me while I shopped at the Chinese grocer.

I turned and found myself looking into Mustapha's handsome face. "Hello," I managed. Then getting control of myself I said, "I haven't seen you for a while." I wanted to sound casual, but felt unsuccessful. His sleepy hazel eyes, his thin lips, his black hair that fell into his face sent prickles down my neck, and I needed to look away. I busied myself with selecting from the sweets a *pisang bol* and *kueh mangkok,* to hide the blush I felt creeping into my cheeks.

"I've been out of town visiting family."

My heart bounced, and I prayed he would not notice my nervousness. I nodded, searched desperately for something to say. "I enjoyed your soap."

"I have more if you need it."

"Does it still have a special price?" The half joking comment slipped out before I could stop myself.

His already smiling face brighten more. His sleepy eyes opened and revealed stars. "Yes, it still has your special price."

I returned his smile, then walked over to select a bunch of green beans. I felt tiny beads of sweat form at the nape of my neck and roll down to collect on the collar of my dress. I picked through the old beans, gathering a handful of the youngest. He picked through them with me, surprising me with his eye for selection. "It's difficult to find fresh food these days," he said, tossing his few beans in with mine.

We moved to the cashier, paid, then walked out together, dodging the first cloudburst of rain, as the humidity gave way to cool dampness. Huddled under a bamboo awning our conversation blossomed and we talked until the downpour became a drizzle. He was easy to talk to, charming, and had a quick smile. We talked of my job and his store, of pre-war days, and where we lived as children.

Bicycling home, I delighted in a new sense of excitement. I had found the courage to invite Mustapha to an office entertainment evening, at the *societeit,* and he had accepted without hesitation. I touched the gold bracelet in my pocket. The spirits were looking after me.

"You're late," Aunt Menny called from the front door, even before I came to a full stop.

I clenched my jaw. My aunt thrived on treating me as if I were a child, making me accountable for every minute. "I ran into a friend," I explained. "He and I are going out tomorrow evening."

"He? Who is he?"

I sighed. "His name is Mustapha." I purposely kept my answer short.

"And who is this Mustapha? Where did you meet him?" And what makes you think—"

"I met him a few weeks ago," I interrupted, as I came up the steps. "His family owns a shop near my work."

"Son of a shop owner? What is he? Chinese?"

"No. He's an Arab, if you must know. "

"An Arab! No niece of mine is going out with an *Arab Djin-Djin!* " Aunt Menny snapped. "You will not go. You promised to crochet me a new blouse. I've waited for weeks, and it's still not finished." Her masculine frame towered over me, as we stood facing each other on the small veranda. Her hands were firmly planted on her hips and her face was contorted in an ugly scowl.

I stood silently with my mouth half open, not believing the derogatory comment she used toward Arabs. I scolded myself for again saying too much, but regaining my composure, I lifted my chin, and told her I was not asking for permission. That said, I walked into the house, slamming the door behind me.

"Henriette, you come here!" I heard my aunt through the door. "You come here. I'm not done talking to you."

The next morning Aunt Menny turned a cold shoulder to me. I went off to work, hoping she would calm down by the time Mustapha came to pick me up that evening.

Time, however, did not assuaged Aunt Menny's disapproval, and she was horribly cold and silent when Mustapha arrived.

"Why do you live with that woman?" Mustapha inquired, when we were safely away from the house.

"At first I thought it was a good idea. Now, I'm stuck. And I'm afraid the next place might be worse."

"Why don't you ask at work? Find some young people to live with." He took my elbow and guided me over a gutter in the darkening streets. "Make sure you see the place before you commit and don't share a room if you don't have to."

We followed the gathering crowd into the *societeit* building. For now, I was content to enjoy the entertainment. I would worry about housing later. The last time I had gone out in the evening, I held my father's hand. Now an exciting young man walked beside me. I would not allow anything to ruin the evening.

The large assembly hall, exclusively attended by Japanese officials and their designated guests, hummed with anticipation. Japanese of all ranks, some with painted Eurasian women on their arms, many alone, filled the hall. I felt a little guilty taking part in the Japanese social event and if Mustapha hadn't accepted, I wouldn't have gone. But the island's best performers were invited to participate in the program, and I yearned to feel and hear a pre-war world.

Mustapha and I took our seats just as the lights dimmed.

The *gamelan* orchestra began to play and the deep rhythmical gong, accenting each musical sentence, seemed to electrify parts of my body. I felt as if in a trance. I stole a sideward glance to see if the handsome young Arab was really there, or if I were dreaming.

Mustapha sat erect, his hands folded in his lap and his eyes riveted on the stage. His straight black hair, at first slicked back, already hung sheepishly over one eye. His nose looked as though it had been shaped by Greek gods, and his chin too, I noticed, was strong. But his skin looked soft and delicate, and the expression on his face was kind, gentle, almost like the the *Warjrasattva* Buddhas at the Borobudur.

The orchestra, joined by a singer whose sing-song voice pierced through the reality of war, placed me in another time. A misty euphoria spread over me. Mesmerized, I watched the graceful dancers. They were *Rama* and *Sita* incarnate. I found myself lost in their slow, rhythmical movements. Their elongated fingers accentuated not the beat of the *gamelan* orchestra, but the shadowy pauses in between. It was as if to draw attention to the less obvious in life, to what lay hidden in the shadows.

TWELVE

WILLIE, LUKE, AND BOBBY

While making my way among the throngs of people at the end of my work day, I heard someone calling my name. I turned, but could find no one I recognized.

A young woman waved and rushed to catch up to me. "I'm Dora," the woman said, catching her breath. She was tiny, with a high forehead and straight black hair that she tied severely off her smooth moon-shaped face and let fall down her back. "Hassan pointed you out to me. I understand you're looking for a place to live." Her brown eyes were dull, her mouth expressionless. "I can offer you a room, but it's only a converted garage."

I looked at her critically. I didn't want to make another mistake. "Are there others?"

"My sister and her two children, and another friend."

Her eyes betrayed nothing, but I thought I caught a slight hesitation.

"My house isn't far from here. You could come and see if it suits you."

We found our bicycles, and I followed Dora. Divorcing ourselves from the crowd, we made our way down quieter streets.

"The Chief of Police lives here," Dora pointed out, as we passed a colorful yard with a well-kept cottage-like house. "And my home is just up the street."

The walls of Dora's house were gray and dirty and the yard wild, with a mind of its own. Only a small section of flower bed, under the front window where I could see a woman and two small children working, was groomed.

As we rode up, the kneeling woman turned. Smiling, she brushed the dirt from her hands and approached us, the children following behind her.

"This is my sister Dien," Dora introduced. "This is Henriette. She's come to look at the garage."

Dien nodded, her full lips curving pleasantly, her eyes slowly moving from me to her sister, then back again.

"Nice to meet you. And this is Anneke. She's two. And Piet is almost four."

We stood awkwardly for moment, as if waiting for something. The two sisters exchanged looks. I knew a secret language passed between them. They no doubt had to be careful of who they rented to as well.

"Please, come in." Dien finally said. "We'll show you the room."

We entered the garage from a separate door at the front of the house. A slight odor of mildew suffused the area, but otherwise, it appeared comfortably arranged with a cot, a reading light, and a place for my meager belongings.

"This takes you into the main house," Dora explained, showing me through a door at the far end of the garage.

I stepped inside, scanning the interior. Nothing suspicious caught my eye. It was dark, but then, no one threw their windows open anymore. Along with the need for blackout security at night, most people were unsure of who their enemies were and preferred to avoid nosy lookers.

The house appeared neat and tidy and from where I stood, I could see two servants busy in the kitchen and in the back yard, a small vegetable garden grew in straight rows beside a stone well.

"Where are you living now?" Dien asked.

"With my aunt, but—we don't get along."

"You don't have any other family in the city?"

"Some, but their homes are full, and I was looking for a place with younger people."

Another curious look passed between the sisters.

"We can only offer the garage," Dien smiled, "but of course you may join us in the house whenever you like. We really try to be a family."

"What do you think?" Dora asked.

"It's fine. It's just—" I looked at the two smiling children. Surely nothing could be wrong if these children looked so happy.

"Just, what?"

An image of Aunt Menny came to me. "Nothing. I'll take it."

After an ugly scene with my aunt, I let myself into my new home through the garage door. In the darkening room I turned on the reading light. It cast an eery yellow glow around the garage and for an instant I didn't feel apart of this world. I imagined *Oma* Saitem's jasmine infiltrating the room, obliterating the smell of mildew. I imagined my father kissing my cheek.

"Can I come in?" A voice startled me as if my ghosts had come alive. A young woman peeked around the corner of the interior door. "I'm Marie, one of your house-mates."

"I'm Henriette."

"Yes, Dora said you were coming."

I placed my few articles of clothing in the chest of drawers. "I brought my ration of rice, and some fruit and vegetables."

The girls' eyes lit up. "We'll take them to the kitchen. Minah can prepare it with the rest, unless you'd rather not."

"That would be fine." I handed Marie the groceries.

"When you're done putting your things away, come join us in the house. We're reading post cards and talking."

"I'm done now," I laughed. "It's not like I have a lot." I pushed my empty overnight bag under the cot, and followed Marie.

Dora and Dien were sitting in the living room, a room in the center of the house with no front windows opening from it. Beside them, a dim light barely revealed their faces.

"Settled in?" Dora asked.

"Yes."

"There's. There's something we want to tell you."

I slid into a chair. My stomach tightened. My senses had been right. There was something.

The girls eyed each other.

Dien nodded.

"It's—" Dora began, but before she could say any more, three shadows materialized on the wall in front of me and I spun around, ready to jump from my chair. Three young men stood behind me. No, boys. Eurasian boys.

"It's about us," one of the boys whispered. "They haven't told you about us."

"We didn't know how to tell you," Dora apologized. "Willie, Luke and Bobby are only seventeen. They live in the third bedroom."

I stared. I knew the danger in hiding men, and the Japanese considered anyone over fifteen a man.

"Swear that you won't tell anybody," Dora pleaded.

I took a deep breath and let it out slowly. My stomach relaxed.

"I'm sorry. Did we frighten you?" Luke asked, stepping forward with the others to sit down.

"A little."

The boys were pale and thin, with eyes that looked out from dark sunken sockets. I wanted to cry, scream. An image of my father passed before me. If I couldn't help him, I could at least help these boys.

"I swear. I won't tell a soul." I looked from one grateful face to the other. "But how do you keep from being discovered?" I whispered, afraid that even the walls might hear. "The Japanese patrol regularly and what if they search the house? And the Chief of Police!" I turned to Dora. "You said he lives down the street."

"The Japanese are not so smart," Luke said. "We can hear their squeaky boots a house away. When we hear them, we hide in the well."

"The well?" My glance went to the dark pit in the back yard.

"We've chipped steps in the rock," Bobby answered.

I shook my head in disbelief.

"And having the Chief of Police down the street makes things even better," Dora snickered, her dull eyes coming alive. "Who would be so stupid as to hide men in their home with the police so close by?"

"What about the servants?"

"The two of them have been with me for a long time," Dien answered. "They can be trusted."

The servants' loyalty was easy to understand. At first, many natives thought the Japanese were their liberators, but they now didn't particularly trust them. They too, saw the food surpluses diminish and heard the rumors of young native girls being abducted. Many natives stayed faithful to their Eurasian masters, content with the security of familiar people and a place to stay.

"There is one problem," Willie, the tallest of the boys, spoke up. "We don't have registration numbers. That means we don't get any rations. The girls have been sharing their food with us. Even the servants have been sharing."

"I'll share."

THIRTEEN

ALL INDIA RADIO

I walked into the cool darkness of Mustapha's store and sat down beside him on a lopsided three-legged stool. He sat hunched over the counter, an issue of *National Geographic Magazine*, some of the pages worn and frayed, spread before him. The radio was softly tuned to the local station.

"What's new?" He asked, smiling.

"I took your advice. I found some girls to move in with. It's working out nicely. Thanks for the push." I didn't mention the boys. I agreed with Dien, the fewer who knew the better, the safer.

"I'm glad." Mustapha glanced back down at his magazine. "Some day this war will be over. Then I'm going to travel, see the places like the ones in this magazine." His long fingers tapped the page. It lay open to pictures of grass covered mountains, icy blue lakes, and giant redwood forests.

He looked like a little boy with a big dream. His lazy half-closed eyes seemed to take him to that distant land as we stood there.

"Is it time yet?" Darsan called.

"For what?" I asked.

"For—" Mustapha began.

"Our news station," Mr. Banawei answered, approaching from the back with a tray of tea and cookies. He put the tray down, seating himself beside me. "How are you my dear?" He patted my arm.

"Fine, thank you. But why all the excitement over the news? It's always the same. The Japanese are winning victory after victory.

"Ah, that's what they want us to think," Mustapha said. "But," he winked at me. "Darsan, watch the front and give me a sign if the *kempetai,* the Japanese secret police," he explained, "or any strangers come." He stood up, fine-tuning the radio, his long fingers gently fingering the dial. "I've located another station," he whispered, not taking his eyes of the radio. "It's broadcast in English. It's the Allies News Service from All India Radio in New Delhi." Static hissed then diminished slightly.

"English? How's that possible? Isn't your radio sealed?" I leaned toward the wall, looking at the back of the radio.

"It's sealed. Those Japanese don't miss anything. Registered and sealed a long time ago, like everybody else. But by luck, or maybe magic, I somehow am able to pick up the Allies News Service, when Radio Tokyo is relaying their news to the Japanese military here. According to the other station, the Japanese are not having such an easy time of things."

"I don't believe you." But I leaned closer, trying to listened in between the static. I could only catch the Japanese station coming in.

"Honest," Mustapha said, when I looked at him with doubt. "I found the station a few days ago. Just by chance. The reception is poor, but someone out there wants us to know the truth. There is much more happening then we know."

"You're taking a big chance. You could be arrested, shot," I whispered, automatically look toward the entrance for spies.

"We're careful."

His father nodded his agreement.

"You know what we've heard?" He stopped adjusting the knob for a moment. "The Japanese are not winning as many victories as they claim, and the Americans have started to counterattack."

I thought about this possibility. The only source of information I had was the local paper and the local radio station, both censored and operated by the Japanese. Sometimes I heard rumors from the Chinese, but I could never be sure if their underground news was true or not.

"Are you understanding the English correctly?" I asked. "Maybe they're just more rumors."

Mr. Banawei gently slapped Mustapha on the back. "My son is excellent in English. There is no mistake. The Japanese are fooling us. They never mentioned the American raid on Tokyo on April 18, or the heavy losses the Japanese sustained in the Battle of the Coral Sea. They only say they are in control and winning."

Mustapha went back to his tuning. "Shhh," he leaned close to the radio. "I found it." His eyes were wide and alert, excited.

Still full of static, I could make out an English broadcaster.

Darsan, who had been rearranging shelves at the front of the store, while keeping watch, could not resist and joined us. He couldn't understand English, but he listened anyway, watching his brother's eyes carefully, then running to the front of the shop to scan quickly up and down the street.

"They're talking about a battle at Midway," Mustapha interpreted.

I tried to listen, but couldn't catch all the words; the station was faint and my English poor. Mr. Banawei and I sat quietly as Mustapha plastered his ear to the radio, giving us translated bulletins.

"The American's won the battle at Midway," Mustapha whispered. "First the Japanese thought they won, but then a third wave of American bombers surprised them."

"Do they say anything about how bad the Japanese naval losses are?" Darsan wanted to know.

"Very bad." Mustapha kept his ear to the radio. The sound began to fade, and the static grew more intense until the station faded to an inaudible hiss.

When tuning didn't return the station, Mustapha moved the radio one way, then the other. Nothing. The local station relaying the daily news broadcast from Radio Tokyo could be heard. The English voice was drowned out completely.

Mustapha turned off the radio with a quick snap. "I wish we could learn more."

"My father said we masses never know the whole truth," I said.

"Your father is a wise man," Mr. Banawei nodded. "But come, let us sip tea while it is still warm. Let us forget the war for a while."

I took a sip. It was good and strong, unlike the weak brew I drank at my place.

"Doesn't your wife ever come into to the store?" I asked, assuming she had prepared the tea and cookies. I had long been curious about Mustapha's mother, but lacked the courage to ask about her.

Mr. Banawei laughed. "I'm not married."

I felt my face flush. "I'm sorry. I didn't—I mean I thought maybe—"

"No need to be sorry. For a time I was married to Darsan's older sister, but she found she had another calling, and left. She left Darsan as well, but by then, Mustapha and he had become too close to be separated anyway."

"And she doesn't care to see her own son?"

"She isn't my mother!" Mustapha answered.

I was confused and must have looked it for Mustapha then explained that his mother lived in Lawang along with his two sisters and two brothers. His natural father had lived there as well, until he passed away a few years ago.

"I don't understand. Mr. Banawei isn't your father?"

Mustapha laughed. "I guess it does sound confusing."

"You see," Mr. Banawei explained, "It all really began in Jeddah."

"Saudi Arabia?"

Mr. Banawei pulled at his beard. "Many years ago, as you know, Saudi Arabia was part of the Ottoman Turkish Empire. Mustapha's father and I worked for the administration. I received information of British arms shipments to some of the Arab tribes. There were a lot of arms, a lot of money that came into play for the purpose of undermining the Turks, who were battling the British and the Russians. I could see it was a no-win situation. I begged Mustapha's father to leave, but he insisted on remaining loyal to Sherif Hussein. I fled Jeddah with my mother. By the time it was obvious that Hussein was being manipulated by the British, the situation was beyond help and only by the will of Allah did Mustapha's family escape to Java as political refugees." Mr. Banawei paused, no doubt images of the past flew into his thoughts. "Mark my words, the Middle East has not seen the worst. Imperialism, or Colonialism, whatever you want to call it, always takes its toll." He looked into my eyes, then into Mustapha's. "Even here, the trouble is only beginning. One people cannot look down on another people without expecting trouble."

I was reminded of *Opa* Pierre-Jacques. This was what he had foreseen. He knew about colonialism. He knew what it would do. He tried to warn me.

"After his family arrived," Mr. Banawei continued, "they had a difficult time financially. My mother and I lived next door and because we had an established business, when Mustapha was born, we offered to take care of him. He has remained with us ever since."

"So you and Darsan are not really related?"

"Not in blood, but he is more then a real brother," Mustapha gave Darsan's shoulder a squeeze. "He was my friend and playmate. If it wasn't for him, I would never have finished school."

Mustapha and Darsan smiled at each other like school boys keeping a secret. "Darsan and I grew up together. We did everything together. Even after his sister left, and I don't remember her very well, Darsan and I were best friends. I wouldn't go to school unless he went also. *Abuya* had to send both of us."

"*Abuya?*"

"*Abuya* is Arabic for father." He looked to Mr. Banawei and I could see the love and admiration he had for this man, this adopted father.

"I am lucky," Darsan said, pouring more tea. "Now I have an education that most natives do not."

"But I don't understand why you didn't go with your family when they moved," I said to Mustapha.

"Because," Mr. Banawei answered, "Mustapha was only three and attached to us, as we to him. When they found wealthy suitors for his sisters, then twelve and sixteen, the family moved away. We begged them to leave Mustapha with us."

I was thirteen when *Abuya's* mother died," Mustapha said. "I had always thought of her as my mother, but *Abuya* explained everything. After that, I took the train to acquaint myself with my family. They are wonderful people, and I visit them often, but *Abuya* will always be my father."

I sat silently absorbing Mustapha's childhood. I could sympathize with his mother's hardships. I could almost see her, baking Arabic pastries and sending the two older brothers out to peddle them. But I could not understand how she could marry off her daughters for financial security, and I could never understand abandoning a child, her child. My children would come first. I would never leave them behind.

"Enough of this," Mr. Banawei slapped his hands on his knees. "I am hungry. Come, Henriette, it is late, join us for dinner."

I didn't want to impose, but Mr. Banawei was insistent, so I graciously accepted, secretly happy there would be more food at home for the boys.

I followed the three men to the back of the store, where a door led to their living quarters. The pungent odor of curry assailed my nostrils, as I walked past colorfully carpeted sofas to a long dining table. I stood staring as if in a dream. White pearly rice took the place of the bug-infested reddish-yellow *kampung* rice that my ration card bought. Chicken coupled with potatoes in a rich curry sauce, and vegetables swam with tofu in a spicy soup. A hunched native woman, gray and wrinkled, bowed as we entered, then exited through a back door. I had not seen anything like this since before the war.

"Do not be deceived, my child," Mr. Banawei said, as he bade me eat. "It is only sometimes that the black market is so good to us."

FOURTEEN

PIANO

"On the days I visit Mustapha," I told Dora and Marie as we bicycled home from work, "if I'm not home by six o'clock, you can give my share of the rations to the boys. You don't have to save it for me."

"I hope Mustapha offers you dinner often," Marie said.

I laughed. I liked being with Mustapha, and could easily make excuses to visit him daily, but I was afraid of enjoying anything too much. I feared that such thing wouldn't last.

"What's Mustapha like?" Marie asked.

"All we know is that he's handsome," Dora said.

"He didn't like school much, but he taught himself English, and Arabic, plus he speaks many of the island dialects. He reads a lot, mostly American magazines and books, like the *National Geographic*, Zane Gray novels; and I've seen several Karl May adventure books."

Dora wrinkled her nose. "A bookworm."

"I love his eyes," Marie said. "He always looks like he's dreaming."

He did have that quality, I agreed, and wondered what he dreamt about.

At the well we washed the sticky heat of the day from our bodies before going inside. Dien and the children had prepared glasses of coconut milk, sweetened with tiny globs of young coconut meat.

"How was your day?" Dien asked, helping little Piet to pass out the drinks.

"The usual. Nothing great," Dora answered.

"I got asked out by a Japanese officer," Marie said.

I gasped. "What? Why didn't you say something earlier? What did you tell him?"

"What do you mean? I said no, of course!"

"I told you something like this would happen," Dora scolded. "You have to be more careful. Don't smile. Don't talk. Make yourself ugly. Do you want to get picked up for a 'comfort girl'?"

"Calm down, Dora," Dien said, patting her sister's shoulder. "She can't help it if she's pretty. Marie is careful."

Dora took a deep breath.

Marie hugged her. "I'm sorry. I didn't mean to upset you."

"I guess you can't help it." She gave her a forgiving hug. "Just please be careful." She picked up the mail and began shuffling through it.

"But you know," Marie said, "not all the Japanese are bad. Some of them aren't any different from us. They have feelings too."

"You're a fool if you believe that," Dora said, then held out a post card to me. "Henriette, your mail."

I looked at the card written in Malay. "It's from my mother." I read through the lines. "She says she sold my piano. I guess she needed money."

"What use is a piano to you now, anyway?" Dora consoled.

"None," I answered, but I envisioned the days when my father listened to my practicing. I began to hum softly to myself, seeing my fingers glide over the ivory and ebony keys.

My father, with smiling eyes, stood beside the dark mahogany piano, watching me. His image seemed so real, it was as if he were beside me that very moment.

"Hey, you," Dora nudged. "Stop dreaming. It's getting dark and it's our turn to check the house."

I got up and together we walked around the outside of the house, making sure no lights were visible. Everything had to be covered with dark paper; openings at the roof line, windows, cracks around and under the doors, even the key holes. We made small adjustments with meticulous care. We wanted nothing to do with Japanese patrols, and the possibility of air raids at night were always in the back of our minds.

Only when we were sure that we had secured the house did we allow Willie, Luke and Bobby out of their bedroom. Then, in the dark silence of the living room, we sat together in a circle, sharing the same food we shared day after day. Minah and Suli diligently sorted out the bugs from the stale rice and served the meager portions with boiled yucca root, shredded jack fruit or any other vegetables, either grown in our tiny garden or cheaply purchased. We washed down our meal with weak tea or coffee.

FIFTEEN

KING DJOYOBOYO

That was fun!" Eddie said, wiping the sweat from his brow. "I'm glad the Japanese still allow us to play soft ball."

"And we almost beat you today," I teased.

"It wasn't that close," Eddie laughed.

"We would have won if Marta hadn't pulled something in her neck so she couldn't hit in the last inning. She always hits a home run."

"That was bad luck." He seemed to remember something and a broad smile broke across his thick lips. "Did you go to the *wayang* show last night?"

"No."

"Marta's neck," Eddie laughed. "Her neck reminded me of the skit Semar did."

"I don't like to go to the *wayang* shows anymore." My seriousness made Eddie stare at me. "The Japanese use them to propagandize."

"I know, but much of the time, we end up laughing at the Japanese. Like last night. Semar, Petruk, and Gareng were exercising, like the Japanese make us do every morning, with their *taiso*." Eddie tried to keep a straight face. "You know how big and fat Semar is? Well, he was telling the people how good exercise is for them, and then he got stuck." Tears formed in the corners of Eddie's eyes. "Really, Henriette, it was funny. Everyone laughed. Semar twisted his head and got it stuck in one position and Petruk had to help untwist him."

"I don't like Semar giving in to the Japanese," I answered dryly.

Eddie wiped the tears from his eyes. The smile on his round almost black face disappeared. "Semar is watching over his Java. It's good for the people to laugh. They're not laughing with the Japanese, they are laughing at them. You should go, see for yourself."

"Japanese security is everywhere at night. They make me nervous."

"It will not always be like this, Henriette." Eddie said. "Many are talking again about the prophecies of King Djoyoboyo."

"What prophecies? Who is King Djoyoboyo?"

"I'm not surprised you haven't heard of him. The Dutch never wanted his name mentioned either."

The sudden hostility in his voice took me by surprise. "I don't know what you're talking about."

"No, I don't suppose you do. You're *Indo,* not native and your Dutch roots and education did not show you what lurked in the shadows of pre-colonialism."

"I thought we were friends," I said. "How can you hold against me what I don't know? Tell me about King Djoyoboyo."

Eddie stood quietly contemplating me, then deciding he trusted me after all, he began to explain. "According to an ancient legend, this king lived in Kediri around 1157. That's according to the Javanese calendar. He was a very unusual king, not only a good warrior and administrator, but also a gifted poet and astrologer."

"Get to the point. What did he have to prophesy?"

"Like a prophet," Eddie continued, "the king received inspiration from God, and predicted the whole history of Java. It is all beautifully written in Javanese *pantun.* His predictions were so accurate that the Dutch authorities banned his writings, and I'm sure the Japanese have done the same."

"What did these predictions say?" He had me curious.

"He predicted," Eddie looked mysteriously around before he began in a barely audible whisper. "He predicted, that a 'yellow peacock' from the northeast would come to drive away the 'white buffalo with blue eyes' from our island." Eddie crossed his brown muscular arms and nodded his head, as if he had said something of great importance.

"Eddie, what is that supposed to mean? Yellow peacocks? White buffaloes?"

"Shhhh," Eddie placed a calloused hand over my mouth. "Trust me, do not mention this in front of the Japanese."

"Well, what does it mean then?" I kept my voice low.

"The yellow peacocks are the Japanese. The white buffaloes with blue eyes are the Dutch. Translated, that means that the Japanese will come from the northeast and drive out the Dutch."

"So if that's true, why should the Japanese ban his prophecy? Those predictions don't threaten them?"

"The predictions go on." Eddie moved closer. His thin eyebrows were arched and his already large brown eyes became larger. "They also say that 'black ants will lay eggs on fine ashes.'"

"And what does that mean?" Eddie's riddles were beginning to annoy me.

"It means, that the island people will achieve independence through revolution."

My eyes must have grown large, for Eddie nodded his head with satisfaction, "ah, now you are surprised."

"Eddie, you must be careful of what you say and to whom. The Japanese might kill you, and those natives who believe you might start fighting we don't need."

"The fighting will come anyway. There are experts who have studied the King's writing. I hear even Sukarno believes it."

"But Sukarno acts as if he's friendly with the Japanese. For all we know, he could be their puppet."

"I think Sukarno has an agenda of his own."

SIXTEEN

BEDUK

I sat on the train heading for Semarang. The slow chug-chug reminded me of a year ago when mother and I went to Bandoeng in hopes of finding Father. So much had happened in a year. So much had changed. I was eager to see my mother and sister. Eager to tell them about Mustapha. Eager to take my childhood wood *jepara* box back to Bandoeng with me. Unless disturbed, it still contained *Opa's* candle, *Oma's lereng* print batik, my sketch pad, and Tjeng's gift— a book of Javanese *Pantun*. Could the flowery words I had such difficulty understanding be King Djoyoboyo's?

From Semarang I rode by oxcart up the mountain. There were many more Japanese then I remembered, but I bowed to the soldiers. I answered their demanding questions in Japanese, which put a proud and arrogant smirk on their face and a bitter taste in my mouth, but it made them feel some kind of misplaced comradeship with me which kept me safe.

Approaching my house I imagined my father coming out to greet me, hugging me, kissing me. I pictured my mother happy, busy with a ladies' luncheon, and Angelica helping her. My heart leapt and my breath caught in my throat, as the front door opened, but it wasn't my father. It was Angelica.

She looked taller, thinner too. Beside her stood a little boy, William no doubt. When she recognized me, she swung William up into her arms and rushed down the steps of the veranda.

"Henriette! What are you doing here?" She wrapped her free arm around me.

I hugged her back. I did not realize how much I missed her. "Just visiting," I said. We stared at each other, taking in the many changes. At sixteen, Angelica had an aura of maturity about her. People grew up quicker in wartime, I guessed.

"And look how William has grown," I said, taking his little hand.

William retreated and hid his face in Angelica's neck.

We laughed.

"Is everything all right here?"

"It's all right. Nothing special. We eat. We sleep. We watch the children. It's boring. What about you? You've changed. You look different."

I rubbed a roughened hand over my arm. "The days of Boy running behind us with a parasol are gone," I said. "But I'm fine. And some things in my life are pretty terrific." I winked and gave her a mysterious look.

"Tell me."

But we had reached the house and I teased, keeping her in suspense a little longer.

"Mama, Henriette's here," Angelica called, as we walked up the steps.

Mother came from around the side of the house, at first slowly, then quicker. For a moment she was speechless, then she threw both her arms around me, giving me a quick hard hug.

"Are you all right? Are you home for good? Tell me." She looked me critically over. "You've let your skin get dark."

I laughed at her old concerns, explaining I was home only for a visit. I sat down in one of the veranda chairs, my father's rattan rocker. I inhaled the coolness and freshness of the mountain.

"Let me clean up real quick," Mother said, brushing dirt from her hands. "I was working in the garden. And Angelica, you go change William first."

Angelica sighed but did as she was told. Some things never change I thought, but felt comforted by the pre-war sameness.

I ran my hands slowly over the smooth finish of the chair, my fingers feeling for a lost time.

"Come on, Henny," my father called. "I need your help."

"Why don't you let Kromo drop the fruit off for you." Mother suggested. "That basket of papayas is too heavy to carry all the way up the hill."

"Not if Henny and I carry it between us."

My father believed in exercise and he did not like using the car if he could avoid it.

"Why don't you come with us," he said to my mother. "Mr. and Mrs. Klomp like visitors. Their boys have been in school in the Netherlands for two years and they're lonely."

"She offers us tea and cookies," I said. "And last time they gave us a big basket of their tangerines to take home. Remember how good they were?"

Mother waved her hand at us. "You two go. I'm too old for all that exercise. Besides, I have some ladies coming by to discuss a luncheon we're planning."

My father and I lifted the basket between us and headed up the mountain road. Villagers and passersby greeted us with smiles. Half-naked native boys waved cheerfully from where they played between the tall bamboo. Men and women glanced up from their gardens of *cassava* and yams. Older natives, resting in the shade, managed toothless smiles and bowed ceremoniously.

"*Selamat pagi,*" a young man called, from a seat on a narrow, rough-constructed bridge, that spanned the gully between the road and the cluster of huts.

"*Selamat pagi,*" my father and I returned the greeting.

"Please, come and cool yourself with a drink of water," the young man offered, indicating his hut.

"Come, Henny," my father urged, as he put aside the basket of fruit.

"But I'm not thirsty."

"Neither am I, but we mustn't offend him by refusing. He has nothing but water to offer us."

I followed my father. The man proudly lead us to a large wooden rain barrel stationed outside his humble home. Resting next to the barrel, a hollow coconut shell served as a communal drinking cup.

"Please, drink," the man offered.

I scooped out a cupful of water, then gasped. Tiny insects squiggled and wiggled in the water. I tugged quietly at my father's shirt.

"Papa, we can't drink this water. Look!"

"Mosquito larvae," my father told me calmly. "Here, let me show you." He took the coconut scooper from my hand. "First you have to blow the water gently. See? All the mosquitoes in the barrel move to one side. Then, before the larvae can swim back, you quickly scoop out the clean water." My father demonstrated once again, then drank down a cupful.

With some trepidation, I followed his example, managing a sip or two.

The native smiled with obvious appreciation.

Returning to our fruit basket, my father selected a ripe papaya and gave it to the man.

"*Terima kasih tuan,* thank you," he bowed to both of us.

By the time my father and I reached the Klomp's plantation, I was genuinely thirsty, hot, and sweaty.

"You poor dears, walking all that way," Mrs. Klomp crooned. "You two sit down here and we'll have something cold to drink."

We sat down in a shaded outdoor patio, where a gentle breeze sang through giant red hibiscus plants. From where we sat, I could see the wide expanse of the tangerine plantation. Bright green-leafed trees with decorations of brilliant orange lined the hillside.

The servant boy was sent to fetch Mr. Klomp, and he arrived just as the servant girl brought in a tray of cookies and glasses of my favorite drink, *stroop soesoe*. While I sipped eagerly at the sweetened milk with rose water essence, Mr. and Mrs. Klomp talked of their sons.

"When will they be home?" My father asked.

"Not for another year," Mrs. Klomp answered, "but with Hitler on the move, I'd rather have them here now."

"There's nothing to worry about dear," Mr. Klomp said. "The Netherlands will stay neutral. All will be well with our boys."

Mrs. Klomp sighed and a tremor seemed to shake her body. She managed a weak smile and nodded. "Yes, of course, they will be fine.

I noticed the look of concern that passed between my father and Mr. Klomp. I wanted to ask what they knew about the war, but the distress on Mrs. Klomp's face stopped me.

For over an hour my father and I talked with the elderly couple. They showered me with treats and promised to have more goodies the next time I visited. They wanted very much for both of us to stay for lunch, but Mother was expecting us, so we graciously accepted the basket of tangerines and made our way back down the mountain.

"Hurry along, Henny. We're going to be late," my father said, when I began dragging my feet and allowing myself to daydream.

"How do you know?"

"Listen. You can hear the sound of the village *beduk* calling the Muslims to their noon time prayer."

I stopped to listen. From a distance came the deep sound of a drum.

"How can you tell they are calling Muslims to prayer?"

"Practice. Every village or town has a *beduk*. It's used for many things: fire, earthquake, volcano eruption; but I learned the call to prayers, because those particular drum patterns coincided with our Catholic prayer time—at dawn, noon, and evening vespers. Of course, it also became a convenient reminder of lunch and afternoon tea."

I laughed.

"So, we better hurry because you know how upset your mother can get when we're late."

My thumb slipped into a worn spot in the rattan, making smooth circular movements. The slamming of the screen door jarred me back to reality. Mother and Angelica pulled up chairs to sit with me.

"Did the Klomp's boys ever come back from the Netherlands?" I asked.

Mother looked at me, confused.

"You know? The Klomps? Up the hill?"

"Yes, I know. What made you think of them?"

"I don't know. Just sitting here, thinking of old times. Did they get back?" I took a sip from the fruit juice.

"No. Their sons never came home. Who knows where they are."

I felt sad for them, but maybe their sons were somewhere safe. "How is *Oma* van Zeel?"

"Fine. She's resting."

"And everything else?"

"Well, not as good as it used to be, but we manage." Mother shifted in her chair. She looked from me to Angelica. An awkward smile pulled at her lips. "The trees give us plenty of fruit. We still have enough to give baskets away to the natives. Poor people. They're having a hard time too."

"And you should see how large our garden has become," Angelica added.

"It gives us plenty of vegetables." Mother shifted again. She threw a curious look over her shoulder into the house. Something bothered her, and I was about to ask, but Angelica wanted to know about my boyfriend, and Mother's eyes grew wide.

I felt my cheeks turn pink. "Well, sort of boyfriend."

"Oh? Who is this young man?" Mother asked.

"His name is Mustapha." But then I didn't know what more to say. Saying he was handsome, sweet, and kind, all seemed so ordinary. I took a deep breath. "He's very special."

"Is he cute?" Angelica wanted to know. "What does he look like?"

"He's tall." I held my hand above my head. "About so much taller than me. His eyes are hazel and dreamy looking. He's—"

"Mustapha?" Mother interrupted. "Has he always lived in Bandoeng? What's his last name?"

"Mama!" Angelica wanted to hear more.

"Well?" Mother ignored her. "What's his back ground? Do we know his family?" Her voice had become short, abrupt.

"No, we don't," I answered. I felt my stomach turn into knots. He's an Arab and—"

"Arab? No, no. I don't think I want you involved with an Arab." Mother waved her open hands before her face as if to wipe away any image she might have been conjuring up.

I didn't expected this from her. "You haven't even met him."

"Arabs are a very different kind of people," she said, still shaking her head. "They're not like us. They're—well, they're foreigners. They have strange ideas, strange habits, strange food. I don't think you should encourage him. Your father would not approve."

"I think Papa would like him." I spoke through clenched teeth, but before I could plead my case further, Enna appeared carrying a whimpering infant.

"He's eaten plenty. I think he just wants to be with Mama," Enna said, placing the baby in my mother's lap.

I looked at the dark-haired, dark-skinned infant. His oriental eyes stared back at me. "Who's this?"

"Walter." Angelica glanced at Mother. "I thought you wrote Henriette about the baby."

Mother's mouth twitched. "It never seemed the right time."

"You took in another baby?" I asked, but the look on their faces said something else.

No one answered.

"This is your baby?" I looked first at the baby, then at my mother, then at Angelica.

"Yes," Mother answered.

"And who is the father?" I asked. An uncontrolled shaking began rocking the already-formed knots in my stomach. My fists closed tight, then feeling my nails dig into my skin, I released them.

"It's none of your business!" Mother retorted, bouncing the baby up and down. "There are things you don't understand. In war things happen. You don't know how, but they do. All you think of is taking care of yourself and the family. You're still—"

I cut her short. "I don't believe you! How dare you sit there and tell me I can't be interested in an Arab because Papa wouldn't approve. Do you think Papa would approve of this? How are you going to tell him about this?"

Angelica looked frightened, sitting round-eyed and very still. William clung to her.

Mother opened her mouth, but I gave her no chance to speak.

"Let me tell you something. If Mustapha asks me to marry him, I will. And you have nothing to say about it. Do you hear me? Nothing!"

My face felt hot and I could feel my neck veins pulsating. My breath caught in my lungs. I gave my mother my most disappointed glare, then ran off the veranda, to the stream in back of the house. I could feel the bile of disgust choking me. I sank to my knees in the cool mud, and cried into the river, my flood of tears carried off to the spirits.

"Oh my God. Papa, I'm sorry," I wept. I could not imagine what my father would say when he returned, and even worse, how could I tell Mustapha of my mother's shame. My shame.

SEVENTEEN
WEDDING PLANS

December 1944

"Y"ou're awfully quiet," Dora said, as she and I stopped our bicycles. "You've hardly said a word since you returned from Oengaran yesterday.

I shrugged my shoulders. "I'm just tired." I secured my bicycle in the decaying rack, and made my way to where other workers were gathering for the morning exercise.

"Are you sure it's not something I did?" Dora hurried after me.

I slowed. "No, it's not you. My visit home didn't go as well as I hoped, that's all."

Dora nodded in understanding and we continued on in silence.

We had almost reached our position in line, when I heard someone calling my name. I turned. Samsu was rushing toward me.

"I must speak with you, Henriette." Samsu bowed his greeting. "I've been watching for you," he paused, catching his breath. He glanced at Dora then looked back at me. "I've prepared a letter of resignation for you."

"Resignation? From what?"

"Your work."

I looked at Dora. Her round surprised eyes looked back at me.

"While you were gone," Samsu continued, "Mr. Yamacura promoted you. He's made you his personal secretary."

I thought of the sweaty man with the leering eyes.

"Henriette, this is not a job your father would want you to have." He lowered his head. "It is not just a secretarial job."

Hot flames licked my face. Sweat formed on my upper lip. The thought of a liaison with a Japanese made my stomach sour.

"Please, Henriette, I could never face your father again. Sign the resignation paper."

"What if I refuse the promotion? Can't we tell him I want to stay where I am?"

Samsu shook his head slowly. "I tried. He does not take no for an answer." He held the papers up to me.

"Sign it, Henriette," Dora urged.

"But how will I—"

"It doesn't matter. Dora took the pen and handed it to me. "Sign it."

I signed, fighting back tears of anger.

"I'll give it to Mr. Yamacura," Samsu said. "No need for you to be harassed." He waited for a moment, looking at me as my father might have. Then, without another word, he turned and hurried away.

"You did the right thing," Dora said.

"But what am I going to do?"

The loudspeaker hissed, crackled, then blared. The Japanese soldier's voice called the workers to line up. I backed away, while Dora hastened to her place.

"Will you be all right?" She called over her shoulder.

I nodded, continuing to back away until I stood alone, watching Dora and the others.

Slowly, I crossing the street to Mustapha's store. At my back I heard, *"ichi, ni,* one, two." I hurried my step, brushing the tears from my face.

Inside the store Mr. Banawei sat on his customary stool, behind the counter, sipping coffee and eating slices of crisp *salak,* his favorite fruit.

He motioned for me to join him.

Mustapha smiled and bobbed his head at me, but continued with his customer, a Japanese soldier. "These are nice cups. Look, I still have four that match." Mustapha displayed blue and white cups and saucers on the counter.

"I don't need cups. I need a bicycle," the soldier answered in a combination of Malay, Japanese, and hand gestures.

Mustapha smiled. "I told you, I can get you a bicycle, but you must wait a few days. But these cups —well—" Mustapha cajoled the soldier, his voice pleasing, his smile genuine. He demonstrated how the saucers could be used to keep the bugs out of the tea. Before long he had not only sold the set of dainty Delft-blue cups, but the teapot that went with them.

"My son is a good salesman," Mr. Banawei whispered.

"But I will be back in two days for the bicycle," the soldier said.

"I will have it, Mr. Kamezawa."

The soldier paid Mustapha, then took his package and marched out of the store, giving the two of us a nod as he passed.

"Good morning," Mustapha smiled, joining us. "He seems like a nice man. He wants me to teach him how the speak Malay better."

I made a face. "Humph, the Japanese."

"They're not all bad," Mustapha said. "Say, aren't you late for work?" Through the front door the station workers could be seen doing jumping jacks to the count of the Japanese drillmaster.

"I don't have any work. I resigned."

Mr. Banawei stopped chewing. He looked at me with one eyebrow arched.

I explained, desperately trying to control the tears that threatened.

"You did the right thing," Mr. Banawei reassured. "I know Samsu. He is a good, wise friend."

"But I don't know where else to look." I could feel my lower lip tremble and bit down to hold it still. I would have to figure out something. I knew that I could never go home again. I could never forgive my mother, and could not imagine what life would be like when my father returned.

In the silence, Mr. Banawei's eyes moved slowly from me to Mustapha then back to me.

"Forget about work. Marry my son and we'll take care of you." He offered the suggestion as naturally as if he had just offered me a cup of tea.

Mortified, I glanced at Mustapha, his face, the same color flush that I felt creeping into mine.

"I, I think if I were to get married, I would like to wait until my father returns."

"But that may not be until the war ends, and that may be a very long time," Mr. Banawei said. "Haven't you heard of the Hundred Years War?"

I couldn't bring myself to look at Mustapha. His silence was as embarrassing as Mr. Banawei's forwardness.

"I better go. If you hear of anyone who has work, please direct them my way."

Mustapha walked me to the door, but neither one of us said anything except a quick good-bye.

I gladly escaped to the street. How insensitive of Mr. Banawei to suggest marriage in such a manner. What if the thought had never occurred to Mustapha?

My legs felt heavy on the pedals of my bicycle. Marriage to Mustapha had crept into my romantic day dreams many times, but my father had always been there too. Still, Mr. Banawei was right. Who knew when the war would end? I could feel a smile spreading across my face, then wondered again what Mustapha's silence meant.

The next day, Dien and I were amusing the children outside, when Mustapha came up the street on his bicycle. Because of the small Turkish flag that flapped on his handle bars, I recognized him from a distance. My heart fluttered like a butterfly, but I composed myself enough to let him into the house where we could talk in private.

"Henriette," he began slowly. He took my hand in his. "My father is right. It could be a long time before the war ends or your father returns." He cleared his throat. "I love you." He cleared his throat again. "You must know that." He looked sheepishly into my eyes and took a deep breath. "Will you," he paused, "marry me?"

I felt the butterflies in my stomach spread their wings, rise to my heart, wanting to explode from inside me. Saitem was right. The spirits never close one door without opening another. I wanted to fly into his arms, but suddenly I remembered Mother. Would he still marry me, if he knew of my shame?

I slipped my fingers from his grip. "I have to tell you something." My voice faded and I had to force it out. "It's about my mother. You see, the last time I visited—"

"Yes, just a day or so ago."

"Yes, well, it seems she has had a baby."

"You mean she's taken in another child?

"No," I turned, took a few steps away. I kept my back to him. "I mean she's been with another man. She's had his baby." I spun around, facing Mustapha. My jaw clenched. My muscles twitched. I sucked in my lower lip, and crossed my arms in front of my chest, as if to shield me from the pain to come. I looked Mustapha in the eyes, waiting for him to say something.

When he didn't speak, I blurted out, "She's been unfaithful to my father. Don't you understand?" The tears spilled, and I turned my back again, trying to gather my strength.

Suddenly Mustapha's arms were around me. He turned me around so we looked into each other's eyes.

"I'm not marrying your mother," he whispered. "I'm marrying you."

For one startled moment I froze, then I threw my arms around his neck, and the tears of sorrow became those of joy.

"Does this mean yes?" Mustapha laughed.

"Yes! Yes! Yes!" I cried.

"For a moment, I was worried." He kissed the tip of my nose.

Then I remembered something else. "There is one other thing," I said, searching his face.

"What's that?"

"No other wives! I know you Muslims can have four."

Mustapha laughed.

It was agreed that the wedding would take place in Lawang, the small town near Surabaya, where Mustapha's mother and sisters lived. With relative ease, Mustapha was able to obtain travel passes from the Japanese military authorities, but train tickets to Surabaya were nearly impossible. It took him days before he was able to find two third-class tickets.

"Thanks be to *Allah*, we got seats," Mustapha said, waving the tickets.

"When do you leave?" *Abuya* asked.

"On the thirtieth! Are you sure you won't come, *Abuya*?"

"There will be plenty of time for us to celebrate. You two enjoy your family."

"I hope the family likes me," I said.

"Daughter, what is there not to like? I love you already."

"But I'm not Muslim."

"That is of no great concern," *Abuya* answered. "It is not forbidden for a man to marry outside the Muslim faith."

"And the woman may retain her faith," Mustapha added.

I was surprised.

"But," Mustapha continued, before I could say anything, "a Muslim woman must marry within her faith."

"Why is that?"

"Because the children are always raised in the faith of the father."

"That doesn't make much sense. How can a mother raise her children in the faith of the father, if she doesn't know it?"

"There is always the family to help," *Abuya* answered.

I felt a twinge of concern, but Saitem and Pierre-Jacques had managed. So would I.

"I know a little about Islam," I said. "My *Oma* Saitem followed some of the practices. She prayed five times a day, never drank alcohol, and didn't eat pork. She even made the servants hang their pork pan on a pole outside her kitchen."

Abuya smiled. "Islam is a very simple religion. Mainly it is important to know that we believe in one God and that Muhammad is his Messenger."

"Do you believe in other prophets?"

"Yes, of course. Abraham, Moses, and Jesus being amongst them. And we believe that every human being is created equal and born without sin, and that we are all accountable for our deeds on the Day of Judgment."

I pondered on what he had said about being born without sin. How different from my Catholic belief.

"Religions have many similar aspects," *Abuya* continued. "You have Lent and fasting days. We have the month of *Ramadan,* when we fast from food and water from sunup until sundown."

"Oh yes! I remember my *Oma* Saitem would celebrate its end with a fine dinner. *Eid,* she called it."

I almost laughed out loud remembering Saitem waving an ax-size knife, saying a few mysterious words, and then slitting the necks of two of her best chickens. Islamic law required the animals to be drained of blood, which Saitem carefully observed. But she did not discard the blood. Instead, she fried the clotted red blob and shared the delicacy with me. The chickens later appeared prepared the way grandfather enjoyed them, accompanied with a host of vegetables and a mountain of saffron rice. In one holiday, she managed to involve Islamic, Catholic, and her old animistic ways.

"See, my child. You know more then you think."

"Is it difficult to become a Muslim?"

"All that is required is a true and honest belief in the Islamic way. Then, in the presence of an Imam and witnesses, you pronounce the *Shahada:* 'I declare that there is no deity but *Allah* and Muhammad is his Messenger'."

"That's all?"

Abuya took a worn book from beneath the counter, "Understanding is important, before commitment." He opened the book. "This is the Qur'an, holy book of the Muslims. It is the last of the holy books to come to man. It is believed that God intended this to be a continuation of the religion already on earth. So you see, we accept everyone."

I looked down at the book.

"Sit closer. I will teach you."

December 30th came quickly. Mustapha and I picked our way through the dark rain-soaked streets to board our night train to Surabaya. Muddy puddles reflected the rising moon peeking out from behind lingering rain clouds. Throngs of passengers crowded the station, elbowing their way onto the train, but I was too excited to feel any annoyance. I was *Sita* and Mustapha was my *Rama*.

Except for the occasional appearance of the moon, we boarded the train in total darkness. There were no exceptions to the Japanese blackout rules. We maneuvered slowly through the stuffy cars, Mustapha carrying our one suitcase and me hanging on to a bag of *Abuya's* specially-baked pastries.

Searching for seats, we soon found the train so crowded that the only available space was on a platform between cars. Even here we were jammed with six other people. Mustapha placed the suitcase on the floor, end up.

"Sit on this," he told me. "You can lean against the wall. We have a long trip ahead of us."

"What about you?" I glanced at the other passengers who stood leaning against the walls.

"I'll stand next to you."

The small case barely sustained my weight, but with Mustapha smiling down at me, I was content. As the train pulled out, I felt only joy. The strictly-enforced blackout rules, calling for every train window to be tightly closed and covered with black paper, did not concern me. The heavy canvas stretched over the landing we occupied robbed us of fresh air, but I breathed in excitement and anticipation.

For hours the train made its slow dark sojourn through the mountains. My body responded rhythmically to the train swaying along the old tracks. I couldn't see the curving mountain sides or the lush jungle forests, but my past experiences painted pictures in my mind.

The hours ticked by. Conversation was scarce and there was nothing to see but darkness and the shadowy silhouettes of the other passengers. Occasionally, teeth or eyes were visible when a passenger jerked awake.

After a while, oppressive, stale, motionless air filled the tiny space. My back ached and my legs cramped. My thin buttocks pressing on the suitcase felt numb. I wished I could trade places with Mustapha, but he was too heavy for the suitcase and there was no place for me to stand, no place for me to stretch my legs, no place to put my hands except in my lap.

I sensed Mustapha's discomfort, as he placed one foot on the edge of the suitcase, leaning on his elbow to rest his back. I patted his leg, looking into his barely-visible haggard face. A gleam of white smiled at me, giving me new strength.

At dawn, as the train descended toward the junction at Kroja, blasts of tropical heat increased our discomfort. Sweat trickled down my face, neck, and back. To ward off motion sickness, a couple of the native passengers applied citronella oil to their foreheads and stomachs. The putrid odor hung in the airless space. I threw back my head, hoping to get some air from a small separation in the canvas. I could see Mustapha's face. His lips were moving in silence, while the train jerked his body one way and then the other.

At noon the next day, the train pulled into Solo, a small city where many passengers disembarked. Exhausted, our legs swollen, Mustapha and I quickly grabbed two vacated seats. There, we drifted in and out of sleep during the five hours' ride to Surabaya.

From Surabaya we still had to take the local train to Lawang. It waited with windows and doors thrown wide open.

"It's not a long ride from here," Mustapha smiled. He touched my cheek. "Before the war, the trains never seemed so tedious. It was always a pleasure to make the journey."

"I'll be all right. There aren't many passengers yet, but let's get on and find seats. My legs hurt."

"Mine too. And I'm hungry." He paused, sucking in a deep breath of fresh air. "For a while, when that smell of citronella oil floated around, I thought I was going to die."

"I saw you mumbling."

"I wasn't mumbling. I was praying. Hoping I wouldn't get sick."

We laughed, sitting down on the hard benches and stretching our legs.

I opened the bag with *Abuya's* pastries. "Ohhh, they're all spoiled."

Mustapha reached inside the bag and withdrew a half moon. Green mold grew on the beautiful shape.

"I'll go get us something," he said, replacing the pastry.

I put my hand on his. "I can wait. Better rest your legs."

He shook his head. "I need something to settle my stomach. Save my seat." Mustapha hobbled from the train and disappeared down the platform.

As the minutes passed, people began boarding, and the seats filled up quickly.

"Is this seat taken?" a young man with brown wavy hair and blue gray eyes asked.

I nodded, instinctively spreading my hand out on the seat I saved for Mustapha. "I'm sorry."

"Would you mind if I sit here then?" The man placed a hand-held stool beside my legs, and sat down before I could stammer out any objection. Other passengers began dotting the aisle with their portable stools, as well.

The man sat with his back to me, but turned frequently to smile. I avoided his glances, not wanting to encourage him, and hoping he might go away. With drooping eyelids I watched through the window, the bag of moldy pastries now holding the place for Mustapha.

Finally, I spied him approaching, his hands filled with wrapped banana leaves. I relaxed.

Mustapha took his seat and just as he did, the stranger turned to look, surprise spread across his face and he leapt to his feet.

"Mustapha!" He shouted.

"Ramzie!" The stranger embraced Mustapha, wrapped banana leaves and all.

I stared with a mixture of relief and confusion.

"This is my brother, Ramzie. And this is Henriette, my bride-to-be."

"Your brother?" I laughed, bringing my hand up to cover my mouth.

Ramzie broke into laughter with me.

"What's so funny?"

"Nothing really," Ramzie answered. "I think I scared her."

"You did."

The train hooted and the engine rumbled. Mustapha and his brother took their seats.

"What are you doing here?"

"I'm going home. Even though the Japanese have taken over the family textile mill and we have no say in the product distribution, we still run the plant. I commute to Surabaya everyday." He looked back at me. "The family is so excited. They're all waiting at Mother's house for both of you. We are eager to meet the woman who stole the heart of the baby in our family."

EIGHTEEN

NIKAH

"Welcome, my child, welcome," Fatima, Mustapha's mother greeted me in a mixture of Arabic and Malay. She took me by the shoulders, gazed into my face, then smacked a kiss on each cheek. "We're glad to meet you, my dear," she smiled. She dressed in a *kain* and *kabaya,* and a sheer white scarf covered her bun of graying hair. Alert hazel eyes peered out from thick glasses.

"Musy, you've found yourself a beautiful girl." Fatima clasped Mustapha's face between her hands, then delivered multiple kisses to his cheeks. "And fair too."

At the front door, I was showered with more kisses and excited greetings. Nine and thirteen years older then their baby brother, Mirna, his widowed sister, and Halema, his married sister, fluttered like nervous chickens. Ed, another brother, the spitting image of Ramzie but older, greeted me with a smile, and a shy hug.

"We're so happy for you both," Mirna said, smiling, while Halema nodded in agreement. Both women, in their early thirties, were beautiful, with soft ivory skin, green eyes, and dark red hair. Izzet, Halema's round-faced, round-eyed husband was the last to greet me. He was a gentle-looking man with a soft voice, who clearly adored his wife.

The sisters guided me through the house, blasting me with questions as we went; "Are you going to become a Muslim? How many children do you want? Where will you live? Are there many sons in your family?"

"Don't trouble her with all your questions now," Fatima scolded. "Let us sit outside where it is cool. They need to refresh themselves. They need to rest." Fatima turned to Mustapha. "The *Imam* arrives tomorrow."

"Tomorrow?" I said, unable to hide my surprise.

"Mother doesn't believe in long engagements," Ramzie grinned.

In the back yard, I sank into a deep cushioned chair, my back happy to be caressed by its soft contour.

"Put your feet up, child," Fatima clucked, looking at my swollen legs. She indicated a small low table and I gingerly stretched my feet upon it. Mustapha put his feet up on Mirna's chair, and she immediately began to massage them.

Fatima glanced in the direction of the kitchen, and as if reading her mind, the servants arrived with cool drinks, assortments of cookies, pastries, and a platter of papaya, guava, pineapple, and mangosteen.

My exhaustion temporarily fell away as Mustapha and I gave in to the party atmosphere. I watched the family laugh, talk, and tease each other. Mirna told stories of when Mustapha was young; how he loved the camera she had given him, and what a wild and adventurous youngster he had been. Halema said Mustapha was gentle and sweet, and Ed and Ramzie laughed at their sister's motherly appraisal of their youngest brother.

I didn't expected such closeness towards a brother that *Abuya* had given the impression they had abandoned.

The joking and eating went on until Fatima suggested Mustapha and I rest. "Sleep for a while. We will wake you for dinner. We can talk more then. Henriette, you will share a room with Mirna and me until you are married."

Ed and Ramzie beamed at their little brother, causing a blush to spread across Mustapha's face.

He elbowed his brothers playfully. And they elbowed back as they got up and walked with him to his room.

In Fatima's airy room I lay down on the bed, my aching body welcoming the soft cool mattress. I closed my eyes and for a moment my father and Saitem seemed to be standing before me. Then I lost myself to the arms of slumber.

The next morning, I awakened to the Muslim call to prayer. *"Allahu akbar—Ashhadu all ilaha illallah*—God is the greatest. I bear witness that there is no God but God. I bear witness that Mohammed is the Messenger of God. Come to prayer." I lay quietly listening to the melodic voice of the *Muezzin*. Soon Fatima's and Mirna's shadows stole across the foot of my bed. I observed their images bow and prostrate in their pre-dawn prayer. I didn't join them. I was not a Muslim yet. I lay there watching the sun rise, its rosy fingers touching soft billowy clouds. I prayed in the way I had often seen Saitem pray, quietly to herself, without ceremony or ritual.

When Fatima and Mirna finished with their prayer, they tiptoed out of the room.

I stretched. This was the first day of my new life. I examined my legs. The swelling was almost gone. I rubbed them, then slipped out of bed, washed, dressed and joined the family on the patio.

Birds chattered in the cool morning air, and the aroma of fresh coffee spiced with cardamom filled my nostrils. It hardly seemed possible, that there was a war going on. Here, all was quiet, peaceful.

"Good morning," Mustapha said, a broad smile on his face. "Did you sleep well?"

"Very. I don't think I moved all night."

"You look rested. How are your legs?"

"Better. Much better."

"Mine too." He held up a sandaled foot.

Ramzie pulled out the chair beside Mustapha, but before I could sit down, Fatima told me to sit beside her.

Out of respect, and wanting the family to like me, I took the seat Fatima indicated.

Mustapha winked from across the table.

"The *Imam* will be here by noon," Fatima told us. "The wedding will not be until the evening, but the *Imam* will want to talk with all of us."

"Don't worry," Halema said. "It's just an informal talk. Muslim weddings are a simple affair. Only the family will be there."

"But tomorrow," Mirna said, "we will feast with friends and relatives."

I nodded my understanding and at the same time, consent. Anything was all right with me. I didn't know what to expect from a Muslim wedding, and I was happy to have Fatima take charge.

"Is there anything we can do for you?" Mirna asked.

"I was hoping you would have some *kabaya* pins."

"I have pins you can borrow," Halema offered, while she poured more coffee for her husband. They're—"

"Shhh." Ramzie held up his hand for silence. "What was that?" We froze in our positions, coffee cups suspended in air, heads cocked to one side. "There it goes again." We glanced from one person to another.

The deep boom came several more times. I looked at the sky. It was clear with patches of slow-moving clouds. No planes were visible. No sound hummed from the sky. Nothing but booms far off in the distance.

"I've never heard those sounds before," Ramzie said, sipping once again on his coffee. He looked at Ed and Izzet, then Mustapha, who looked back at Ed.

"That's the sound of bombs," I whispered.

"Could be a lot of things," Ed answered. "Maybe when the *Imam* arrives he'll have news."

"I'm sure they're bombs."

The morning drifted into noon, then afternoon, with no sign of the *Imam*. Clouds of smoke meandered in the distance, and eventually, word arrived that Allied planes had bombed Surabaya harbor and the surrounding military installations in an attempt to reclaim the islands from the Japanese.

"No doubt the *Imam* is stuck in Surabaya," Ramzie said.

Mirna looked at me with soulful eyes. "We'll have to postpone the wedding until he can get here."

"Ya Haram!" Fatima declared, resorting to her native Arabic, as she clutched her chest, one hand upon the other.

For a moment I thought she was sick, but she continued in such an excited voice it became clear she was upset about something. "It is not proper for an unwed couple to be together alone. It is un-Islamic. Temptation—"

I glanced at Mustapha. I hoped no one noticed the bubble of laughter threatening to explode from within me.

"Mama, really, it'll be all right. After all, we're not alone," Mustapha consoled.

She patted his hand, but continued to shake her head. "What are we going to do? What are we going to do?"

"We're going to send the servants out to let our friends know that the wedding has to be postponed," Ed answered.

"And tell the cook not to start preparations until we know when the wedding will be," Halema added. "Come now, Mama, it will be all right."

But Fatima would not be consoled and she fretted all day. By dinner time, I wasn't laughing anymore. The situation had become so stressful I was prepared to call off the wedding and go home.

As we entered the dining room for dinner Mustapha seated himself next to me and put his arm around my shoulder. "Everything will work out," he told me.

I tried to smile.

"She is not lawful to you yet, Mustapha," Fatima glared from her seat at the other end of the table. "Respect her."

Mustapha jerked his arm away.

"Henriette, come sit next to me," Fatima ordered.

"Mama, this is not necessary," Mustapha objected.

"Yes, it is! Why give temptation a chance?"

The elderly had such strange ideas, but I got up and I walked to the chair Fatima indicated, while Mustapha shook his head.

"I know!" Ramzie declared. "Why not call in an official from the village to perform a *nikah*."

"A *nikah*, yes, that is a good idea," Mustapha agreed. "What do you think of that idea, Mama?"

Fatima remained silent, but her eyes became thoughtful. "Yes, that is a solution."

I looked questioningly at Mustapha, but he was busy staring down his mother.

"A *nikah* can be performed by a village *Imam*," Ed explained. "The ceremony is usually done for engagements. This way the couple would be absolved of punishment should their passions run away with them, but Islam does not believe in long engagements, so a consummated *nikah* is a marriage."

"Yes, it is the only solution," Fatima agreed. "Send a messenger at once. The *nikah* must be performed tomorrow."

First we must measure your corset," Mirna laughed, as she and Halema helped me dress for the *nikah*. Halema handed her sister a corset made of white cotton and multiple long stays. They placed it around my waist, cinching it up as tight as they could.

I knew the tradition. The strings would be cut at the last hole of the corset, then knotted with new string. After each child I bore, it would serve as a guide to return me to my present form.

"You are so small," Halema said. "It will not be easy to get back to this slim figure after a baby."

"Can't you give me a little extra room? I'm not always this thin."

They laughed. "Yes, it would be better if you were a little more fleshy."

"Like us." Halema laughed, cutting the strings where they were, then slipping the corset off me and proceeding to help me with my *kain*.

"Are you sure you want to wear this batik?" Mirna asked. "I have others that are more festive."

"No, thank you," I said, fingering *Oma* Saitem's batik. "This one is very special to me." I felt in wearing Saitem's batik, her spirit would be with me. Images of my father also appeared and I was convinced, he too, was thinking of me. Only for a second did thoughts of my mother intrude. I pushed them away.

Halema wrapped the *kain* around my hips, the delicate fan pleats in front dancing seductively open with each move I made. An aged lace *kabaya* top, pinned with Halema's pearls, added a touch of antiquity that made me momentarily feel lost in some other time. My hair, scented with the fragrance of jasmine, I wore pulled back and up off my neck, and coiled around my wrist was Saitem's gold serpent.

When Halema and Mirna were satisfied with their work, I tiptoed into the living room in my bare feet. Mustapha waited for me, dressed in long cotton pants and a white shirt. He stood opposite the village *Imam*.

As I entered, Mustapha turned. His mouth opened slightly, and his eyes lingered on my shoulders, then met my gaze. A tremor ran the length of my body, and from the look in his eyes, any doubt that had remained in me, disappeared.

He held out his hand for me to join him. I licked my lips nervously and stepped closer.

The *Imam* motioned us to sit. With Mustapha's help, I kneeled, then shifted my weight to sit as gracefully as I could on one hip—native fashion. Mustapha sat crosslegged beside me.

"You are both here of your own free will?" The *Imam* asked.

Mustapha and I whispered, "Yes." It was as if we both had something stuck in our throats. Mustapha's left knee, which just barely touched my right one, moved, and pressed ever so lightly against mine.

The *Imam* nodded and smiled at both of us, then turned his attention to me, asking if my decision to become a Muslim was my own, without coercion, without threat.

When I swore that it was, we continued with the ceremony.

"*La ilaha ila Allah, wa anna Muhammad A Rasul Allah,* I believe in only one God and Muhammad is his Prophet," I repeated three times. My voice trembled, but I said it with conviction.

The *Imam* nodded his encouragement, then began the reading of the *Al Fatiha*. I didn't understand the words of the prayer, but *Abuya* had taught it to me, and it was beautiful to listen to. The *Imam* then spoke of our duty as a married couple.

We listened, our eyes occasionally wandering to each other. The *Imam* talked of harmony, of honoring God, his prophet, and each other. He talked of children and being guided by the Qur'an.

I listened but my mind swam in a hundred directions. Not until Mustapha took my hand, placing five *rupiahs* into it as a gift, did I realize the ceremony had ended.

"I'm sorry it can't be more," he whispered. "But some day—"

I looked into his face. "I know."

We signed the official papers, then hand-in-hand faced the family's glowing faces. I was married. I was a Muslim. But I felt no different, and had no ring to remind me I was married. Rings were not part of the Muslim custom, Mustapha had explained, and with the war, impossible anyway. I didn't mind. I was with my *Rama*.

Amidst laughing, we were led to the dining room, where the cake was cut and coffee served. I handed a generous portion to Mustapha. How handsome he looked. How wonderful to have someone to comfort me, be with me always. How wonderful to be in love, married.

He took the plate, his eyes seeming to caress me. Our fingers touched and then he turned and followed his brothers and the *Imam* into another room, while I was detained by Fatima and my new sisters-in-law. I swallowed my disappointment, remembering I would have to get used to new customs, at least in the presence of his family.

The evening wore on and the childish romantic images I had of marriage dulled, but eventually Mustapha returned, and the family could not follow us or dictate customs in our bedroom.

The following day, the guests began to arrive just before noon. The servants were busy all morning. A freshly-slaughtered sheep lay roasting over an open fire. Garlic, onion, cloves, and cumin wafted through the air. The cook, with her extra help, steamed green beans, sorted stones from rice, and watched over her many simmering pots.

Mustapha and I stood, dressed as we had the night before, greeting our guests and making acquaintances.

"How lovely you are," one old women crooned. "And is that the blush of a fulfilled wife? You are a lucky girl. A lucky girl."

I glanced quickly at Mustapha. He acted as if he hadn't heard the woman. I hoped that no one else had. Comments like that were not considered polite in my upbringing. The old crone moved on.

Like the night before, men gathered in one room, while the women gathered in another. Dumb as I perceived the custom, I abided. The women I was introduced to seemed kind and Mirna and Halema stuck close to my side. During dinner, conversation ranged from Arab cooking, to children, to the importance of boys to carry on the family name and traditions.

After the dishes were cleared away, I heard music coming from out doors.

"Two of our friends always bring their *oud* and drum," Fatima explained. "Come look." I peeked from behind the wooden partition that shielded us from the men. The *oud*, a sixteen-string instrument, had a mellow sound; the small drum, held under a man's arm while he beat the goat-hide top with his free hand, had a deep primitive beat. The men clapped. Then one or two stood up, stamped their feet, and danced.

The dance steps were simple. They had no special form, and each dancer seemed to improvise steps to the beat of the drummer, who in turn synchronized his beat with the melodious voice of the *oud* player.

"It's an old Yemenite song," Halema whispered at my shoulder. "They are singing of almond-shaped eyes, and lips the color of pomegranate. It is a desert love song."

It sounded lovely, but what good was a love song if you couldn't gaze into your lover's eyes? I continued to watch while one of the guests pulled Mustapha to his feet. At first hesitatingly, then clumsily, Mustapha improvised a few steps. The guests were delighted and clapped louder. The women crowded around me to peek at what had caused the commotion.

"What a fine young man that Mustapha is," one of the women sighed, then began clapping her hands to the rhythm of the drum. The rest of the women joined in and some began to dance. I watched, feeling for the first time a little stab of discomfort, as the women lost themselves to their culture.

Dutifully I learned how to say my prayers in Arabic. I did not want my new family to think Mustapha had not married the right woman. I washed my body as Mirna instructed and covered my head and arms with the special prayer garment before prostrating myself on the prayer mat, in the direction of Mecca.

I prayed together with Mirna and Fatima in the privacy of our home, unlike the men, who went to the Mosque. It did not take long, only five or six minutes, once we were properly washed and dressed, but I always took care to finish my prayer by looking to one side of me and then the other. Mustapha explained that all Muslims finish their prayer with this gesture. It was to greet the angels that sat on either side. I liked this belief and never failed to greet my angels.

Patiently I listened while Fatima explained how to prepare Mustapha's favorite dishes; how he liked his rice, his lamb, his coffee, and what fruits to have on hand. I accepted the advice, knowing this was not how he ate at *Abuya's*. Also, I said nothing of the separate dinning arrangements, which didn't happen nightly, but always with company. Nor did I complain of the time Mirna and Halema insisted on spending with their brother. I recognized the closeness of the family and wanted to learn to be a part of it, but for now I only felt left out.

Three lazy weeks passed before we were reminded of the war.

"The Japanese have confiscated the trains from Surabaya to Bandoeng," Ramzie told us at dinner. "How long do you have on your permits?"

"A week or ten days."

Ramzie frowned. "Something's up. If you two intend to get back to Bandoeng in time, you'll have to leave now. Go north. Take busses and small trains."

I slipped my hand into Mustapha's.

"We'll start first thing in the morning." Mustapha looked at me. I'd never seen him so serious.

"Why not stay here?" Mirna suggested.

"We can't. We have to get back to *Abuya*."

NINETEEN

GAJA MADA KRIS

June 1945, Bandoeng

I quickened my steps, as the sound of an airplane spilled from the scattered clouds, then appeared low over the city, an uncommon occurrence. People stared up. Some ran for cover while others watched, waiting for something to happen. Pamphlets rained from the plane's hold, drifting down to the damp streets. Onlookers ran to examine them.

Japanese soldiers dashed after the pamphlets, clubbing the fingers and striking the backs of those who dared to pick up the messages. With screams of confusion at my back, I fled, not daring to touch or even look at the scraps that continued to rain down.

At *Abuya's* store, I found Mustapha, his father, and Darsan sitting in the back. I rushed to them, but before I could speak, I saw that Darsan had a pamphlets in his hand. His usually soft brown eyes were stern, angry, and the veins in his neck bulged.

"The Dutch again! Always the Dutch!" Darsan's normally timid voice erupted.

I blushed inwardly, wondering if I had judged him wrong and that he secretly grouped me with the *Belanda totos* who held his kind in low esteem.

"This will bring the prisoners and the Dutch hope," he shouted. "Hope that the islands will be again the paradise they thought it was. But too much has changed. It can never be the way it was before." He paused, glaring at the paper in his hand. "And thank God for that!"

I shuddered at his vehemence, sitting down without saying a word.

Darsan looked at me. His eyes softened. "Please," he said. "Forgive me Henriette, I think of you as one of us. But you must understand the harsh realities. The way we natives think and feel. And this!" He shook the pamphlet above his head. "This is an insult!"

"I don't know what it says," I said.

"It gives vague promises of a new relationship with 'friendly' Indonesians, but it threatens Sukarno and those who collaborated with the Japanese."

"Maybe it will be different this time. Maybe the Dutch have learned their lesson."

"It will be no different," Darsan answered. He lowered his voice. "I have no fondness for the Japanese, but their motto, 'Asia for the Asians,' has been heard for years now, and we Indonesians believe it. This is *our* country."

Thoughts of Eddie came crashing into my head. Could it be that the prophecies of King Djoyoboyo were coming true? I had read Tjeng's book of Javanese *Pantun*, but without someone to translate the meaning, they were just lovely poems. Did what was happening now mean there would still be years of revolution? A feeling of helplessness seized me. My dual heritages seemed to take up arms within me and I felt myself being torn apart.

"Do you think the natives will fight the Japanese and the Dutch?" I asked.

"To get their independence? Yes."

"Darsan is right," Mustapha said. "You can never go back. History has shown that time and again."

Abuya nodded in agreement. "It is no different than when the Ottoman Empire began to crumble. We must be one, or be torn into little pieces by the vultures of other countries."

"Maybe the Dutch and the natives can begin over— have a new kind of government." I suggested. I hesitated. "My father talked of that; letting the natives have more power, granting them the vote."

"That might have worked once," Darsan said. "But now it is too late. We do not want to share anymore. We stand behind Sukarno. We will unite our islands and become a strong nation of our own. Diversity will add to our strength." Darsan caught his breath. He lifted his chin. "Sukarno is in possession of the Gaja Mada kris."

"A belief in that alone will give the natives inner strength," Mustapha agreed.

I remembered the legend of the famous kris. It belonged to the great Buddhist prime minister during the ancient Majapahit kingdom. The supernatural kris became a symbol of authority. Anyone who had the kris had supernatural power.

TWENTY

TISNAWATI

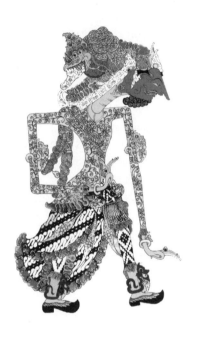

Two months dragged by and nothing more was heard of the pamphlets or of the returning Dutch. Every night I went to bed wondering how much longer I could endure another day, but lying in Mustapha's arms eased my anxiety. I was not alone. Mustapha was with me and his vision of a bright tomorrow never faltered. He believed there would be better days and he made me believe.

When the daylight came I had new strength. I took one minute, one hour, at a time. I filled my day with as much as I could. When Mustapha left for work in the morning, I began by cleaning our tiny living accommodation. The single room, within a house originally used as part of an internment camp, was located on the edge of town, where *Abuya* insisted it was safer. Often I wondered what happened to those Europeans who had been interned there, but images of Aunt Nora, Uncle Kees, Marie, and Jantje appeared, and I quickly forced the images out of my mind. I didn't dare think that something might have happened to them. They were fine and I would see them when the war ended.

When I finished tidying the room, I made my way to the long rice-ration line. Every day was the same. All of us stood with our registration cards. No cards, no rice. And rice was what sustained us. For more than an hour I waited, listening to people complain, or speculate about the future. Sometimes I stood in the rain with my old umbrella. More often, I stood in the heat, sweat stinging my eyes and blurring my vision, so that I would imagine dim shadows and they would take form in my mind.

Barechested young native men plowed glossy mud behind teams of gray, or sometimes white, water buffalos. Adjacent to the muddy newly-prepared rice paddies lay paddies of gold maturing rice. And bordering each were walkways lined with banana and coconut trees.

"Oh look, Papa, what are they doing over there?" I pointed. A procession of villagers were making their way around one of the mature paddies. They had come from a small hut, from which emanated a steady plume of smoke.

"That's a *selametan metik*," Father answered, slowing the car. "A ritualistic harvest of first-fruits. They are paying homage to the Rice Princess."

"Who's the Rice Princess?" Angelica asked, sitting up quickly to look out the window.

"The Rice Princess," he explained, "was a beautiful goddess by the name of Tisnawati who fell in love with a mortal on earth. This made her father very angry and he demanded that she return to the heavens. When she refused, he turned her into a rice stalk."

"Why a rice stalk?" Angelica asked.

"Well, in the heavens Tisnawati was adored for her graceful form. Angry as her father was, he could not deny her everything. He turned her into the spirit of the rice plant, the most lovely and precious of all the foods on earth."

"What about the man she fell in love with?" I asked.

"The old king watched the young lover gazing at Tisnawati, gathering the rice plant into his arms, and swearing that he would never leave her. When evening came, he played his flute softly, as the rice plant danced in the gentle breeze."

"That's sad," I said.

"The king thought so as well, so he turned the young man into a rice stalk too. The harvest ritual re-enacts their marriage and asks for their blessing so that their harvest will be fruitful."

"What about the fire in the hut?" Angelica asked.

"It's not a fire. There is a shrine in side the hut. Fruits and flowers are offered and incense are burned."

I turned for a last look at the procession. The people were silhouettes against the gold of their ripe harvest.

"Card." A Japanese voice shouted.

I blinked. Realizing I had reached the front of the line, I quickly produced Mustapha's and my registration cards. Without emotion, the Japanese poured two cups of poor-quality rice into the tin I held out. In better days, I would not have stopped to even consider such rice; but now, carrying the precious staple food, I headed for the market.

Bargains were available at the flea market to someone with a keen eye. Old clothes, from men long gone into the camps, were easily made into new slacks for Mustapha or a dress for myself. My worn dresses I turned into underwear and socks.

A lovely batik print caught my eye, but I cringed when I realized it had been cut and sewn into a skirt. There were blouses and shirts made of batik as well. I fingered the material, but the memory of Saitem's painted prayers made me walk on.

Completing my rounds of the flea market with little success, I took a *dokkar* to *Abuya's*. I arrived to find Kamazawa there. Personally, I had not seen much of the Japanese soldier, but I knew he had become a friend, and often came to the store for lessons in Malay, or just to visit. Today he appeared very serious and by the look on Mustapha's face, I could tell something was wrong.

"Turkey has joined the Allies in declaring war on Japan and Germany," Kamazawa told Mustapha.

"I don't believe it," Mustapha answered. "They were adamant about remaining neutral."

Kamazawa shook his head. "It is hard to believe. I'm only telling you, because that is what my superiors have told me."

"What does that mean for Mustapha and *Abuya?*" I burst

out. Then realizing I had intruded on their conversation, apologized, and stood with my hand in Mustapha's.

Kamazawa bowed a greeting to me. "It is not certain what will happen," he answered. "But be prepared for eventualities." He was silent, thoughtful. "Most sad of all, is that I can no longer visit you."

"Why?" Asked Mustapha. "Nothing has changed."

"It is an order. In my heart I sense there is more, but I am not being told. I am only an officer."

I understood, and for a moment my hate for the Japanese lessened. Individually, they too walked in the shadows.

"I am leaving my bicycle with you," Kamazawa said. "It is in much better condition than yours. You may need it more than I." He bowed, and left, his shoulders hunched as he crossed the store and slowly stepped out the door, hesitating, almost as if he wanted to say more, but then didn't.

A few days later Mustapha and *Abuya* were ordered to the office of the local Japanese army commander. There, with some twenty other European residents—citizens of neutral countries—they were told that their respective countries had declared war on Japan and Germany. As such they were now considered citizens of enemy countries. Rightfully, they should be placed in camps for civilian prisoners. But in his generosity the Japanese commander would forgo that, provided they would promise not to undertake any hostile and subversive actions.

"Everyone in the room agreed," *Abuya* explained to me. "Then they informed us that our travel passes, identification tags, and radios had to be handed over to police headquarters."

I stared at Mustapha, my eyes filling with tears. "It's always one awful thing after an other. How long can we survive?"

Mustapha put his arm around my shoulder. "It is in the hands of *Allah*," he said. "We will prepare for the worst and hope for the best." He looked from me to Darsan. "If we get arrested, you take care of Henriette and the shop."

Darsan nodded. "It goes without saying."

TWENTY-ONE

SURRENDER

The next few months passed slowly. If possible, food became even more difficult to obtain. Many tried to survive on the black market, or by bartering goods for food, but it was clear that supplies were diminished. Peasants had been forced to give their entire rice crop to the Japanese and those who held back were punished. Natives wore rags, and some even wore jute rice bags that barely covered their emaciated bodies.

The local paper reported Japanese victories, but what filtered through the rumor mill was that the Americans were advancing in the Pacific. New fear of bombs being dropped when the Americans landed on Java filled every home. Some people fled to the mountains, most stayed and prayed.

August arrived with beastly heat. There had been no rain for several days. People were restless, confused, suspicious. I felt nervous and worried too. There were changes going on around me, but I couldn't see them. I only felt them, as if spirits were speaking, but in a language I couldn't understand.

"There's something odd going on," I finally said, as I joined Mustapha at the store, early one afternoon. "I can't put my finger on it, but I passed a Japanese soldier in the street and he responded to my bow with a smile."

"You're an attractive woman," *Abuya* said.

"No, it's not that. And it wasn't just one soldier. It's almost as if they are not so arrogant anymore. They carry themselves differently. There is another look on their faces."

"She's right," Darsan agreed. "The other day, I saw a prisoner being brought into the hospital. Who has ever seen a Japanese bring a prisoner to the hospital?"

"And there's food at the market. Not much, but more than normal," I said.

We stared at each other wondering what all this could mean.

Happy birthday," Mustapha awakened me with a kiss. I wrinkled my brow, stretched and smiled.

"August 17. You're twenty-one today. Come on, *Abuya* is preparing a surprise."

I hurried and got dressed.

Sitting sideways on the back of the bicycle, I held onto Mustapha's shoulders as we rode through the streets. Traffic was still light and the morning air, cool. Not a bad start for my birthday, I thought, considering. Then it occurred to me there weren't any Japanese guards. Oddly, the disappearance of the enemy frightened me.

"Mus, what's happening?"

He didn't know either. We looked up and down streets, a feeling of panic setting in.

"Look," I pointed at the government building. The red and white Indonesian flag flapped in the breeze, where once the Japanese flag stared down on us and before that, the Dutch tricolor.

"Must be flying for your birthday," Mustapha teased, but both of us knew the Indonesian flag had never flown there before. We stopped to ask other passers-by, but no one seemed to know. More people gathered in the street, pointed at the flag, asked questions, but there were no answers. We got back on the bicycle and hurried on to *Abuya's*. Maybe he or Darsan would have an answer.

Abuya and Darsan only knew what rumors they had heard from the Chinese underground: the war was over, the U.S. had destroyed Japan, the Japanese had lost.

By afternoon the news arrived: The war was indeed over. Japan had surrendered to the Allies and Sukarno and his nationalists had proclaimed independence for Indonesia. Loudspeakers on street corners and in the *aloon aloon* blared the announcement. The previously-controlled public radio station reported Sukarno's triumph, and even the *Tjahaja* newspaper boasted bold headlines. Celebrations popped up in the streets and shouts of "Freedom! Liberty! Independence!" rang out.

I felt hot tears burn my cheeks. "The war is over," I whispered, letting the tears fall freely. My thoughts filled with my father. "Papa will be coming home now," I said, squeezing Mustapha's hand. "Papa's coming home. He'll be so surprised."

Mustapha put his arms around me and hugged me close. "What a birthday gift, ehh."

"The United States ended it," Darsan said. "With their new atomic bomb."

Mustapha nodded his head. "What do you suppose an atomic bomb is?"

"Must be big. They only dropped two and the Japanese surrendered," Darsan answered.

"Thank God for the Americans," I said.

"There must have been tremendous casualties for the Japanese to surrender so quickly," *Abuya* lamented.

"No reports yet," Darsan answered. "Only that Hiroshima was bombed on August 6 and Nagasaki on August 9."

Abuya sighed. "Violent death is ugly. No matter whose it is."

A small contingent of Allied troops arrived almost immediately. They arranged for the release of all interned Europeans and checked their health status. Camp gates were thrown open, and I watched emaciated, unrecognizable Europeans and Indo-Europeans walk free. With toothpick bodies, they wobbled toward vendors gathered outside the camp. Hollow eyes searched the crowd for a familiar face, for family, just as I searched for my father.

British troops began arriving, bringing with them scores of Dutch and Dutch ex-POWs from the prison camps in Thailand and Indo-China. The Red Cross tried to alleviate the confusion and hysteria brought on by so many missing persons. They tried to restore order and bring a sense of hope, but it was slow in coming. Thousands of people, myself included, had to fill out forms on missing family members if we hoped for information.

TWENTY-TWO

REBELLION

T he fighting is not over," Darsan said, as we sat eating dinner around Abuya's big table. His face was dark with premonition. "There is trouble ahead. The natives have been patient. They have listened, and waited for the Japanese to come through with their promise of helping them attain independence. But now it is clear that it was only a wartime ploy."

"But Sukarno has proclaimed Independence!" I said. "What more do the natives want?"

"Declaring Independence and getting it, are two different things," Darsan answered.

Mustapha put his spoon and fork down, leaned his elbows on the table and rested his chin on his hands. "You're right. What do you think the Indonesians will do?"

"They are doing it all ready," Darsan answered. "Native soldiers, who were trained by the Japanese, have organized and proclaimed themselves freedom fighters. They are ready to oppose the British Gurkha troops that try to re-enter the city to claim it for the Dutch."

I felt numb. My body trembled so that my insides shook. "Is there ever going to be an end? Will there ever be peace?" Hot tears formed in the corners of my eyes.

"Don't cry," Mustapha consoled. "It will be all right. *Allah* will watch over us."

But it seemed that *Allah* would have chaos. Darsan was right. Previously meek natives turned renegade, went on rampages of fire-bombings and killings of people considered Dutch or pro-Dutch. Home after home was gutted by fire. Those who stayed either died in the scorching flames, or were shot, or worse, hacked into pieces.

In defense the British troops secured the airbase and were forced to set up a stronghold on the north side of the city to protect the newly-freed Europeans and Indo-Europeans. The freedom fighters responded by organizing their own troops on the city's south side.

"Henriette, if you and Mustapha intend to stay here, it is not safe for you to dress as you do," Darsan told me. "Hostilities are increasing."

"But I'm Javanese."

"Half of you. Angry mobs are not going to take time to think if they see someone who looks like you. You look more Dutch than you realize."

Darsan's eyes frightened me; dark, piercing, focused, and somehow knowing.

But even dressed as a native, I discovered the extent of the unrest.

"Go away. We cannot sell to you," the storekeeper said to me, as I shopped for vegetables. The brown eyes of the familiar storekeeper were down cast, apologetic.

"But I am Javanese!" I pleaded.

"And what else?" An angry man in the corner snarled. "Get out!" He was a small man, dark, with a square head and round black eyes. His hair hung shoulder-length, his dirty body dressed in rags.

I could see the long years of pain and deprivation had turned to hatred. Saitem's Javanese blood had kept me from being interned. Now I didn't understand why that same blood wouldn't protect me from the natives.

"Get out," the man shouted again, raising the club like stick he held in his hand.

Slowly, I backed out the door. I held my chin high. I would not allow them to see my pain, but when I reached *Abuya's,* I broke down on Mustapha's shoulder.

He held me in his arms, patting my back, as my tears flowed. Then gently he reminded me of the baby. I hiccoughed and dried my eyes. My hand went to my stomach, where I rubbed the little bulge. Only a week ago I had felt the first stirring of life.

"What are we going to do?" I asked.

"I'll do the shopping from now on," Mustapha answered.

"But you don't look like a native either."

"But they know I'm not Dutch! Turks, Arabs, we've always been neutral. They have no grudge with us." Mustapha paused, seeming to think. "I can't believe we actually let the Japanese trick us in to thinking the Turks had entered the war." He held my face in his hands so that we looked into each other's eyes. "Most shop owners around here have watched me grow up. They used to laugh at me and my little Turkish flag. You know, the one I always have on my bicycle. It won't be a problem for me to do the shopping. They know I wasn't a part of the colonial rule."

"It's not the shopkeepers," I said. "It's the rebels."

"It'll be all right."

"No, Mustapha! You have all ready waited too long," Darsan's voice came from behind us. "You must take Henriette to where she can be safe."

Abuya, his face sad, stood beside Darsan. "He is right, my son. Too many innocent Europeans have been killed."

"The hostility is growing as more British Gurkha and Sikh troops arrive," Darsan said. "It is all ready impossible for you to reach the north side of the city. The sniper and rocket fire is out of control."

"Then what—?"

"Move to Kencana Street," Darsan answered, reading my mind. "It has been declared a safety zone for Europeans. You will be away from the demarcation line where much of the shooting is going on, and it is protected by Japanese troops."

"Japanese?" I stared, unable to understand Darsan's rational.

"They are under orders of the Allied command now," Darsan explained.

I looked hesitatingly at Mustapha. His eyes looked thoughtful, but I could see he was at a loss for answers.

"There is nothing to think about," Darsan continued. "You must go. No one knows how long this will go on. It is not just for yourself. It is for your baby too. How long is it since you have seen a doctor? I know the native doctors will not see you and the European doctors are all in the north."

Abuya nodded, stroking my cheek. "We cannot deliver your baby. In the compound there will surely be someone who can help you, a midwife, or maybe even a doctor."

"It will be a dangerous walk to Kencana Street," Mustapha said. "It's more than six kilometers and the guerrillas are everywhere. We'll need protection."

"I am sure the Arab Red Crescent Society will help," *Abuya* said.

Darsan put an arm around Mustapha's shoulder. "And I will walk with you."

TWENTY-THREE

KENCANA STREET

Dawn of our designated moving-day brought word that the Tjikapoendoeng River, running through the city, had flooded. Numerous houses along the banks were washed away and with them, people. It was believed that during the night Dutch saboteurs had blown up a dam in the mountains, at the head of the river.

Mustapha and I had to postpone our departure for another day. Flood victims took precedence.

Early the next morning four members of the Arab Red Crescents arrived with a *grobak*. They loaded our mattresses, clothing, bicycle, and books into the rickety cart.

"You are in *Allah's* protection," *Abuya* said, as we started off. "Take care of her, Mustapha." He kissed both my cheeks, hugged his son, and then we departed.

I dressed in a sarong and *kabaya,* with a scarf on my head, and walked behind the *grobak,* flanked by Mustapha, Darsan, and two Red Crescent volunteers. The road was empty and an eerie quiet settled around us. Without stopping we plodded through the mud-covered streets. My shoes sank into thick ooze, and I had to pull my sarong higher so as not to get caught in the mud.

As we came closer to the safety zone in the Papandajan area we passed familiar homes of my European relatives and friends. I placed my hands over my stomach, wanting in some way to shelter my unborn child from the ugliness of war and hate. Broken windows and doors gaped open, exposing ravaged and burned interiors. Some homes lay entirely in cinders. We passed block after block of shadowy memories. I felt like my happy youth, my carefree life, my world had been bombed away and a feeling that it had never even existed spread over me.

The anger unleashed in the natives, the people I thought I knew and understood, was more then I could bear. But I didn't cry. Tears had no place now. I suspended my feelings. I locked them up in my lock-box. I refused to feel anything, or to speculate on whatever fresh anguish might lay ahead.

"Take care of *Abuya*," Mustapha told Darsan when we had safely reached the compound.

Three Japanese guard approached us, and for a moment I could feel the steel grip of the Japanese guard at Tjimahie, feel the dry kiss of my father. But these Japanese soldiers only asked questions, then let us pass.

"Take care of yourself." Mustapha's voice cracked, as he hugged Darsan.

"I will. You take care of each other."

For a moment, Darsan watched as the Red Crescent volunteer helped roll the *grobak* into the compound, then he slipped away.

I felt a little more at case now that we were safe again, but a knot of discomfort and uncertainty remained in my stomach. The street seemed so quiet with only the sound of the *grobak's* wooden wheels grinding down pebbles and dirt. I reached for Mustapha's hand and together we walked, not certain where we were walking to or what we were looking for.

Before we had walked a full block, a familiar voice called from one of the houses. I looked up to see my Aunt Marie rushing at me. "For heaven's sake, are you all right?"

Before I could say a word, her arms were around me. Then, suddenly aware of my condition, she stepped back for a better look. Her eyes went from my abdomen, to Mustapha, then to each of the Red Crescent volunteers.

I could read her mind. "I'm married," I said, introducing Mustapha.

Aunt Marie examined him with cautious eyes before extending her hand slowly. By that time Uncle Peter and their three daughters, all close to me in age, joined us.

The girls greeted me with hugs and kisses and concern for my condition, and probably some jealousy of having found such a handsome husband in these troubled times. In our school days, my three cousins were far more popular than I and often gloated over the men they would end up marrying. I felt my gold serpent in my pocket. It brought more good luck than I realized.

Uncle Peter clasped Mustapha's hand with vigor. "Nice to have another man around the place," he laughed. He looked thin and wasted.

"We're staying in the garage of this house," Aunt Marie said. "There is still an available *gudang* in the back. Let's take your things there."

The volunteers steered our load in the direction Aunt Marie pointed.

"We have no idea where anyone is," Uncle Peter sighed, as we walked. "We just sit and watch as new people enter the compound."

"We passed your house," I said.

"Bad?"

"Burned," Mustapha said.

Uncle Peter shook his head. "What will become of us? What will become of our paradise?"

The *gudang* was one of four small rooms, that in better days were used for storage. They were located behind the garage, facing a stone well and a makeshift lean-to, where Aunt Marie did her cooking over an open fire. After the volunteers helped unload our belongings, Mustapha and I joined the family at the garage. We sat outside, leaning against the wall and shaded by a small flamboyant tree. From there we could watch the street.

I breathed out a sigh of relief. "I'm glad we're safe now."

Uncle Peter gave his head a slight nod. "Safer, not safe. We still have to take turns keeping watch at night."

"Why ?" I could feel my teeth clench and my jaw tighten. "I thought the Japanese were guarding the compound. We saw them as we entered."

"They do, but this house is on the outside perimeter. We're in constant danger of attack by infiltrating *pelopors.*"

"Why don't we move closer to the center of the compound?" Mustapha suggested.

"There's no more room," my cousin Dolly answered. "We've tried."

"The *pelopors* intend to kill anyone who looks European," cousin Reka said, her voice rising and her eyes resembling those of a frightened cat. "At night you can hear gunfire. They kidnap, shoot, burn down houses, and murder whole families in the compound before the Japanese guards have time to respond. They're barbarians! They've learned nothing from Dutch rule!"

I wondered why it was safer here then with *Abuya.* Fear was everywhere. It walked with us by day, and slept with us at night. We had no freedom. We were under blockade and under a food boycott. Confined to the relative safety of the compound, if it were not for Aunt Marie's two servants, we would have gone hungry.

The servants secretly roamed outside the compound in search of food; picking fruits, digging up potatoes, and locating duck eggs in the walls of rice paddies. For the rest of us, there was nothing to do but sit and wait. We talked with neighbors of bygone days and hopes for the future, but it was always the same and soon there was nothing to talk about except fear. It got so that I could not stand talking anymore. There was no use dreaming that the past would come again. I had grown up that much.

TWENTY-FOUR

THE CONVOY

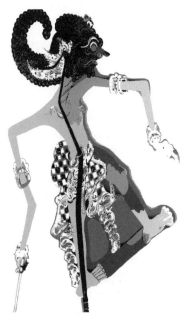

Confined for more then two weeks, Mustapha grew restless; round and round the compound he bicycled, magazine after magazine he read, until he had read all his magazines at least three times. He was not accustomed to sitting idle, or wasting his time in empty conversation. He needed to be doing something.

"I'm going to visit *Abuya*," Mustapha finally told me one morning.

"Go out of the camp? Are you crazy?"

"We moved here for your safety. I'm not in any danger."

He said it sweetly, but I sensed his resentment. If not for me, he would have stayed with Darsan and his father. There was nothing I could say, but I was afraid, and if something happened to him now—the thoughts were too awful. "Please, don't risk it."

"I'm going crazy here. I'll be all right. I promise. If I feel it's dangerous, I'll come right back. Besides," he smiled, "Abuya and Darsan will want to know that we've located a midwife and that you and the baby are in good health. They were both very concerned." He patted my cheek and gave me a quick kiss. Then got on his bicycle and rode down the street, his tiny red flag with the white star and crescent, flapping prominently on his handlebar.

I bit my lower lip, praying that his stubbornness wouldn't get him killed.

When Mustapha returned, less then two hours later, he brought good tidings from *Abuya* and Darsan.

"Really, no one paid any attention to me," he told me. "And look, *Abuya* has sent you some pastries. Don't let anyone see them. Save them for you and the baby." He kissed me, and I forgot how angry and afraid I had been.

From that day on Mustapha took daily trips out of the compound, bringing news to *Abuya* and Darsan of our condition and life in the compound. We soon realized that having Mustapha watch the activity on the streets was an asset to all of us. Uncle Peter encouraged him to keep his eyes open for any changes that might signal danger.

"We're one of the last European compounds in the south," Mustapha informed us several weeks later, as we sat in what had become our gathering place; under the shade of the flamboyant tree and leaning up against the garage wall.

"Do you think we're in danger?" Uncle Peter asked. "I mean more so than usual?"

"I don't know. The streets surrounding us are quiet."

"Maybe too quiet?" Reka asked.

"They're going to attack the compound. I know it," Aunt Marie whispered. She clenched her fists but her eyes remained calm, as if resigned to her fate.

"What are we going to do?" Cousin Dolly asked. "We can't just stay here and die."

"We're not going to die," Mustapha said. He said it calmly as if he knew for sure. "But I agree, we need to do something. We should try to move in closer to the Japanese barracks."

"Great! How do we do that? Everyone would like to get closer." Reka scoffed.

"We must devise a plan," Uncle Peter murmured.

"Are we so sure we can trust the Japanese?" I asked. "Just a few months ago they were our enemies."

"We have no other choice," Uncle Peter said.

We sat for some time, each thinking to himself, while tracing designs in the dust around our feet and occasionally looking up to see what was happening in the street.

"There's only one way." Mustapha broke the silence. "We have to make a ladder to scale the compound wall, then lay long planks across the ditch extending to the other wall."

"But that's nearly a five-meter drop!" Aunt Marie gasped.

"It will be all right," Uncle Peter said. "Once the planks are in place, we can use them as a bridge, crossing the ditch and descending into the Japanese camp."

"It's only about a three-meter crossing," Mustapha encouraged.

"It's a good idea, unless someone has something better," Uncle Peter said.

No one said anything.

"Now the only question remains, when?" Mustapha pulled at his upper lip.

"It can't be in the black of night. We'll never be able to see what we're doing," Carol, the youngest cousin, said.

"It will have to be at dawn or twilight," Mustapha answered. He and I exchanged looks. We both had the same concern. I was now seven months pregnant.

Two days later Mustapha announced that we would have to go over the wall the next morning. All of us exchanged nervous looks.

"I'm ready. I can do it." I wouldn't allow myself to believe otherwise. We all knew what was expected of us. We accepted the risk.

"No one takes more than one overnight bag," Uncle Peter said. "We'll start just before dawn."

That night, the 22nd of December, we all lay cramped together in the garage. Mustapha took the first watch, and Uncle Peter the second, but no one slept. From the tiny window on the side of the garage we could see the flicker of rocket fire, and the rumble of guns seemed closer and heavier than ever before. I wondered if the first glimmer of morning would ever come. The moon rose slowly, and just when it had ascended to its place, there came a loud knocking at the door. The silence in the room filled with terror. All of us sat up. We were silhouettes of fear, shadows clinging together.

Repeated banging rattled the door.

I grabbed Mustapha. "We're too late! They're going to kill us! We should have gone over the wall yesterday!"

Mustapha muffled my sobs. "Shh—Shh—" He crept to the door.

All eyes were on him. No one breathed.

"Open up," came Uncle Peter's voice.

Mustapha opened the door but stood ready to slam it shut again should he need to.

Two Japanese stood next to Uncle Peter. "You get ready, now!" They ordered. "We are taking you by convoy to the north side of the city. Soon the trucks will come. Get ready." The harried Japanese soldier delivered their orders, then turned and headed to the next house.

"Quick, get up. Let's start cooking whatever food we have," Aunt Marie ordered, already making her way to the lean-to. "There is no sense in leaving food behind if we don't have to." We jumped from our mattresses and followed her orders. "And we don't know when our next meal will be."

Mustapha stopped me. "I'm going by bicycle to the north. I'll be back in an hour or so."

"No, don't. Why? Wait, we'll all go together."

"I'll be back before the convoy comes. Someone has to find a place for us to stay."

"We can find a place when we get there. They'll put us up somewhere. Don't go!"

"There will be too many of us. They're moving the entire compound. That's several hundred people. I don't want you to have to be in one room full of strangers. I'll be fine." He patted my hand. "You go help Aunt Marie and the others. I'll be back before you know it."

I walked with him to get his bicycle. The full moon drifted behind a storm cloud.

"Please *Allah*, don't let it rain now. Not for awhile anyway, please," Mustapha prayed out loud, then kissed my cheek. "Don't worry."

I watched his shadow ride down the deserted street. Don't worry. I couldn't remember what that felt like.

With full daylight Mustapha returned. People gathered in the street. They were frightened, worried, hopeful, all at the same time.

I rushed to Mustapha, even before he stopped his bicycle. "I thought you would never come back."

"Finding a place wasn't as easy as I thought. But at least I didn't have any trouble going back and forth past the Gurkha guards."

"What did you find for us?"

"It took some banging on doors, and waking up of people who weren't yet aware of the situation, but I finally found another garage. It's small, but it will hold all of us. They're readying schools to use as temporary shelter for the others. Everything is in order."

"I'm scared. What if the convoy is attacked?"

Mustapha held me close. He was damp from his hurried ride on his bike and the moisture in the air, but his heart beat strong and steady. "Everything is taken care of, I tell you. As I came back, I saw armed Japanese taking their posts. We will be well protected. Come on, let's get our things together. When do we leave?"

"We don't know. They keep telling us to wait. All we can bring is our mattress and one bag."

"What about my books and magazines?"

"We have to leave them. We can't even take the woven baby bed."

"What?" He became silent. I could see him thinking, as he pushed his bicycle along, back to the *gudang*.

"We would have had to leave them if we climbed over the wall," I said.

"This is different." His eyes rested on the baby basket, then on the box of books.

I could tell by the look in his eyes that he had an idea, and I knew I wasn't going to be happy with it. "What are you doing?"

"I'm going to strap the baby bed onto the bicycle and put the books and magazines inside. Since the convoy isn't here yet, I'll bicycle them over."

"Oh, no, please, not again."

"It was no problem the first time. Really. It'll be all right. We need the bed. What will our baby sleep in? I'll hurry. It won't take as long this time."

Mustapha kept his word. He made the round trip in under an hour, but when he arrived his face was drained of color.

"Are you hurt?" My hands flew to his body, touching, groping, looking for blood. I found none. "Something's wrong, I can tell. What?"

He eased his bicycle to the ground and took my hands in his, shaking his head. "I'm not hurt." He sat down beside the bicycle and put his head between his knees, taking a few deep breathes.

I must have looked frightened because my aunt and uncle came rushing over. We helped Mustapha to the shade and sat with him.

"I got to the north with no problems," Mustapha began, "deposited our things—but on the way back—" He stopped, wiped the sweat from his forehead and swallowed hard.

"What, what did you see?" Uncle Peter demanded.

"The Japanese. Those same Japanese that I saw coming back the first time? The ones I told you were taking up their posts for the protection of the convoy?"

"Yes, yes, what about them?" I urged.

"They've been killed—all of them. I saw them lying in pools of blood. Shot! Stabbed! Their eyes wide open. Some didn't have heads. Others didn't have legs or arms." His color seemed to pale more. He took a few gulps of air. "I've never seen anything like it." His eyes filled with tears and he rested his face in his hands.

I had never seen him cry, and my eyes filled with tears for him, for myself, and for all of us.

The morning stole away slowly. Noon came and then afternoon. Japanese guards patrolled. Their faces were as tense as the people who waited.

The trucks will come, the soldiers kept telling everyone, but nothing came. Mattresses and suitcases cluttered the street. People whispered, waited, prayed.

It was after four o'clock in the afternoon when the ground rumbled and dark shadows appeared in the distance.

"The trucks! The trucks are here!" Someone shouted. People swarmed around the open bed trucks that rushed into the compound.

The Japanese tried to maintain order. "Ten people to a truck," they shouted.

Like frightened children, we obeyed our former enemy. We loaded a truck as best we could. Mattresses, suitcases and Mustapha's bicycle went in. We sat on top of the mattresses, cradling a few additional belongings. Mustapha insisted on lying close to the floor hidden under clothes. He told me he was afraid of being recognized by the gurkha guard.

Awkwardly, I tried to climb into the back with the rest of the family, but my swollen stomach made it impossible. A Japanese guard helped me into the front seat next to the driver, then positioned himself on the running board, his gun at the ready. Above me, on the cab, I heard the clank of steel on metal. The muzzle of a machine gun appeared at the top of the windshield.

I looked at the driver, his face a mass of rigid muscles, his dark narrow eyes darting from one side of the street to the other, from one house to the next. While he waited one hand rested on the butt of his side arm, the other on the steering wheel. Sweat poured from his temples, and he repeatedly mopped his face with his shirt sleeve. The stillness was oppressive, and just as I thought I would scream, the truck rolled forward.

Up and down the compound streets the trucks began to move, gaining speed slowly. No sooner were the trucks in motion, then Chinese families, like vultures descending upon the spoils, moved into the vacated houses.

"We watch for you. We watch house for you, *njonja*," they grinned.

I didn't care. I felt for my bracelet. "Please, help us," I prayed.

The trucks picked up speed, one following close upon the other. I couldn't tell if my heart had stopped beating or if it was just beating so fast I could no long feel it. I couldn't even tell if I was breathing. I felt numb. My eyes were riveted to the scene in front of me. I had no choice unless I closed my eyes, and the unknown or unexpected was more frightening to me.

The convoy didn't take the expected route, but stayed along major streets, preceded by a military escort. We saw no dead soldiers, but lurking behind houses and trees I thought I detected long-haired *Pelopors*, armed with guns. In the distance, I heard the revolutionary cry, *"Merdeka"*. It was ironic that no matter where I looked, I was keenly aware that anyone could be my enemy; from the Dutch who felt superior, to the Japanese who hated the Europeans, to the Indonesians who now hated everyone.

After what seemed like an eternity, the railroad crossing came into sight. I could see machine guns positioned on sand bags. Less then a block, and we would be safe, but then a shot rang out. Then another. The Allied guards across the tracks went into alert. Another salvo of gunshots exploded. The truck lurched forward, engine straining. Somewhere people screamed. I held my stomach.

The next thing I knew, we had crossed into the safety zone. We were safe. I could feel myself breathe again. The driver too, ventured a smile; and as other trucks dropped their evacuees off at a local school, he offered to drive us to the garage Mustapha had rented.

"I know it's small," Mustapha apologized.

"It's fine," Aunt Marie said. "Anything is better then a schoolroom of forty or more."

Mustapha and Uncle Peter unloaded the mattresses with the aid of the servants. My three cousins and I constructed partitions in the garage by throwing clothes over suspended rope, while Aunt Marie prepared dinner behind the garage over a small charcoal fire.

"What's this?" Mustapha asked, when we all gathered to eat. He was looking at the can my aunt handed him.

"They gave it to us as we came in. They're British rations," Aunt Marie answered. "And don't throw away the cans. We can use them to heat other food. We don't have any pans."

Mustapha took a bite of the dark mystery in the can. "What is this?" He repeated.

She looked into his can. "They call it mutton," Aunt Marie answered.

Mustapha chewed, then chewed some more and then some more.

I laughed. "Here, try mine. This is corned-beef hash." We shared.

Reka traded some green beans.

That night I lay on my mattress close beside Mustapha. The garage was quiet except for the sound of breathing, the song of crickets, and the scurrying of wall lizards. I thought of my father and felt his nearness. I felt certain that I would see him soon. Perhaps he was all ready here.

"My father will love you," I whispered to Mustapha. "He will be so surprised."

"He'll be even more surprised to know he's a grandfather," Mustapha answered, placing his hand across my abdomen.

The baby stirred.

TWENTY-FIVE
NILOFAR

January 1946

I sat reading in the shade of a papaya tree, its skinny trunk offering a little support for my back when I looked up to find Mustapha rushing toward me. He had a wide smile stretched across his face and even before he reached me he began shouting his news.

"Guess what? Mr. Billyard, the old man we see on our walk every morning offered us a room in his house. He felt sorry for you in your condition."

A real room. Just for the two of us. I could hardly believe it.

Mustapha sat down beside me. "We can move in any time we like." He took my hand. "And there's more. This must be our lucky day."

My thoughts flew instantly to my father. I felt his presence. I waited patiently for news from the Red Cross and checked the registration of new people entering the city almost daily.

"I found a job."

Mustapha, Henriette, and Nilofar. Henriette is wearing Kian and kabaya in order to look more Indonesian.

I hid my disappointed. "That's wonderful. Where?"

"At the airport. While I was at the registration office, I heard they needed workers. The Dutch can't hire native people, because they don't know who they can trust."

"But how will you get there? The roads aren't safe." I felt the familiar knot in my stomach. Even with the baby I could feel the knot of fear, as it twisted and work its way into my chest.

"They'll pick me up in an army truck. We'll go by convoy. I start tomorrow."

"It sounds dangerous."

"It'll be safe enough. I have to work. We need money. There is rent to pay, rations to buy, and we'll be needing baby things soon. Trust me. Everything will be fine." He gave my arm a squeeze. "*Allah* is watching over us."

Come in, come in," Mrs. Billyard greeted us. "We are so glad to be able to help you two children." Mrs. Billyard's loose-hanging dress told of a once-stouter figure and her diamond earrings suggested wealthier times, but she apparently wasn't a woman trapped by the past. Friendly and enthusiastic, she made Mustapha and I feel at home.

It took no time to put away our belongings, and then Mrs. Billyard was calling us to tea and cookies. They were really dry crackers, but dipped in tea, they became edible.

"Put your legs up, dear," Mrs. Billyard said, bringing a small cushioned seat for me. "When are you due?"

"Not for another month or so."

"Ahh, babies," Mrs. Billyard sighed. "Remember when Hans was born?" She said to her husband.

"I remember a noisy little monster," Mr. Billyard teased.

"Oh, men! What do they know? You'll meet our Hans later. He works at the newspaper."

I awoke in the middle of the night. Rapid salvos of artillery fire rattled the house, and through the laced curtains I saw flashes of light. I got up to get a better look and found the night sky bright with fire. Indonesian guerrillas were no doubt attacking somewhere along the demarcation line. I crawled back into bed, praying that the British Gurkhas could hold them. As I lay back, pulling the single sheet over me, I felt a pain start across my stomach and spread over my abdomen. The muscles tightened and a dull ache stretched around to my lower back. I took a couple of deep breaths. The pain went away. But the same cycle started again some ten or fifteen minutes later. I lay awake for nearly an hour, waiting, counting the contractions, watching the glow through the window.

Mrs. Kamps, the midwife, warned me about the onset of labor. I knew the baby's time had come. But why now? Curfew wouldn't be lifted for several hours. I turned on my side and watched Mustapha. He looked like a little boy, his hands tucked under his cheek and his hair hanging in his face. His breathing was even and undisturbed. I hated waking him.

"Mus?" I whispered, not wanting to startle him. "Musy?"

He stirred, opening his eyes slowly. "Hum?" They fluttered closed again.

"Mus, I'm in labor."

"Hum?" He moaned in his sleep.

"Mus, the baby!" my voice louder, with the onset of the next contraction.

"What?" Mustapha sat up. "Now? What do I do?" He ran to the window. "It's still dark outside." He paused for a moment. "Oh, my God. The guerrillas are at it again." He spun back around to me. "How will we get to the clinic? The curfew. The blockades. Are you sure?"

My stomach began to relax again. "Yes, I'm sure."

Mustapha pulled on his clothes, stumbling once or twice as he searched for his pant leg in the dark. "I'll wake Mr. Billyard. Stay where you are. Don't worry. Everything will be just fine. Just fine." He ran to the Billyard's bedroom door, knocking like a wild man.

"Who's there?" I heard Mr. Billyard's voice.

"It's me, Mustapha. Please, my wife—the baby—" Mustapha could not get his sentences straight. Within seconds I heard a door open, and then Mrs. Billyard was rushing into our room.

"I'm sorry," I said, "my timing's so bad."

"It is all right, dear. When babies want to come into the world, they don't bother to look at the clock."

"But what are we going to do?" Tears filled my eyes as I looked out at the night.

"Don't you worry." Mrs. Billyard patted my hand. "Johann, get the car ready," she ordered her husband. "We're going to have a baby!"

"Come, Mustapha, you help me. My wife will help Henriette," Mr. Billyard said, taking Mustapha by the arm.

"And wake up Hans. We'll need his help too," Mrs. Billyard shouted.

Within a few minutes they deposited me into the back seat of the car. Mrs. Billyard got in with me and ordered Mustapha to sit in front with Mr. Billyard.

"Hans, carry the lantern and walk in front of the car. Keep swinging it back and forth," Mrs. Billyard instructed.

"The Gurkha soldier will shoot me!" Hans protested.

"No one is going to shoot you," Mr. Billyard assured him. "They won't shoot if we explain our emergency. Now hurry!"

Hans took the lantern and began to walk nervously in front of the car.

Mrs. Billyard held my hand. "It is going to be all right, dear. Breathe deeply and try to relax," she instructed.

"Stop! Who goes there?" came a voice, as we approached the first barricade.

Hans waved the lantern back and forth. "*Hospital, hospital.*"

"We have a mother about to have a baby here in the car," Mr. Billyard added, sticking his head out the car window.

The soldier approached the car, took the lantern from Hans and held it up to the rear seat window.

I tried to smile through the pain of a contraction that had started just seconds before.

"Go on," he said. "Looks like you better hurry." He waved

the car ahead and we passed through two more barricades before reaching the clinic.

Mustapha and Mrs. Billyard helped me inside, where I was immediately attended by a midwife.

"You'll have to wait here," the midwife said, when Mustapha wanted to follow me.

"We'll wait with you," Mr. Billyard said. "I don't want to break the curfew twice, anyway."

Mustapha kissed my cheek. "I'll be here if you need me."

The midwife took me by the hand. "No need to be afraid child."

All during the night artillery fire rumbled and sometimes shook the hospital, but the midwife didn't let on if she was as frightened as I was. She stayed with me, soothed me, told me how to breathe, and kept me relaxed. With the first glimmer of daylight streaking the night sky, the baby made its way into the world.

Amidst loud wailing, the midwife bundled my baby and placed her beside me. She was a bald little thing with big black eyes and a round mouth. I opened the thin blanket and examined her fingers and toes. She was perfect in every way.

"Please tell my husband," I sobbed, taking the baby, my baby, in my arms. I felt weak and sore, but excited, and could not take my eyes off the miracle in my arms. "Tell him we're both well. He was so nervous."

The midwife smiled. "I'll tell him, but I'm not letting him in. You need your rest. He can see you in the afternoon."
***

When Mustapha returned, I was awake, the little bundle snuggled beside me.

"It's truly a miracle!" he whispered, peeking at the tiny sleeping face.

"It hardly seems possible that this was really inside me all this time." I stroked the red wrinkly fingers. "What do you think we should name her? Frieda? Anneke?"

Mustapha didn't answer.

I looked up. "You're not disappointed she wasn't a boy, are you?"

"No, no, not at all. I was just thinking maybe we'd like a more exotic name. I've been thinking of names ever since the midwife told me you had a girl."

"We," I corrected.

"We," he smiled. "I kind of like the name Nilofar. Nilofar Farhat."

"Nilofar Farhat," I repeated. It conjured up images of the *Arabian Nights*, flowered patios, lily ponds, and peaceful gardens. I liked it. "Does it have a special meaning?" I asked repeating the name to myself several more times.

"It means water lily," Mustapha answered. "She is our little flower."

Nilofar opened her eyes, seemingly staring at us.

"I think she likes her name," I laughed.

TWENTY-SIX

DUTCH ARMY

April 1946

Motherhood became a happy deterrent for me. It kept me from dwelling on Red Cross slowness in reuniting families, and also from worrying about Mustapha. I hated that he worked at Andir Airbase. The road to the base ran parallel to the demarcation line, and sniper fire from Indonesian guerrillas had increased, but I understood the importance of the airbase as the only life line between Bandoeng and Batavia.

"What's in there?" I asked as Mustapha arrived home carrying a small green duffel bag.

"Rations and some clothes."

"Clothes? What kind of clothes?" I emptied the duffel bag onto the bed. A few tins of mutton, corned-beef hash, and beans fell out, along with a khaki shirt and trousers. "It's a uniform! Have you joined the Dutch army?"

"Of course not. I'm not Dutch. They wouldn't allow it."

I held up the khaki shirt and inspected it, then laid it down on the bed next to Nilofar. "I don't know. This looks like a uniform to me."

"You're wrong," Mustapha insisted. "Remember when I wanted to join the Dutch Air Corps? They wouldn't take me. I wasn't Dutch. I tried to join with two of my classmates, Saltikoff and Pan Huyzen. I told you."

"I remember, but why would they give you these clothes then?"

"To identify people working at the airbase. They have to take every precaution."

"I suppose." I examined them, front and back. "Try them on. Let's see how they look."

Mustapha complied.

"Turn around so I can see the back," I said, spinning my hand in the air, and trying not to break out laughing.

Mustapha turned.

"The shirt fits fine, but the slacks look like they belong to a short fat man."

Mustapha looked down at his protruding ankles, while he held the pants up at the waist. We both laughed.

"I still think you're in the army."

"Well, you're wrong."

I shrugged my shoulders. "Go ahead and take them off, I'll see if I can fix the pants for you. But later. Let's eat. I have a surprise."

I was proud of having discovered a Chinese couple on Dago Street who made *tofu* and *tempé*. I wanted to surprise Mustapha with a good meal, instead of the horrid canned mutton.

While Mustapha watched Nilofar, I hurried out to the kitchen and returned with the food.

He stared, his mind seeming to need time to register the sight . He took a bite, savored it in his mouth, smiled with his lips tightly closed over the spicy *tempé*.

"I'm in heaven," he said, taking another bite. He licked his lips and swallowed slowly. "Isn't it funny how it's the little things you miss?"

We sat at our small table that served as dining table, dresser, and desk. Mustapha told me of his day, while Nilofar made cooing sounds from the bed and exercised her legs by stabbing the air.

"They've asked me to join a training class for air traffic controllers," he said, but before I could ask what that would mean we were startled by a round of artillery fire.

Nilofar's arms and legs jerked, then she burst into tears. I picked her up, drawing her close, rocking her, telling her not to be afraid. Mustapha blew out our lantern and rushed outside with neighbors. I followed a little behind. The horizon toward the Indonesian sector glowed red and purple with the unmistakable smell of smoke blowing our way.

"What is it?" I whispered.

"I don't know. Looks like the south side is on fire," Mr. Billyard answered from the group standing outside.

I stepped closer to Mustapha. I watched the smoke billow and form dark, red-rimmed cloud shapes in the sky. I touched Mustapha's arm.

"May *Allah* watch over them," he answered my silent question. "It's been seven months since we've seen *Abuya* and Darsan."

For more then an hour the artillery barrage continued and when the firing ceased, a red, hot glow continued in the distance.

The next morning we learned British forces had attacked a large concentration of Indonesian militia, who were poised for an attack on the northern sector.

"Don't go to work today," I begged.

"We can't let every little thing scare us."

"Little thing? I'm not complaining about little things. It's getting more dangerous out there. You know members of the Colonial Army have rearmed themselves and that means more killing."

"It won't be like this much longer. Even now the British are attempting to mediate between Sukarno and Hatta's government and the Dutch Colonial government."

"With no success." I spat the words out. I was tired of war. Tired of uncertainty. We had a family now. I wanted safety.

"It takes time," he sighed. "Both sides know whoever controls Java, will control Indonesia. Neither one wants to give Java up."

TWENTY-SEVEN

WILLIE

A few weeks later British forces repaired the power station damaged by guerrillas, and electricity was miraculously restored to the compound. With this came the lifting of the curfew and the opening of a movie theater. More Dutch and Eurasian evacuees were reunited with family and friends, and the atmosphere became almost euphoric.

Having light and the relative feeling of safety again calmed my fears and we settled into a routine. Mustapha even managed to take in a few movies; but not enjoying many of the thriller-adventure pictures he did, I preferred to stay home with Nilofar.

One morning I sat rocking the baby on the veranda when a gaunt skeleton of a woman walked by.

"Hello," she said.

There was familiarity to the stranger's sunken face, but I could not recall where we had met.

"It's been a long time, eh, Henny?"

The voice, although raspy, sent shivers down my spine. I knew this person. I stared. "I'm sorry. Do I know—Willie?"

She nodded, smiled, and walked toward me.

"Willie!" Baby in hand, I rushed to my childhood friend. She was so thin I was afraid to hug her, but held out my free hand to assist her. "Come sit down."

Willie's eyes were sunken dark circles, her cheeks and jaw so devoid of fat that the outline of her gums could almost be seen through the paper-thin skin. Her wrists and ankles were no bigger than a broom handle and her shrunken waist and hips lay hidden in a frayed dress.

"I've changed a little," Willie joked. "But you look good. And who is this?"

"This is my daughter, Nilofar. But Willie, let me get you something to eat."

"No, thank you."

"It's no trouble. I have something all ready prepared," I said, rising, wanting to feed her, needing to feed her.

"Henriette, I can't. I had something before I came. My stomach can't handle too much at one time. Please, sit down. Let's visit. Tell me about your husband, how your family is."

I felt instantly guilty. I thought I had had such a difficult time, but I could see that luck had been with me all along. Unconsciously I touched the serpent bracelet, now back on my wrist. I told Willie what twists my life had taken, what horrors I had seen, but I sensed they were nothing compared to my friend's.

"So you don't know one way or the other about your father?"

"Not yet." I shook my head. "Soon, I imagine. It can't be that much longer."

"My father died," Willie said. "I never saw him after they took him away from us, but I received word. And my mother— I watched her suffer. At the end they took her to a hospital, but it was too late. She had beriberi, and her body became so swollen that she died in her own fluids."

"I'm so sorry," I whispered. I wanted to say more. But what? The knot in my stomach twisted again, rose to my chest, then fell from my eyes in large tears.

"It's horrible to see your family suffer," Willie said. Her eyes became glazed and I knew she no longer saw me, but the nightmares she lived. "I don't want to think about it, but I can't help myself. The images come night after night." She took a deep breath. Her brown eyes stared like a crazy woman's. "The camps were awful. At first, they fenced off streets and let you live with your family, but very soon the Japanese moved us from one camp to another. They separated the men from the women and children. They fed us less and less, slowly starving us. Children cried at night. I cried listening to them. I helped scrape the white-wash off walls to give to the children. We hoped it would give them calcium."

I rocked Nilofar back and forth, more to shield myself from the horrible pictures Willie painted, than from the infant's fussing.

"We survived on one small cup of rice and two teaspoons of vegetables a day," Willie continued. "Even that was rotten, but we ate it anyway. Many of us suffered from dysentery and malaria because there was no medicine. We did whatever the Japanese wanted. They treated us worse than animals. If we didn't bow to them, they kicked us. If anyone was caught trying to sneak out of the camp, as some tried through the underground sewer, they were caged for days in the sun. And if they suspected you of having information they wanted, they pumped your stomach full of water and forced you to tell. Those who gave in were left alone in their misery. Those who didn't, were stomped on until their stomachs exploded on the inside."

I felt the bile crawling up my throat. I swallowed, trying desperately not to vomit. I took several deep breaths, pushing away the images that pressed forward.

Thankfully, Nilofar began to cry, and Willie was startled into the present. I soothed Nilofar with soft words.

"I'm sorry," Willie said. "I was rambling again. Sometimes I wake up and I don't know where I am, and I cry thinking the Japanese are going to torture me, but then I remember I'm safe. Safe, unless—" Her voice crescendoed, became hysterical. "Unless the Indonesians get us!"

"Willie, stop! We are safe. Put the past behind you. It's over. You can't change what happened, so just look to the future. Make yourself well. To live in fear is to be dead." I dabbed at the corners of my eyes. I refused to allow Willie to frighten me. "When it's your turn to die, you die whether you like it or not." My words surprised even me.

TWENTY-EIGHT

LOSSES

Late one afternoon, while cleaning bean sprouts on the veranda, and listening for Nilofar to awaken from her nap, I must have fallen into daydreaming, for when I looked up I found my mother standing in front of me. She wore a tired half-smile and her long, almost totally gray hair was unfashionably knotted at her neck. Her clothes hung on her hunched shoulders. William, now four, was small although he showed no signs of malnutrition, and Walter stood on healthy but unsteady legs behind his older brother.

My mother and I stared at each other in silence. Neither one of us seemed to know what to say. I shifted my look to the boys. William and Walter smiled angelically up at me, and I could not help but smile back. They were children. They didn't ask to be born illegitimately. The guilt was not theirs and I could not place it on their little heads. I stepped off the porch and gave them both a hug and kiss. I could not bring myself to do the same for my mother, and my mother let it be.

"I had a hard time finding you," she said, her voice cracking. "I didn't know you got married. Did you marry the—"

"Arab? Yes."

"As long as you're happy."

"We're happy," I said, sensing a resignation in her. She looked years older, helpless, and suddenly I felt sorry for her. "I'm glad you're all right. Come sit down. I was just waiting—" Suddenly aware that Angelica was not with them, I panicked. "What's wrong? What happened? Where is Angelica?"

"She's fine. She's also married. A lot has happened."

"Yes, a lot," I relaxed back into my chair. "I have news." I paused, watched her critically. I wanted to see her reaction. "You're a grandmother!"

"What? You have a baby?"

"Yes. Come see. She's sleeping right inside."

"You boys stay right there. Mama is going into the house for one minute." The boys paid little attention. They were happily playing in the dirt.

The eagerness with which my mother followed me into the house dissipated some of the bitterness I felt. Time had passed. She would have to carry her own guilt and face my father. I didn't accept her shame anymore. Nothing could change what she had done, but she was still my mother.

"She's beautiful!" Mother whispered. "What's her name?"

"Nilofar."

"What kind of strange name is that?"

"Mustapha named her. And Mother, don't start. You'll like him. Just wait. You'll surprise yourself."

"Can I hold her?" She reached for the baby.

"Not now," I stopped her. "She'll be up soon and you two can get acquainted then. We have some catching up to do. I want to know about Angelica, who she married, where she is. How is *Oma* van Zeel? Where is she?"

Together we cleaned bean sprouts and sorted rice, while William and Walter were content to play in Mrs. Billyard's yard. Angelica had married a Dutch policeman. She had met Bob while he was imprisoned at Ambarawa, where she and other young women routinely pretended to be someone's fiancé in order to bring extra food to the starving POWs, my mother told me. She apparently had made such an impression on the young man, that as soon as the POW camps were opened he rushed to Oengaran to visit her.

When it was discovered that Oengaran was a major Indonesian guerrilla base, Bob rushed to evacuate them to Semarang. He had planned to return for Mother and Walter, but the guerrillas had already blocked the roads. It was then that the toothless native whom we used to give our fruit to— and buy our charcoal from—warned Mother to leave the house on the next British convoy. Mother did as the native insisted.

"I saw the roof of our house burning as we drove off," Mother said.

"Our house is gone?"

"I don't know what's left. I don't want to think about it. I don't want to think what must have happened to the people who stayed."

"Mr. and Mrs. Klomp?"

"They were afraid to leave. What if their sons should return and find them gone."

"And Angelica, *Oma*, William, were fine when you got to Semarang?"

"Yes, they were all waiting at the Red Cross with Bob. He's a nice young man. They managed a quick civil service wedding before he was sent to New Guinea for training."

"New Guinea? Does Angelica know what it's like there?"

"They had no choice. That's where the Dutch troops are regrouping."

"Poor Angelica." I wondered if Mother might have urged her into marriage. One less to worry about. A Dutchman to take care of her.

"She's stronger than you think, Henriette."

I picked at the bean sprouts in silence. "And *Oma*?"

"*Oma* went to Borneo with your aunt. They need each other."

Nilofar's cries reached the veranda and I went inside, returning with the baby.

"Oh, look at her. Come here, boys. Come look at your little niece," Mother smiled, taking Nilofar in her arms.

The two junior uncles looked up. They took a moment from their play to look at Nilofar.

"Are you really happy, Henriette?"

"Yes. Really."

Mother stroked Nilofar's little pink toes. "Your father would love her."

"Mama, have you heard from Papa?"

Mother didn't look up. She swallowed several times. I could see tears forming in her eyes. "Your father's gone, Henriette. He's—dead," she whispered, her voice so low I couldn't be sure I heard correctly.

I touched her arm. "What did you say?"

"He's dead, Henriette," she repeated louder, wiping away the tears that escaped the corners of her eyes. "He's dead," she whispered again. "He died in 1943. I only just found out myself. The Red Cross letter just arrived one day."

Our eyes met briefly, before Mother looked back down at Nilofar.

I squeezed my eyes shut. My chin trembled and a solitary tear rolled down my face. So many times in the last few years I had felt my father's nearness, as if he had been standing next to me.

"There must be some mistake!" I whispered in a voice I hardly recognized as my own. "It can't be! He's so strong! Mama, are you sure?" I gripped her arm hard. "Maybe they're wrong! Mama, there is a chance they are wrong."

"No, Henriette. It's true. The Red Cross told me he died in Burma near the river Kwai. Many of our POW's were sent there in transport ships. One ship was torpedoed by an Allied submarine and sank. The ship your father was on made it to Burma where the POWs were forced to work on the railroad." Mother's tears flowed freely now and she reached for a well-used handkerchief in her pocket. "He died with many other good people. Your *Oom* Piet too. I'm sorry, I know how much you loved him. We all loved him."

There was a long silence. I felt a gush of coolness on my cheek. I couldn't imagine my father dead. The Red Cross had to be wrong. People made mistakes. Somewhere he was still alive.

I took a deep breath. "I remember the hikes we took in Oengaran. The stories Papa used to tell. Life seemed so perfect then. I can't believe it's all gone now. The house, Papa." I choked back a sob. "I never got to say good-bye." I touched my cheek. I felt his last kiss.

"None of us said good-bye," Mother said. "Thousands of others did not get to say good-bye." There was another long pause before she continued. "Your *Oom* Kees and *Tante* Nora never made it out of the camp either."

Tears began to pour down my cheeks. There was no controlling them now. "And Marie and Jantje?"

Mother shook her head, holding the handkerchief over her eyes with a trembling hand. "Gone. May they rest in peace."

I remembered them saying good-bye to me. They were so confident they would be taken care of, protected. My hand went to my bracelet and I thought of how I had touched the Buddha at the Borobudur and Marie had not. I shivered at my own superstition.

TWENTY-NINE

"SANITIZING"

When Mustapha returned from work early that evening, he found himself head of an expanded family. At first worried, I discovered not only could Mustapha charm my mother, but he readily took her and the boys in. I was learning what a huge heart Mustapha had. He forgave easily, harbored no hate, and liked everyone. He encouraged me to talk about my father, but I couldn't. I couldn't believe he was dead. I wouldn't.

On borrowed mattresses, the six of us spent a very uncomfortable night in the Billyard's small room. The heat and humidity seemed more intense, and my sleep was troubled with dreams. Dreams of my father, Marie, little Jantje, my aunt and uncle, countless others. Dreams of Angelica, whom I needed to see, to convince myself she was as strong as Mother made her out to be.

By afternoon of the following day, Mustapha had located a large home on Riouw Street, with several available rooms. Uncle Ambon, as the owner of the house wished to be called, expressed his delight in having young people at the house.

Currently his only occupants were Rudolf Ceunick, an elderly Dutchman, and his two spinster sisters, Jo and Weiss.

Rudolf, a sixty-one-year-old former tea-plantation owner and real estate man, lost everything during the Japanese occupation. Internment had cost him his wife's life, and he was now trying to put his life back in some kind of order. He tried to pick up the loose pieces, but his tea plantation on the slopes of Mount Malabar was in Indonesian territory and lost to him with the Indonesians in revolt. His houses, as well, were in the outskirts of town and not in the protected area.

Jo and Weiss were delighted with the diversion the children brought into the household. They gladly assumed the role of aunties to Walter, William, and Nilofar.

After many delays Mustapha's air-traffic-control training class began, and ten weeks later he found himself officially assigned to the control tower.

"You know, when I'm up in that tower, so high that I can see the city on one side and the mountains on the other, I feel like I could reach out and touch God. It must feel like that in the minarets of the mosques in the Middle East."

I smiled. The war had not changed him. He was still a dreamer. "You'll continue to have a military escort when you go to and from the airbase, won't you?"

"Yes, and that reminds me. The captain called an important meeting. All the tower personnel are confined to the base overnight."

"Why? What's going on?"

"He didn't say."

Early the following morning I heard the steady drone of airplanes. I knew one after another were landing at Andir. Only later did I learn they were C-47 military transport planes carrying Dutch troops and supplies. Mustapha had counted over one hundred landings carrying thirty men per plane.

"The Dutch are bringing in reinforcements," he told me.

"They're not going to let the Indonesians have their freedom, are they?"

"Not without a fight."

I didn't care who won anymore. I just wished the fighting would stop and life would have some normalcy.

A few days later a new barrage of artillery and rocket fire was heard on the south side of the city. Rumors flew, but within a short time, we learned the Dutch had began what they called "sanitizing" the southern half of Bandoeng.

Mustapha and I didn't know exactly what that meant, "sanitizing", and our concern for *Abuya* and Darsan grew. Mustapha tried to get permission to cross the demarcation line, but with no success. We would have to wait.

More than a week passed, before the Dutch announced they had gained control by forcing native guerrillas to flee into the jungles. Mustapha was one of the first to cross into the old section of town.

"Praise be to *Allah,*" he said joyfully, when he returned from the "sanitized" area. "They are both well."

I breathed a sigh of relief. "And the store? Is it damaged?"

"I didn't see any destruction of buildings. Some minor damage to brick and plaster of stores and office fronts, but otherwise nothing. It's very quiet. People aren't moving around like they used to. *Abuya* looks well and sends his love. He'll come see the baby soon."

"And Darsan?"

"I didn't see him, but *Abuya* said he had been through Dutch lines just yesterday to check on him."

"He's one of the guerrillas, isn't he?"

Mustapha nodded. "A captain."

"I'm not surprised."

"Nor I. He's hiding in the jungle with his companions. But we must keep him in our prayers. "

Sew this on my uniform when you get a chance, will you?"

I examined the emblem. "Do you know what this means?"

"It means I've been promoted to senior traffic control officer," Mustapha answered. He didn't look at me as he changed out of his work clothes and dropped his shirt on the bed beside me.

I didn't say anything. I watched him from the corner of my eye, as I pulled my sewing box from beneath the table and pinned the emblem in place.

He walked back and forth a couple of times. "Okay, okay, you were right." He threw up his hands. "I'm in the Dutch Service. I don't know how it happened."

We looked at each other, then both laughed.

"What are you going to do?"

"I have to tell them I'm not Dutch. I don't want people to think I'm deceptive or dishonest. I'll tell my superior tomorrow. They'll probably discharge me."

"Then what?"

"I'll find something else to do. Maybe I'll go back to working in the store with *Abuya*."

A few days later, Mustapha returned with another emblem. "They've made me a corporal."

"How can that be? You told them you weren't Dutch?"

Mustapha nodded. "I don't understand. I never signed any enlistment papers and the closest thing to military action I've experienced was when the British needed a translator and ordered me to warn the villagers near the airbase that any hostilities carried out by them would be punished. Their villages would be burned and the populace executed. I still shiver when I think of it. It was the most difficult thing I've ever had to do."

"It must have been frightening for the villagers."

"And they made me carry a gun."

"I didn't know you knew how to shoot."

"I don't. I've never touched a gun before that, or after."

"You'll have to tell them again. Maybe they didn't understand what you meant."

THIRTY

MERDEKA ATAU MATI

December 1946

As months went by, I watched Rudolf take a paternal role with William and Walter, and my mother seemed to enjoy the attention she got from the still-handsome widower. She appeared less haggard and a new sparkle shone in her eyes.

"They're two lonely people. They need each other," Mustapha told me, when I raised objections to my mother and Rudolf wanting to live together as husband and wife. "A legal marriage would cost them your father's government pension, and that's all they have to live on."

"And what will people think?" I asked.

"That they're married," Mustapha answered. "It's between them and God."

"And what if the Red Cross made a mistake and my father is alive? What then?"

Mustapha took my hand.

"It is possible," I insisted, then turned away from the expression in his eyes.

"Yes, it's possible," he said. "But you can't live on 'ifs'. It's something your mother will have to deal with. You can't make decisions for her. We all have our choices to make."

Choices echoed in my head. *Opa* Pierre-Jacques certainly was right about difficult choices.

In the weeks that followed, the Dutch consolidated their position in Bandoeng. Although in the jungles the rebel cry remained *Merdeka atau Mati*—Liberty or Death—the city became safe, schools reopened, food was more abundant, and Rudolf's house, on Peltzer Lane, became available.

Immediately the family moved in: Rudolf, my mother, the two boys, plus Mustapha and me with Nilofar.

The spacious house offered more individual privacy, and without our knowing it a new life emerged. Rudolf and my mother were happy in their role as husband and wife, and the two boys thrived under Rudolf's discipline.

Abuya visited regularly, taking great pride in bouncing Nilofar on his knee; and often stayed to tea and supper. Darsan crept back into the city to help manage *Abuya's* store, but not for one minute did I believe he wasn't still in touch with the jungle rebels. It gave me a sense of security, however, to know if hostilities should erupt, Darsan would know and protect his family, warn us.

Postal services were also restored and with it came a letter from Angelica. She had given birth to a baby girl, Erika, and she and Bob were confident they would return to Bandoeng soon.

I had visions of my sister and me taking walks with our daughters. The girls would grow up together, be best friends. Maybe the hard times were finally over.

What is this?" I unwrapped the square piece of paper. "More stripes?"

"I know." Mustapha answered. "They say they're still processing the discharge papers. In fact—" He hesitated.

He was holding something back. "Now what?"

"They're transferring me to Kamiran Airport."

"In Batavia? We have to leave Bandoeng?"

"It's temporary. Over three hundred planes land at Kamiran. They need help training more traffic controllers."

I was disappointed. I had not seen my sister for almost two years, but the flicker of excitement that passed over Mustapha's face didn't escape me. I sensed his boredom with his life at Andir Airbase, just as he had grown bored with working in *Abuya's* store. I knew he had already accepted the position.

"Listen," Mustapha suggested. "It's only until my discharge papers come through. Why don't you stay here? It'll only be for a couple of weeks."

Mustapha moved into the barracks of the airbase in Batavia, and I stayed on Peltzer Lane. But ten days later, Mustapha arrived home, sneaking through the back door and scaring me to death.

"I hitched a ride with the plane flying the Saturday milk run," he said, his face beaming at having surprised me. "We have until Sunday night, when the plane returns to Batavia."

"What if they find out you're gone?" I asked.

"Then they might throw me out of the service. That would speed things along."

We both laughed at the ridiculousness of the situation.

For the next two weeks, Mustapha arrived as pre-arranged; but on the third Saturday, noon passed and there was still no sign of him. I pushed my serpent bracelet up and down on my wrist, a habit I had developed over the years.

"Something's wrong," I told Mother and Rudolf when they returned from a walk with the boys.

"Maybe he had to work and couldn't get word to you," Rudolf suggested.

"Maybe. I hope you're right." I pushed away images of guerrilla shootings and plane crashes. I busied myself with Nilofar, and then when I thought I could no longer stand it, Mustapha walked through the front door.

Sobbing, I rushed into his arms. "Where were you?"

He patted my back. "I ran into a snag, so I took the train."

"What!" I looked up into his face. I forgot my tears and felt the rush of anger. "You know how dangerous the trains are. You could have gotten blown up." I took a deep breath, trying to sort out my feelings of relief and anger. "How are you getting back?"

"I have a flight. Thank goodness for that." Mustapha walked over to where Nilofar happily mashed a banana in her hands. He kissed her cheek, wiped her hands clean, then lifted her out of the chair. Instantly she scurried toward the back door. Now that she could walk, she was after anything that moved in the back yard.

"Something happened, didn't it?" I asked, opening the back door and following Nilofar out.

"Maybe you should come to Batavia. This discharge is taking longer than I planned."

"What happened? I can tell by your face that something went wrong."

We sat down in the rattan chairs on the porch and watched Nilofar as she toddled about, stumbling over the uneven grass, but delighting in each new texture she encountered.

"It wasn't that anything happened to me, personally." He looked at me with those lazy half-closed innocent eyes. "It was what I saw." He paused, watching Nilofar get back up on her little legs. "I got on the train with other service men and natives. Nothing was out of the ordinary. Actually, all was fine with the train I took. But after we passed the junction at Cikampek, a train going in the opposite direction toward Batavia passed us, and no sooner had it done so, then I heard a loud boom."

I sat silent, my heart beat not quickening. Constant fear had made my body numb I decided. But I wanted to cry from frustration.

"The other train hit a land mine and became derailed. People were screaming, crying out, yelling." Mustapha shook his head. "Those poor people. Why is it always the innocent that have to suffer?" He walked over to where Nilofar was sampling the dirt from the flower bed. He brushed off her mouth and hands and brought her back on the porch, where I tried to interest her in a set of blocks, but she headed back over the grass.

"Can't they protect the trains better?"

"The Dutch try. The trains carry freight cars full of sandbags in front of the engine to absorb the explosion of the mines. It just doesn't always work."

"We can't continue like this."

"You don't mind coming to Batavia then? After the accident all I could think of was finding a place for us. I thought temporary meant a few weeks, but they've dragged their feet on everything else, why would this be any different?"

"I don't mind. We don't know when Angelica will get here anyway."

THIRTY-ONE

OENGARAN

Carrying Nilofar, I disembarked from the small two-engine propeller plane with the assistance of the pilot.

"I figured we'd need transportation," I answered Mustapha's look, when I approached with the pilot pushing his bicycle alongside of me.

"You read my mind." He took over the bicycle and thanked the pilot for his assistance. He flicked the little Turkish flag on the handle bar with his finger. "This bicycle has sure seen a lot of mileage. I wonder what happened to Kamazawa, if he made it back to Japan."

"I hope so."

"He was a nice man."

We reached the street and Mustapha hailed a *betjak*. Nilofar and I sat with our two suitcases, while Mustapha bicycled beside us. We made our way through the noisy city to Lembang Street, where Mustapha had rented a room in a home owned by a Chinese herbologist, Mr. Lee, and his wife.

Walking up the rickety staircase and down the dark hall, I wondered what possessed Mustapha to rent this place. But when he opened the door, the light burst through a window, revealing a large cheery room decorated with modest furniture. And from the window, a lovely view of the park and a little duck pond greeted us.

"It's bigger than I first thought," Mustapha commented. With careful arranging, the room held two military cots, a table with two chairs and a playpen which doubled as a bed for Nilofar. "There's no kitchen, but I brought a small portable burner from the barracks and a pot for coffee. Mr. Lee's wife said she would do some light cooking for us."

"You've become a pro at finding places to live," I laughed. "This is wonderful, and Nilofar will enjoy the duck pond."

"Come on. Let's unpack later," Mustapha said. "I don't have much time off and we need to get to the registrar's office."

Nervously, I rode on the back of the bicycle, while Nilofar, propped up and secured, rode on the handlebars. Unable to see if Nilofar was safe, I repeatedly tapped Mustapha's back, but he assured me she was all right and enjoying the adventure.

At the registrar's office Mustapha spoke with the clerk, while I scanned the lists of residents.

"Mus!" I interrupted him and the clerk. "Angelica and Bob are here! They arrived a couple of days ago. They're staying at the police barracks in town."

"I'm almost finished," Mustapha said. "We can go see if anyone's there, if you like."

"You bet I'd like." He couldn't finish fast enough for me. Nilofar and I paced back and forth until the business was finally taken care of. Then we got back on the bicycle and picked our way through the streets to Bob and Angelica's address. I knocked at the door, delirious with the thought of surprising my sister. The door opened, at first slowly, then wide with astonishment.

"Henriette!" Angelica threw her arms around me, breaking instantly into loud happy sobs. "Oh, Henny. And look at your baby!" Her eyes wandered over every inch of Nilofar.

"And this is Mustapha," I said, as we stepped into the small apartment.

Angelica smiled, shaking hands. "Bob will be here soon. Come in. Sit down." Angelica stroked Nilofar's head, kissed her cheeks. "Can I hold her?"

Nilofar tolerated the attention only a short time, before she wanted to be put down.

I glanced around the room. There was no crib. No baby bottles. No toys. No baby. Angelica's eyes met mine.

"We lost the baby," she said, looking longingly back at Nilofar.

Silence filled the room. I didn't know what to say. I took my sister's hand.

"She was only two months old," Angelica said, before tears formed in her eyes, and I felt my own eyes sting.

"But your last letter. It sounded like everything was well."

Angelica took a deep breath. "It was. But one day I noticed Erika drooling, her mouth pulled to one side. It wasn't normal. Then her body began to pull and arch to that same side."

"Was there no doctor?" Mustapha asked.

Angelica stroked Nilofar's thin black hair. "I took Erika to the hospital. It was a horrible place. The floors were dirty and the stench of soiled beds overpowering. Rats ran along cock-roach-infested spaces above the beds." Angelica shook her head and wiped the corners of her eyes.

"What did the doctor say?"

"They couldn't find anything wrong. Her symptoms were intermittent. The next day her right side was completely para-lyzed. Bob and I rushed her back to the hospital. As much as we hated that place, we had nowhere else to go. Tetanus, they said. She died the next day."

Nilofar stood silently watching. Her brown eyes were large and seeming to sense the sadness, she began to whimper.

I picked her up. "Sh, sh, sh, it's all right," I consoled her.

"You know, a strange thing happened while we were in the hospital that night," Angelica continued. "Bob and I were sitting beside Erika's bed. I was afraid to leave her alone. Afraid the rats would come and I—" Her lips trembled and she took a deep breath. "Bob had drifted off to sleep and I was sitting there in the dark by myself listening to Erika's breathing. Then suddenly I saw—" she stopped and took another deep breath. Tears trickled down her cheeks. "I saw Papa, Henny. He came and picked Erika up and carried her away. I quickly woke Bob, but when I turned back to Erika, Papa was gone, and Erika had stopped breathing. Papa's watching over her now."

My tears frightened Nilofar and Mustapha took her onto his lap. I put my head in my hands and cried. I cried for little Erika, for all the pain and suffering my sister had endured, and for my father, whom I missed with all my heart.

"Even before Mama wrote and told me Papa was dead, I knew," Angelica said. "I knew when I saw him carry Erika away."

"I still can't believe he's gone," I said, taking the handkerchief Mustapha handed me.

"They're together now. I know they are." Angelica dried her eyes. "You know, I always thought Papa loved you more. His strictness scared me, and he was always so proud of you because you did well in school, while I could barely get by. I was jealous of you. But when I saw him take my little baby, I knew he loved me too."

"*Oma* Saitem used to say, 'Sometimes it takes only a short time to learn the wisdom of this world'. Maybe that's how it was with Erika."

"Maybe." A faint smile glimmered in her still distant eyes.

We were still wiping away tears, when the front door opened, and a tall man with thick black hair, and a complexion that was more dark than fair, walked in. There was an awkward silence as he took in our tear-stained faces and little Nilofar in Mustapha's lap.

"This is Bob," Angelica smiled and went over to stand beside him.

"The girls were catching up on things," Mustapha said, stepping toward him. Nilofar boldly took in the new stranger.

Bob shook Mustapha's hand, then put his arm around Angelica. He wiped her face.

"Each day is a little better," he said. "Did you tell them that we are going to have another baby? This time it will be born under better conditions."

"You're pregnant?" I looked critically at my sister. Nothing showed.

"I'm not sure yet," she smiled.

"I'm sure," Bob said. Then, apparently eager to change the subject, he asked about Bandoeng and who was this man, Rudolf.

"He's a good man. You'll like him," Mustapha answered.

"Mama deserves someone good," Angelica said, then blew her nose. "She went through hell in Oengaran. You were lucky you were not there. I still have nightmares about it."

"Mama didn't say anything about it. Just that our house might have burned down."

"It's hard to believe Oengaran was a stronghold for the rebels," Angelica answered.

"It's a good thing we always gave those fruits away." I smiled at the recollection. "That's probably why the little charcoal man warned her about the attack."

"Probably, but also because when food got really scarce, Mama let the natives grow food gardens on our land. Things were pretty quiet, too quiet for the Dutch, I guess. They got suspicious and British soldiers started bombing houses. Ours was one of them."

"Why would they bomb our house? Did they think rebels lived there?"

"I don't know, but we woke up one morning with a cannon aimed right at us. The soldier blew a section of the house away before he realized that there were only women and children inside. We were lucky no one was hurt. But you should have seen Mama go out. The things she yelled at those soldiers."

"What did they do when they realized their mistake?" Mustapha wanted to know.

"Nothing," Angelica continued. "They said they were under orders. They searched the house and left, but we could hear gunfire everywhere, so we ran for shelter at the Red Cross.

Mama left me there with William, and *Oma* van Zeel, while she took Walter and went to look for a safe place to stay.

"She was gone for such a long time, and the gun fire had gotten so much worse, I thought something must have happened. When it seemed things had quieted down, I told *Oma* I was going out to look for her. You would not believe what it was like out there. William and I had to step over dead bodies lying dismembered or breathing their last breath. Some were Indonesians—many were British or Dutch. They laid in pools of black blood, all ready dried from the sun. Some bodies were covered with flies. And the smell of rotting flesh is something I'll never forget."

Angelica sat back down next to me and Bob and Mustapha took the empty chairs.

I shivered, swallowed. Mustapha looked pale and I could tell he was remembering his own horror, the sight of butchered Japanese.

"Did you find Mama?"

"No. I returned to the Red Cross. Mama had come back for us, but found only *Oma*. The guard told me we would find her at Anneke's."

My father's peaceful Oengaran with these bloody images. It seemed impossible.

"By the time William and I got to Anneke's, we were all hungry, but there was nothing to eat. Anneke's house doesn't have a garden like ours. And our garden still had food growing at it. There was nothing else I could do, but go back to our house and dig up some of the potatoes."

I had new admiration for my little sister. She had come a long way from the spoiled little *Noni*. Mother was right. She was stronger than I knew.

"I covered my head with a shawl and went the back way through the hills and down by the stream that flowed behind our house. I had no problem getting there. I dug up the potatoes and carried off as many as I could. I hadn't reached the stream yet, when I heard a noise from the bushes. I ran into the stream, trying to hurry across. 'Halt!', somebody called. I froze. Turning slowly, I saw it was one of the rebels. His looks frightened me; tangled hair hung to his shoulder, and his black eyes were sharp and unfriendly. His clothes were little more than rags, but he carried a rifle. I felt numb, sick. I thought I would faint or that he would shoot me. He shouted for me not to move.

I took my sister's hand. "Did he hurt you?"

"I sank into the stream as low as I could, holding the potatoes underneath the water. Fortunately the water in the stream was high from recent rains. 'I'm so embarrassed,' I told him in my best Malay. 'I have to go to the bathroom.' He, and some other rebels that had gathered, looked at me, with my pathetic scarf and my embarrassed state, gave me a curt little bow, and left."

"You pretended to be going to the bathroom?" I couldn't help but laugh. From where had Angelica come up such an idea. It never would have occurred to me.

"Yes. And it worked," Angelica said proudly.

"One thing about the Indonesians, they don't humiliate people," Mustapha said.

"I got home safely, and we all had potatoes to eat." She smiled. "That was the first time I felt happy about our native features."

"Dressed as you were, and at that time of day, many *Belanda* could have passed for a native," Bob said.

I glanced at him. My neck hairs bristled—as if a spirit had walked across or through me.

"And the next day Bob came to get you out of Oengaran?" Mustapha asked.

I rubbed my neck and directed my attention back to my sister.

"Yes," she said. "Mama wanted *Oma*, William, and me to go first. We drove down the street in Bob's car. And you know, as we left, I could see some of the rebels playing football."

"At a time like that?" Mustapha grumbled.

"That's what I thought until I realized they were using a Dutchman's head for a ball."

"No wonder Mama didn't want to talk about it."

THIRTY-TWO

LARA KIDUL

I felt very alone, after Angelica left with Bob for Bandoeng. Nilofar took up most of my day, and while she napped I read, but once in a while it was nice to have someone to talk with. Then I would give in and visit with Marisa. Marisa was a petite Dutch girl who had a baby the same age as Nilofar. We met one afternoon, while walking at the little duck pond. The two toddlers seemed to enjoy each other's company and so a friendship developed.

Not until Mustapha and I met Marisa's husband, Bill, did I back off from the friendship. Bill was tall, with European facial features, but skin darker than most natives, and black hair. He worked for the Dutch Naval Intelligence Service and seemed to relish telling stories of tortured Indonesian prisoners.

With a casualness I found nauseating and Mustapha found inappropriate for mixed company, Bill told us of electric wires being applied to the genitals of Indonesian prisoners. "It's wonderful to watch them squirm," he had said. And after they were interrogated and humiliated, they would be forced to "flee", only to be shot in the back. With a sinister smile, Bill said it was the only way to extract information from those "rebel animals".

Only twice did I allow myself to be put into a position of socializing with Bill. His zeal for torture and killing frightened me, and the fact that he could so cold-bloodedly talk of annihilating his own kind was incomprehensible.

We couldn't understand how the Dutch, who had just suffered the same atrocities under the German Nazis and the Japanese Fascists could carry out the same inhumane acts. From Bill's boasting it became clear that any agreement the Dutch might have signed with the Indonesian Republic was not something they intended to live up to. Bill obviously believed that the Indonesian Republic had been crushed and that the Dutch were back in power.

"I don't believe for one minute that the Dutch will control Indonesia again," Mustapha told me.

"Bill makes it sound like they're already back in power."

"They'd like to believe that. It's not so different from the Japanese boasting of their victories. Remember? But the Indonesians have tasted freedom, it's in their blood now. Furthermore, Indonesia has gained political and moral support around the world. India and Australia have placed the issue before the United Nations Security Council. Speeches critical of the Dutch have been heard in the United States Congress. Egypt and the other Arab states, as well as India and Pakistan, formally recognize the new Republic. No, the Dutch will have to fight the whole world in order to get Indonesia back."

Here they are!" Mustapha rushed into the room waving an envelope over his head.

I looked up from where I was feeding Nilofar at the table overlooking the duck pond. Mustapha's smile stretched across his entire face. He danced around the room, shaking the envelope over his head.

Nilofar clapped, thinking her papa very funny.

I just stared. I had no idea what had him in such a mood.

"They're my discharge papers," he said, when I didn't

make any comments. "I'm out. They've finally let me out. It reads, 'wrongfully drafted'."

"You're a civilian now?" I stood up and reached for the papers. "Let me see." This was news.

Mustapha handed me the envelope, and lifted Nilofar into the air, dancing with her around the room.

She squealed with delight.

I scanned the papers. "Congratulations! Now back to Bandoeng?" My thoughts went immediately to Angelica. Her baby would be due soon.

"Ah, not yet." Mustapha stopped dancing. "They've assigned me to a civilian position with the Dutch Naval Air Service in Surabaya."

"Navy? Doing what? You have to go to sea?"

"No, no," he reassured me. "I'll be doing the same thing. Civilian air controller. They have no one there. And guess what luck?"

He didn't wait for my answer.

"My family is in Surabaya now. We can stay with them. You won't be alone like you are here. And it's been a long time since we've seen them."

Living with Mustapha's family had never occurred to me. I knew it would mean living with their customs. Mustapha would pray in the mosque instead of with me, in the privacy of our room with Nilofar looking on. But he looked so eager, and what could I do anyway?

We departed from Tandjoen Priok, the harbor in Batavia, on an inter-island steamer. It sailed peacefully across the Java Sea for its two-day journey to Surabaya. Nilofar liked the new experience. She wanted to stand out on deck and watch the waves, feel the salty air, watch the birds that flew overhead.

More than halfway through the crossing, beyond Semarand Harbor, an explosion rocked the ship, sending passengers screaming in all directions. The steamer heeled, and with horror, I stared down at the sea. One hand grasped the steel railing while the other wrapped tight around Nilofar's little body.

The black water swirled beneath us and old stories of my youth haunted me.

"What's that?" I asked my cousin, Marie on a visit to the coast.

"It's a shrine. It's for our sacrifice. You always have to make a sacrifice before you can go into the sea," Marie answered.

"What kind of sacrifice?" Angelica wanted to know. "We have to kill something?"

"No, no!" Jantje, answered. "We can make a sacrifice of flowers, coins, or food."

Angelica heaved a sigh of relief, but as we walked past the shrine, she stopped to peek into the little wooden structure anyhow. I knew she was looking for any sign of bones.

"Why do we have to make an offering before we go into the sea?" I asked.

"Haven't you ever heard of Lara Kidul?" Marie asked.

"No!"

"Oh, Papa, we must tell Henriette and Angelica about the Queen of the Indian Ocean."

"Let's put all this down first," Uncle Kees said, but he hurried and I knew he was encouraged by our enthusiasm. He was like my father, his older brother. They inherited Saitem's love for native stories.

We spread out our mats and put up the large umbrella that flapped in the warm wind. We threw off our shoes and flopped down on the mats.

"I'm surprised *Oma* Saitem never told you the story," my uncle said, as he helped Aunt Nora and Mother to be seated on the mats. He slipped out of his own sandals and crawled carefully onto mat. "A very long time ago," he began, "there lived a beautiful maiden by the name of Dewi Srengenge. She was so beautiful that the King of Banyuma, in Central Java, fell in love with her and married her. Of course, she became his favorite wife. This made his other wife, Dewi Kundati, very jealous, so she employed an old wizard to use his magical powers to turn Dewi Srengenge into an ugly and frightening creature. Seeing how deformed she had become, Dewi Srengenge ran away."

"Why didn't she just tell the king?" Angelica questioned.

"She couldn't do that, silly," Marie answered. "The guards would mistake her for an evil creature and kill her before she could enter the palace."

Angelica shrugged her shoulders.

"Let me finish the story," Uncle Kees laughed. "As she wandered around, she met a kind-hearted old man who listened to her story and took pity on her. The old man reported her story to the king, who when he discovered it was true, immediately sentenced Dewi Kundati and the wizard to death."

"And he got his beautiful wife back?" I asked, my sense of romance ignited.

"No," Uncle Kees continued. "That's not the way it happened. No one could give Dewi Serengenge back her beauty. In her sadness, she roamed from village to village, until she finally reached the southern coast of West Java. There, at the beach near Saudra, she heard a voice calling her. 'Come, Dewi Srengenge. A kingdom awaits you. You will regain your beauty and live forever. Come!' Lured by the voice, Dewi Srengenge entered the sea and from then on became known as Nyai Lara Kidul, Queen of the Indian Ocean."

"She died?" Angelica asked.

"Oh, no. She became queen of the sea and lives forever in the water. The legend says that Senopati, king of the Mataram Empire, was sitting by the sea meditating one day when Lara Kidul appeared. He was so struck by her beauty that he immediately fell in love and married her. That's how the great bond was established between the Mataram Empire and Lara Kidul."

"Did she live in the palace with the king?" I asked, still hoping for a happy ending.

"No, she continued to live in the sea, but it is said that the great water palace, here in Djokjakarta, has a secret underground waterway that leads to the Indian Ocean. That's the way the king visited her. She promised faithfully to come to the aid of King Senopati and his royal descendants whenever they desired her service. That is why they still hold a ceremony every year after the birthday of the Sultan of Djokjakarta. It is to honor Queen Lara Kidul and to ask her blessing on the Sultan, his court and his people."

"After you make your offerings, you may go into the sea, but hold hands, because sometimes the lonely Lara Kidul takes someone to the depths of her waters to keep her company. Such people never return," my father warned.

Marie and her brother nodded.

"We've heard such stories," said Marie. "Swimmers, who have disappeared, never to be seen again."

We took a few pieces of fruit to the shrine. Not one of us intended to go into the ocean without paying the expected tribute. After solemnly performing our duty, we held hands and entered the sea, advancing no further than our knees.

We splashed and laughed in the refreshing waters. The horizon tilted oddly, I thought, and the sand beneath my feet pulled away, as if strong hands were grabbing my legs. We held tightly onto each other, fearful lest one of us should fall and join the queen in her kingdom beneath the sea.

I held tight to Nilofar, tossing her biscuit into the sea as a meager sacrifice. I supposed there were many ways Lara Kidul captured her prey.

The next instant Mustapha's arms were around Nilofar and me, ushering us to a place away from the tilting rail.

"A bomb! A bomb! We've been bombed by the Indonesians," someone yelled. I held Nilofar close, staying beside Mustapha, as frightened passengers ran about with no place to hide. The crew tried to calm them, while at the same time look for damage and the actual cause. The panic lasted until an officer announced that one of the ship's boilers had blown up, but that everything was now under control.

With passengers reassured, calm returned, and fear was replaced by joking laughter. The ship continued its journey, limping into port the next day.

THIRTY-THREE

CASBAH

J ust look at this beautiful baby!" Fatima beamed, stealing Nilofar from my arms, and smothering her with kisses.

Nilofar twisted and jerked, but was no match for her enthusiastic grandmother.

"Maybe I should take her. She's not used to you yet."

"Nonsense." Fatima walked off, ignoring my outstretched arms. "What better way to get acquainted?"

I looked to Mustapha for help, but he just patted me on the arm and said all would be fine. I hurried after them, not as confident as Mustapha. But once inside the house, Nilofar's struggles ceased. Fatima placed before her an assortment of pastries and Nilofar's baby hands eagerly grabbed at them. She laughed at the sugar-covered dough that powdered her hands and dusted her dress.

Delighted that her granddaughter was happy, Fatima turned her attention to Mustapha, kissing him with loud smacks and hums as if she were devouring a dessert. He smiled sheepishly, obviously enjoying the attention.

Mirna came rushing from another part of the house, throwing her arms around her little brother. "We're so happy you've come." She hugged and kissed me as well, then pinched one of Nilofar's round cheeks. "And look at his little beauty!" Her voice was loud and high with excitement.

Nilofar dropped the cookie she was eating and glared at her with big uncertain eyes. Her little chin trembled.

"You've scared her." I tried to sound amused.

Mustapha picked up Nilofar's cookie and held it out to her. When she refused it, he picked her up in his arms, took a bite of the cookie and then offered it to her again. This time the smile returned and the chubby fingers curled back around the sugared dough.

Fatima playfully smacked Mirna's shoulder. "Fix a plate of the pastries for all of us and we'll take it outside where it is more pleasant to sit. And send someone to tell your sister that Mustapha and Henriette have arrived."

Tables and chairs were arranged in the shadiest part of the patio, and a slight breeze blew through the palms. We no sooner sat down in the cushioned chairs than coffee arrived, accompanied by tall glasses of cool melon juice, a platter of fruit, and a selection of pastries.

"It's nice here," I said, breathing in the familiar aroma of cardamom-spiced coffee.

Fatima reached for a demi-cup of the thick oriental brew. "It is peaceful in the Casbah. Much better than even the elite European section."

I started to ask about the Casbah, but Mirna anticipated my question.

"The Dutch prefer to call this *Kampung* Arab," she said. "Under their rule, we non-Europeans were discouraged from living in the European section of the city, even if we could afford it. Some of the Arabs and Yemenites who live here have homes much larger than the Dutch ever had. It is not exclusively Arab, but it is very much like our old world. We feel safe here."

"Safe?"

This time Fatima anticipated my question. "The guerrillas are still shooting in Lawang. We had to leave. The countryside is not safe for anyone."

She was right. The war was over, but not the fighting.

Just then Halema came rushing through the back door to join us. I learned she and her husband lived in a home across the way. This family liked to stay together. She too hugged and kissed Mustapha and me; and noticing her, Nilofar left the flowers she was examining and ran to hide her face in the folds of my dress.

Soon after our arrival, Fatima arranged for a *Samrah*. The special evening would bring together family and friends. The night would be filled with music and fine food.

"Mama, make sure we have *madbi*." Mustapha licked his lips.

When I looked at him questioningly he explained, "*Madbi* is not so much a food, as a way of eating. A tradition. It's an ancient method used by the Bedouins of Arabia in which a slab of stone is preheated to just the right temperature, before the meat is roasted upon it. Olive oil, onions, heavy garlic. Ahh, I can taste it now."

"It's different from mutton then?" I teased.

He rolled his eyes, held up his hands. "Please, don't remind me of that stuff."

I looked forward to the new culinary experiences, and also to meeting Ramzie's new wife, Musna. I knew I would have to endure the custom of men being separate from women, but these were only temporary arrangements and I was always glad to see Mustapha happy.

Fatima greeted the guests, directing the women to a spacious room adjacent to the outdoor patio while the men, entered the back yard through a separate entrance.

"You are not used to our Arab ways, are you?" Musna said in her quiet voice.

"Not yet," I admitted. I sat beside Ramzie's pregnant wife. I liked her. She was shy and quiet, not outspoken and self-assured, as Mirna and Halema were.

We sat huddled in a corner, becoming better acquainted as the rest of the guests gathered. I learned that Musna came from a conservative Muslim family. They didn't believe girls needed to be educated beyond elementary school, they arranged her marriage, and their sole pleasure would be for her to have many sons.

I smiled and nodded, pretending to agree with the importance of sons. How silly, who did they think gave birth to these sons? I made a silent promise to myself that sons or daughters, I would treat them equally.

"Men tend to talk about things that are of no interest to women," Musna continued softly. "We are happier sitting with one another and talking women's talk."

I bit the inside of my lip. "Yes, that's true."

"Do you have children?" Another woman, who joined us on the over-stuffed couch, asked.

"My little daughter is fifteen months," I answered.

"Ahee," another elderly woman joined us. She shook her head. "A daughter nearly a year and a half and not expecting a second one yet?" The woman extended her arm to probe my abdomen.

I moved her hand away, fighting the urge to slap it.

"What is wrong, my child?"

I was too startled to comment.

The woman continued. "We know of a good doctor. We can send you to see him. Maybe he can also help you to have a son."

"Thank you. I don't need a doctor." My tone was sharp.

The woman's lips closed over her yellow teeth and her eyes widened just slightly. She said no more and turned her attention to a *Dalala*, inquiring about marriageable men.

"I know of a charming young girl available for marriage," the one woman told the *Dalala*. "She comes from a good home, but they don't have much money. She wouldn't mind being a second wife."

"Fine," the *Dalala* nodded, with a sugar-sweet smile on her lips. "I will begin to look right away. Is she pretty? Is she fair?"

I cringed at the conversation, and rather than listen, got up to sample the *madbi,* tomato rice, and vegetables.

Dessert signaled the beginning of the entertainment. The men began to sing and clap to the sounds of the *gambus,* joined by a drum and violin.

Musna motioned for me to peep through the partition screen. Together we scrutinized the men, Musna explaining that they were dancing a dance that originated in Hadramaut.

"There are Ramzie and Mustapha."

"Do they always dance in groups?" I asked.

"Or by themselves."

"Wouldn't it be nice if once in a while they could dance with their wives?"

The other women heard and laughed.

"We dance with each other also." One woman got up and began dancing around me, her hands gracefully moving above her head, and her hips undulating. The seated women swayed their hands in the air to the rhythm of the outdoor music. If I hadn't been so disgusted with the conversation, I could have enjoyed the music and appreciated the dance.

When the call to prayer awakened me the next morning, I wished I could stay in bed. The guests had stayed late the night before and it would have been rude for me to have gone to sleep before the last one had left. I looked around the room. Nilofar was still asleep in her bed and Mustapha must have already started for the small open-air mosque down the street.

Dutifully I dragged myself out of bed, washed my face, hands and feet, and clothed myself in the loose sarong and head covering that hid my hair. I prayed privately in my room. Some of the prayer came in the learned Arabic, but I finished with a more casual conversation with God in Dutch. Then before getting up I greeted the angels on each side, hoping that they truly existed and would be there to help me through my earthly life.

After a leisurely breakfast with the family, Mustapha left for work and Fatima snatched Nilofar for a walk.

"Go get ready," Halema said to me. "It's time to go shopping. The horse-cart will be here any time now." Mirna and Musna were already getting up from the table.

"But Nilofar?"

"Mama will take care of her. Don't worry. Mama knows we're going."

"But wouldn't she like to come?"

"Mama gets tired. Hurry."

"Give me one minute." I rushed to check on Nilofar, and finding her happily playing with her grandmother, I quickly got ready and returned to where the others waited. I climbed into the cart. Laughing, we made our way to the open market. It had been a long time since I had had a carefree morning.

We pinched and poked at fruits and vegetables, then stopped for coffee, then pinched and poked more food, the patient driver waiting and keeping a close eye on the items we had purchased and placed in his cart. The morning went by quickly.

"Are we done?" I asked. "I should be getting back to feed Nilofar." I was becoming concerned about leaving her for so long.

"Mama will feed her," Mirna said, waving her hand as if to brush away my concerns.

"But—"

"No, no. We're not done yet."

The cart clip-clopped past dead chickens and ducks hanging on ropes from their feet. A native held up slabs of red meat. *"Daging kambing, Njonja?"*

"Do we need meat?" I asked, resigning myself to the situation.

"Ahee," Halema shrieked. "We don't buy meat! You don't know what you're getting. Could be dog meat."

"I've even heard stories of human meat being sold," Mirna whispered.

I stared at the red-brown blobs.

"We only eat the chickens slaughtered from our own henhouse."

"Or our own lambs, on special occasions," Mirna nodded at her sister.

"Good, then we're ready to go home?"

"No, no. We'll send the driver home with the food. We have to stop and have tea with Mrs. Alamudi." Mirna looked at me as if I'd known this all along.

"And I promised Mrs. Baadila too," said Musna. "We'll have to stop there also."

Late afternoon we finally returned. Mustapha was home and entertaining Nilofar on the patio.

"Where were you?" he asked, without getting up.

"Shopping with your sisters. Didn't your mother tell you?"

"Yes, but all this time?"

"We stopped for tea with friends." I thought I detected a frown, but dismissed the idea when Mirna, Halema, and the others joined us, and Mustapha told them how happy he was that I was adjusting to their way of life.

I soon realized that my new social life required me to shop and go to tea on a daily basis. Of course there were days we stayed home, but then we were expected to serve tea to anyone who happened by.

Nilofar seemed to enjoy Fatima and was well cared for, but I felt a responsibility to my child and frequently took her along on our shopping trips. She liked riding in the horse-carts and looking at the bustling market place. She also became my excuse to go home when the others were not yet finished with their visiting.

It was not that I found the Muslim women unfriendly. They were charming, and the wonderful pastries they served with tea or coffee reminded me of the lazy pre-war days. The endless chatter of little else than children and how many everyone had, was what irritated me. I wished I could spend my time with something more rewarding, but I felt trapped by family obligations.

One afternoon I arrived home to find Mustapha waiting for me. He greeted his sisters with a smile, helped them out of the cart, then excused himself, taking me by the arm to where we could talk quietly.

"I was home early today, thinking we could do something," he said. He spoke in his usual calm voice, but I detected an edge. "Don't you find all this shopping, tea, and gossip a waste of time? I didn't think you were the type."

I couldn't believe my ears. All this time I was trying to please him. For months he had said nothing, and I thought I was doing what he wanted me to do, be like his sisters.

Mustapha paced back and forth in front of me, not meeting my gaze. "You used to be here when I came home."

I felt a smile building within me. His jealousy felt good, not to mention I could now give up this charade. "You mean you wouldn't mind if I didn't go with them?"

"No. I'd like it better."

"What I'd really like to do is try to grow some flowers. I saw some beautiful orchids and chrysanthemums. Plus I'd like to make Nilofar some new clothes, she's outgrown most her things, and Musna said I could borrow her sewing machine."

He was smiling. "Then why don't you do that?"

"I thought you expected me to be like your sisters. I didn't want to be rude."

While watering my new chrysanthemums one afternoon an older woman, accompanied by a younger one, arrived for tea— mother and daughter, I assumed. I kept quiet, hiding around the side of the house where my flowers thrived, hoping Fatima would not notice me and bid me join them. Lost in my own thoughts, I cultivated the soil and pulled weeds until I heard Mustapha's name mentioned.

"Young—give sons—*bagus putih*—" I listened more closely.

"For Mustapha?" Fatima asked.

"She will be a good second wife."

"I will talk to my son."

I stabbed repeatedly into the ground, then with an angry thrust over-turned a stubborn weed. My first instinct was to confront my mother-in-law. Confront all three of them, right this second. But I knew that was not their way. They would look at me as if I were crazy. It was not up to me. It was up to Mustapha. I stabbed at a second weed. I would have to wait until Mustapha returned home. He would put an end to this nonsense quickly. I set my jaw and continued caring for my garden, although the beauty had gone out of the day, and the time until Mustapha returned home dragged.

When Mustapha finally arrived, I spoke with him in the privacy of our room. Nervous and shaking with anger I told him what I had overheard. He patted my hand and with a sheepish smile assured me he wasn't interested. Then he kissed me and I wished I hadn't wasted the whole afternoon worrying.

By supper time Mirna and Halema were openly discussing the recent offer to Fatima. Mustapha sat enjoying his meal, as if nothing special were being discussed. I kept my mouth shut. I was angry and hurt that they were so insensitive to my feelings. I felt sick, as if I were suffocating in my silence. I wanted to scream. I wanted Mustapha to put an end to this second-wife talk. I wanted him to explain to his family that he would never take another wife. But he said nothing.

"Why didn't you tell your family to stop this business?" I asked, when we were again alone in our room.

"It's just their custom to go through these rituals. They can't offend the poor woman and her daughter."

"Oh, but they can offend me! Who am I? Some piece of used furniture?"

"It's not like that. Muslim women understand. They think you understand."

"Well, I don't! And I don't want to. Why can't you just tell them you're not interested? Why do you have to play along with the ritual, as you put it? Why do you have to sit there and smile like an idiot? Because it's a boost for your ego?"

"Come on, honey. They don't mean any harm."

"Are you going to tell them, right now, to stop meddling in our personal life or not?"

Mustapha reached over to put his arms around me, but I shook him off and stepped away. His sweet non-confrontational attitude made me more furious.

"Honey, that's just the way they've always done things in my family."

"Are you going to tell them or not? Don't you care about my feelings?"

"Of course I do, but—"

"Fine! Have it your way. Have as many wives as you want, but without me."

"Don't be silly. You'll see it in a better light in the morning. It will all blow over in a few days."

That night I slept with my back to Mustapha, facing the wall. He made no further attempts to talk to me, which only added to my anger and hurt. All night long I tossed and turned. If only he would hold me, assure me of his love, and promise to set his family straight. But none of that happened, and I knew I had to do something. I would never be happy if I continued to let my life be dictated.

By morning, I remembered a distant uncle who worked at the trading company here in Surabaya. I didn't know him well, only having met him a few times at family reunions or weddings, but when Mustapha greeted me in the morning as if nothing were wrong, as if nothing had happened, I made up my mind.

Taking Nilofar with me, I took a *dokkar* under the pretense of shopping, and nervously made my way to the trading company. I asked for him at the front desk and was relieved to find he still worked there.

Sympathetic to my problem, Uncle Roland took immediate action. We left the office in his small two-seater car, driving straight to the Casbah. Mustapha was still at work. Fatima, with no Nilofar to occupy her time, had apparently decided to go shopping with her daughters. The house was quiet. Quickly I pulled my suitcase from the armoire and packed Nilofar's and my things.

My uncle placed the suitcase in the rumble seat as I climbed in the passenger seat, Nilofar in my lap.

"You sure you want to do this?" My uncle asked.

"Yes."

"Maybe you should tell someone where they can find you."

"I left a note for Mustapha that said I was leaving. That's all he needs to know."

THIRTY-FOUR

CHOICES

April 1948

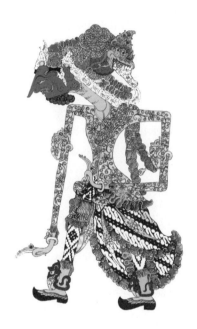

For the next two days I tried to sort out my feelings. Finally I determined that going back to Bandoeng was my best choice.

"Let him know what you plan to do," my Aunt Rosa told me.

"After all my dear," Uncle Roland said. "You haven't given the poor man a chance to come after you."

"I don't want him to," I answered, lifting my chin and pressing my lips firmly together.

"Come, come," Aunt Rosa smiled. "Love doesn't just disappear. Give him another chance. It's not as if he accepted a second wife. Telephone the guard at *Kampung* Arab and have them deliver a message to him. Tell him where you are and what you are planning. Meanwhile, we can make arrangements for you to sail to Batavia."

"Do you have someone with whom you can stay there?" my uncle asked. "It might be a few days before you can get a plane from Batavia to Bandoeng. The countryside is still not safe and they discourage Europeans from taking the train."

"I have friends there."

"Don't leave without calling." My aunt put her arm around my shoulder. "Disagreements in a marriage is how couples learn about each other, but you have to leave room for under-standing and forgiveness."

Her words reminded me of Saitem. Hesitatingly, I agreed. It wasn't that I didn't love Mustapha anymore. I was afraid his family had too strong a hold on him and he wouldn't want to come. That would hurt even more.

After breakfast I walked, with my aunt to give me moral support, to the nearest telephone to make my call. I had no idea when Mustapha would receive the message, or how he would feel when he got it, but I prayed he would understand my feelings and come charging after me as *Rama* had done for *Sita*.

The morning went by slowly and no matter what I did to try and occupy my mind, I could not help but think of Mustapha and what my life would be like if he was not in it. At times I thought maybe I had been too rash, acted too quick-ly, but I had beliefs and I had to live by them.

Just after two o'clock, a *dokkar* stopped in front of the house. Mustapha was in it. I watched from the window as he stepped down and drew forth his suitcase. My first impulse was to throw the door open and run into his arms, but I stopped myself. I got my emotions under control. I didn't want him to think all was so easily forgiven. I wanted him to know there were certain things I would not give in to. Sharing him with another woman was one of them.

THIRTY-FIVE

ABUYA

I've missed Bandoeng," Mustapha agreed, as the plane began its descent. I looked down at the view below. Majestic blue volcanic mountains stretched out to me, their foothills splashed with the bright green of rice paddies. Home, I thought. This would always be home.

"It's been too long since we've seen *Abuya*," Mustapha said, as he placed our luggage in a *dokkar*. I wanted to ask him why we hadn't left earlier then, but I didn't want to start an argument. After all, everything was fine now.

"And we haven't seen Angelica's and Bob's baby." I counted on my fingers. "The baby is almost nine months already." I took Nilofar's little hand. "You're going to have a cousin to play with. Won't that be fun?"

Nilofar's two-year-old eyes were big and round. She was busy taking in the new sights, as the *dokkar* made its way to Peltzer Lane.

When we arrived at the house, we surprised Angelica in the back yard. She was watching William and Walter while her baby slept in a cradle, shaded by wisteria and fanned by the afternoon breeze.

"We're home," I said, hugging my sister.

"We got your telegram. You can have your same room back. How long can you stay?"

"Forever, I hope." I peeked into the cradle. The round, black-haired infant breathed quietly, her eyes moving under their lids as if dreaming of some past life. I felt the sting of tears and sniffed them back. "I'm glad you and the baby are well."

She hugged me. "Isn't she beautiful? And the doctor assures me she's healthy."

"Where is everybody?" Mustapha asked, as we admired little Danielle.

"Bob is still at work, and Rudolf went with Mama to the doctor."

"What's wrong with Mama?"

"Nothing." Angelica seemed startled at my concern. A wrinkle formed on her forehead. She's having a routine check-up."

"Why? What kind of a check-up?"

"Didn't she tell you?" She covered her mouth with her hand. I could see a smile spreading beneath it. She paused.

"I thought Mama wrote you about the news."

"What news? It seems Mother never writes me about important news." I could not keep the anger out of my voice.

Angelica's eyes were big, like when we were children and she ate my candy bar and lied about it.

"She's going to have a baby."

"Baby?" I scrutinized my sister's face, looking for the glimmer in her eyes that said she was lying, but she only laughed, assuring me it was the truth.

"Guess Rudolf isn't as old as we thought," Mustapha joined her laughter.

I gave him a dirty look. "But Mama is forty-six!"

"And Rudolf is sixty-something," Angelica said, "but they are having a baby."

Mother and Rudolf returned less than an hour later. Their transformation shocked me. Mother stood with a girlish grin, and the obvious bulge of her abdomen seemed to contribute to the glow in her face. Likewise, Rudolf strutted around like a proud father-to-be.

"She's happy with her new life," Mustapha told me while we unpacked.

"I know, but it's hard for me to imagine her with anyone except my father. There's a part of me that just can't let him go. Sometimes I feel like he's still out there. Don't you understand how hard it is? I never saw him dead. I never saw him sick. To my mind he's still healthy, alive."

Bandoeng breathed new life into me. I was in control of my own life again. While Mustapha went back to work at *Abuya's* store, Angelica and I took walks together, ate lunch in the park, and watched Nilofar feed the ducks as little Danielle looked on. We frequented the market place, Angelica looking for goodies to satisfy her sweet tooth, and me scanning the materials that were becoming available.

Now and then I bought a small scrap to make something for Nilofar, who outgrew her clothes faster than I imagined possible. I took sewing classes to increase my high school sewing knowledge, and soon enjoyed experimenting with new infant styles fashioned by cutting patterns of my own from newspaper.

Angelica and I visited friends and talked of old times and new, but the war years, the camp years, were never mentioned. Everyone preferred to lock those images away. Even Willie, who had steadily put on weight and now looked almost normal, no longer talked of her family or the camp.

Only the newspapers reminded us that all was not yet well; that in the country Europeans were still not safe, and in the jungles the call for freedom had not died. Only in the cities did we live with the belief that life was returning to normal.

"I have a surprise for you," Mustapha told me one afternoon when he came home from work.

"What?" I looked at him eagerly, but there was nothing in his hands.

"It's outside. Come see." With the help of the *dokkar* driver, he lifted out a piece of furniture and brought it into the house. "It's a sewing machine."

The machine wasn't new, but anything was better than the slow tedious work I did by hand. I pulled over a dining-room chair, sat down and watched the needle bob up and down as I worked the wheel.

"I can make all kinds of things now! Where did you find it?"

"*Abuya* found it. It was his idea."

Dear, sweet *Abuya*. Sometime I believed he understood me better than anyone. "I must go thank him right away."

"Tomorrow will do. He's resting." Mustapha rubbed his temples, a wrinkle of concern spreading across his forehead. "I'm worried. He looked very tired when I left."

"Do you think he's sick?"

"Darsan seems to think so."

"Make him see a doctor?"

"We tried. He won't go. You know how stubborn he can get."

I didn't know how long I'd been sleeping when a noise at our bedroom window awakened me. At first I thought it was just the rain, but the tapping became faster, louder, more urgent.

"Mustapha! Mustapha!" came a strained whisper.

I shook Mustapha's shoulder. "Musy, someone's outside."

"Mustapha," came the voice again. "Come quick. It's *Abuya*."

Mustapha bolted from the bed, almost tripping over the loosened sarong he slept in. "It's Darsan." He ran to the front door to open it.

"What's wrong?" I heard him ask, as I put on a robe and hurried to join them.

"*Abuya* fell. I found him on the floor hardly breathing. I took him straight to the hospital."

"Let me put on my pants. I'll go with you right now."

Mustapha ran past me with a wild look in his eyes.

"What can I do to help?" I asked, when he rushed back out, rumpled, but fully dressed.

"I don't know yet," he whispered in a shaky voice, as he hurried to catch up with Darsan who had already stepped off the veranda.

I watched their shadows disappear down the dark street. The rain came down harder. Thunder rumbled over head.

I arrived at the hospital at daylight. Mustapha and Darsan sat at *Abuya's* bedside. *Abuya* looked pale and helpless, his robust body now frail. His lips were tinged with blue and his eyes flickered now and then, but never fully opened.

"Does he know you're here?" I asked.

"Yes, but he's very weak," Mustapha whispered. "He hasn't said much, but the doctor said he's sleeping easier since we got here."

Abuya's eyes fluttered, then opened very slowly. "My son." His whisper, raspy, almost inaudible, his breathing, short and shallow. He tried to reach out, but Mustapha had to take the shaking hand before it fell to his chest.

"It's all right. We're here," Mustapha told him. "We'll sit with you. Just sleep. Before you know it, you will be better. You need rest."

Abuya's blue lips twitched. "I will not get better." He pointed to his chest. "My heart—bad. I love you." He looked at Mustapha long and hard, then closed his eyes. His breathing relaxed.

For hours we waited, but *Abuya* did not open his eyes again.

"I need to get back to the house for a while," I told Mustapha. "Poor Angelica is taking care of all the kids."

Mustapha followed me outside. "I have to stay. I know he's dying. I can see it, feel it. I don't want him to be alone when he goes." Mustapha's eyes were red and full of tears.

I hugged him. "I know. At least you can be with him. You can say good-bye, be there until the end. I wish I had that chance with my father." My voice cracked.

Mustapha hugged me hard. We sobbed in each other's arms.

I knew Mustapha now understood my pain.

Early the following morning, *Abuya's* breathing stopped. He died quietly, peacefully, holding Mustapha's hand. Darsan and Mustapha, in accordance with Muslim custom, buried him within twenty-four hours and notified his nearest kin, a nephew in Saudi Arabia.

"What happens now?" I asked.

"I don't know. Muslim law stipulates that his property be divided among his living male relatives, but I'm adopted and don't have any legal claim to any of his estate."

"What about a will?"

"I'm certain there isn't one. I would have known about it. Darsan and I checked through all his papers to be sure. There's nothing."

"What are you going to do?" I asked. "That means that the store will no longer be ours?"

Mustapha shrugged his shoulders. "*Allah* is generous. He will provide for us, as long as I have faith and keep praying."

I rolled my eyes. I was a person of action. As far as I was concerned, to have faith is good, but more times than not, faith needed assistance.

"What about the newspaper? You used to work there."

Mustapha made a sour face. "Nah, setting type and getting dirty with ink is not for me." He paused, his eyes taking on that far away dreamy look. "Maybe we should consider moving to Saudi Arabia. My brother, Ed, raves about it, and my mother and sisters will be leaving for Jeddah soon. We could join them there."

"No! I'm not leaving Indonesia. Especially not to live with your family."

"But they understand you better now, and things are still so uncertain here. We need to do something about the future. I don't want my children to grow up in the midst of turmoil and chaos."

"I don't either, but it won't always be this way."

"It's been eight years since this mess started, and it's still not over."

"But it's better. Every day is better."

THIRTY-SIX

ALI

Several weeks passed before Ali, *Abuya's* nephew, arrived from Saudi Arabia. I went with Mustapha to the airport, although he told me Abuya's nephew would not expect it of a woman. This only made me more curious, if not somewhat angry.

Ali was not difficult to pick out. He came off the plane wearing a floor-length white *galabaya*, his head covered by a red checkered scarf held in place by a black band.

"*Assalamu Aleikum,*" Mustapha greeted him in his self-taught Arabic.

"*Aleikum Assalaam,*" Ali answered.

I caught the surprise in Ali's eyes, and the slight twitch in one of his thick black eyebrows. He probably didn't expect Mustapha to speak Arabic. It made me that much more proud of my husband.

Mustapha introduced me, and I extended my hand in European fashion. Ali shook it with a limp grip and sweaty palm. His black eyes had become impassive and his lips barely moved in greeting.

We took Ali to the store and showed him *Abuya's* lodgings.

"Please, make yourself comfortable," Mustapha told him, "rest. I will return for you at prayer time."

"There are sweets and juice on the table with which to refresh yourself," Darsan said, passing his hand over the table where we had so often eaten together.

Ali nodded.

The following morning, I returned to the store with Mustapha. I fully intended on playing the proper hostess by accompanying them to the other properties in *Abuya's* estate, but instead was left at the store with Darsan. Mustapha explained that Ali felt business was not a place for a woman.

"He is of the old world," Darsan consoled me, as I pretended to straighten shelves, jamming things back and forth, and making a worse mess.

"Men aren't any better than women."

Darsan rearranged the shelves behind me. "Prejudice of one kind or another exists everywhere."

I took a deep breath. Looked Darsan in the eye. "You're right." I sat down on the wobbly stool.

When Mustapha and Ali finally returned, they settled themselves at *Abuya's* desk, legal papers spread before them. Ali looked pale. Sweat pored from his forehead, and with a shaky hand he wiped it away. People who were used to dry heat had difficulty with our humidity. I brought a platter of sliced fruits and tall glasses of ice tea, garnished with fresh mint leaves. The mint would help cool Ali.

I kept a low profile, but nothing escaped me. Darsan stayed close at hand also. Poor Darsan. This store was his life too. What would he do? It would be more difficult for him. He couldn't make a living being a guerrilla captain.

Mustapha and Ali spoke in Arabic for several minutes, Ali's color returning with each sip of tea. He scrutinized the papers carefully. Finally he turned to Darsan and said something in Arabic, which Darsan couldn't understand.

"He's asking if you know me," Mustapha translated. "He wants to know who I am."

Darsan shrugged his shoulders, confused, but answered.

"He is Mustapha, son of *luan* Banawei."

Mustapha was about to translate for Ali, but Ali held his hand up. He understood.

Ali stood up, tracing his jet black mustache with his thumb and forefinger. He held up his hand, indicating we should wait. Then he walked outside, returning moments later with Mr. Go, owner of the Chinese batik store across the way. Again, he asked the same question, pointing at Mustapha. Mustapha translated for Mr. Go.

"That is Mustapha, *tuan* Banawei's son," the old Chinese answered. Ali nodded, then went back into the street and returned with a passerby. Again he asked the same question and again Mustapha translated.

"That is Mustapha," the man answered.

Ali said something to Mustapha. "He wants to know if you know who my father is," Mustapha said to the man.

"*Tuan* Banawei," the man answered.

Ali smiled. There was another exchange of Arabic. Darsan and I looked on, impatient to know what was happening.

When Ali finished speaking, the two men embraced as brothers.

"Ali says it's obvious that I'm considered *Abuya's* son, therefore it's only right that I should have the son's share of his estate."

Darsan and I exchanged surprised looks.

"The store and its inventory are ours. The other real estate will be sold and the proceeds will be divided among his relatives in Saudi Arabia."

I could barely speak. "I didn't expect such generosity." From Darsan's eyes, I knew he hadn't expected that either. I thanked Ali.

He returned my smile and then said a few more words to Mustapha.

I looked at him for a translation.

"He said if I ever come to Jeddah to look him up. There are great opportunities there."

Ali then excused himself. He would change clothes so that they could go together to the mosque and pray.

"God rewards the good," Darsan smiled, as he helped Mustapha clean away the legal documents.

"Yes," Mustapha answered. "And you are my brother. Half of everything I have received today is yours."

THIRTY-SEVEN
BOREDOM

Ali's generosity meant more to me than anyone. It meant that Mustapha had no reason to search for a new way to make an income, and there was no threat of leaving Bandoeng. The store provided adequately, and each day business improved. Darsan lived in the back as *Abuya* had done, and Mustapha commuted from the Peltzer Lane.

I had every reason to believe that finally life would be normal, the war would be forgotten, and in a matter of time all would be safe. Eventually, Mustapha and I would find our own home and we would live the life I had imagined in my childhood dreams.

But as the weeks went by I sensed Mustapha did not share my optimistic view. Again I felt his boredom setting in. More and more he let Darsan take care of the store, while he spent long hours taking pictures of nothing in particular or studying magazines and books. Outwardly he didn't appear unhappy, but I knew better.

"My brother, Ed, asked me if I would like to join him on the *Hajj*," Mustapha finally said one evening. "Every Muslim should try to do this at least once in his life time."

"You mean go to Mecca? In Saudi Arabia? I can't do that now. Nilofar is too little and I don't want to leave her behind."

Mustapha scratched his chin. His usually dreamy eyes were alert, alive, but they didn't meet my gaze, and I knew he had more to tell me. I waited.

He waited, seeming to search for a way to speak his mind.

"Oh, I see. You mean, you and your brother." I tried to keep the hurt out of my voice, but I could feel my neck and jaw tighten.

"It will give me a chance to see what my family raves so much about. Who knows, maybe it's a nice place to live."

"And you've all ready made up your mind that you're going?" I bit my tongue. I hadn't wanted to sound sarcastic.

"No, no, nothing's certain yet."

But I didn't believe him. "How long will you be gone?"

"No more then four months."

"Four months! To do a *Hajj?*"

"Maybe shorter," he replied quickly. "I want to work there before the *Hajj*. I want to see and feel what the country is like. And this pilgrimage, you understand how important it is to me. I've dreamed of seeing the *Kaaba*. It's the first temple built by the Prophet Abraham and his son Ishmael, you know." His eyes were like a little boy's remembering a long-lost fairy tale. "And to drink from the well of Zamzam. It's over three thousand years old. Isn't it amazing that it still gives water, when thousands upon thousands of pilgrims drink from it? It's a miracle. You understand why I'm going, don't you?"

"Sure, I understand," I lied. My thoughts went to Saitem, who had always taught me prayer was sacred, but where you prayed didn't matter. "I'll be fine. Take your time."

"I'm going to fulfill a religious obligation but also to plan our future. Trust me. Don't be mad."

"I'm not mad." I knew there was nothing I could do or say to change his mind. It hurt to feel that I was not important enough to share his dreams. It hurt that he could leave his wife and child during troubled times. I wanted to cry, but clenched my jaw firmly shut instead. I still had my lock box of feelings, and just tucked this away with other pains.

THIRTY-EIGHT

HAJJ

The first month Mustapha was gone, I spent most of my time at home. I helped Mother get William and Walter off to school, then took a walk with Nilofar. She liked to race down the street, picking at stones and looking at flowers growing at other homes. When we returned I sat quietly on the back patio sipping coffee and reading Voltair, Emile Zola, or the like, while Nilofar chased after cats or chickens to use as baby dolls in her stroller. When the sun became too warm we went indoors. There, Nilofar entertained herself with little scraps of material and toy scissors, while I worked on my latest project; a new-style dress or pants for myself, or Angelica, and on occasion something for one of the other children.

The days passed slowly but the evenings were worse. After Nilofar had gone to sleep the loneliness would creep in, and no amount of reading could keep my thoughts away from Mustapha.

I pulled out the post card that had arrived only the day before, thirty-four days after Mustapha had left. On the front was a picture of hundreds of tents set up to accommodate the pilgrims of the *Hajj*. I read it out loud to myself.

> *Dearest Henriette,*
>
> *It took twenty-one days for our humble little boat to reach Jeddah. I was welcomed by the local mayor and Ali Banawei. They were extremely gracious and Ali offered to have me stay with him. From the little I've seen of the city, it is very nice. There is a large colony of Indonesians here and I have found one good Indonesian restaurant. Will write a letter soon.*
> *Kiss Nilofar for me.*
>
>
> *All my love,*
> *Mus*

I looked at the picture again, then examined the stamp. It was pretty. I put the card into a drawer and got into bed. I wondered why the mayor had come to greet Mustapha. I wondered if "nice" meant that he was interested in living there. Images of women being offered as second, third, or even fourth wife came to me. I pushed the thoughts away, not only angry at my jealousy, but at a society in which women allowed themselves to be treated in such a manner. I forced myself to remember the stories of the *Ramayana,* envisioning the strong-minded *Sita.* After hours of tossing and turning I finally fell asleep, the shadows of the puppets dancing in my head.

The next day I awoke with a new sense of purpose.

"I've enrolled in a Chinese cooking class," I told my family in the afternoon. "Do you want to come?" I asked Angelica and my mother. "It starts tomorrow."

"Why do you want to cook Chinese food?" Mother asked, turning up her nose.

"Because it's different. It might be interesting," I answered. "Our first lesson is deboning a chicken without breaking the skin, then stuffing the skin and shaping it back into a chicken."

"Sounds like a lot of work," Angelica answered.

"And how often are you going to cook?" Mother asked. "This is not a permanent situation, you know."

Mother still believed things would return to the old way. "It's not just the cooking, but it's a way to meet new people. I'm tired of sitting around."

"I'm having some ladies over tomorrow," Mother answered. "You could join us. You could help Angelica keep an eye on the boys."

"Please, don't take offense, but I want friends my own age."

"You're just feeling lonely because Mustapha's gone," Angelica patted my shoulder. "You'll feel better once he is back and you have a man to take care of again."

"That must be it," I said, walking off, mumbling under my breath. Nevertheless, my sister made something clear to me. Life had to be more than just taking care of a man.

The next day I put on the new dress I had recently fashioned, dropped Nilofar at a friend's house, and went alone to Mrs. Woo's.

There were ten ladies in Mrs. Woo's kitchen. They gathered around with paper and pencils, taking careful notes as Mrs. Woo demonstrated each cut, pull, tug, chop, and stuff. They were a congenial group and easy to talk with. Most of them were Indo-European, like myself, but there were a couple of *Belanda-totos,* who much to my surprise, were friendly, and didn't seem like the snobs of the old regime.

While the stuffed chicken baked, Mrs. Woo served coffee, and answered questions. Helen, one of the *Belanda Totos,* asked if anyone played tennis.

"Cooking questions, cooking questions," Mrs. Woo laughed.

"What do you serve the chicken with?" Rebecca asked.

"Rice, vegetables. We Chinese eat rice with everything, unless we decide to use noodles. Not so different from the Indonesians."

Rebecca made a note in her book. "I play tennis," she said to Helen.

"You do? Anybody else? I thought maybe a group of us could play once a week. I noticed you can rent courts at the hotel."

"I played in high school," I said.

"Great! One more and we'll have a foursome."

"Ladies," Mrs. Woo said. "It's time to do the vegetables."

We dropped the subject of tennis for the time being and took notes on bok choy, black wood ear, bamboo shoots, and the other vegetables Mrs. Woo was placing on the chopping board.

When the chicken was done, and the vegetables properly sauteed, everyone took a small sampling. Among umms and ahhs, the subject of tennis arose again. This time we found our fourth and organized a game for the following Thursday.

My tennis skills were not as bad as I feared. It took a while but my ground strokes soon made their way comfortably over the net, and as long as I didn't try anything fancy, my game went well. My serve was another story, and needed a few weeks to prevent double faults; but Helen, Rebecca, and Joannie had similar problems and no one really cared. All we wanted was an entertaining game, and then to sit and sip iced coffee at some little outdoor cafe.

"I've been meaning to ask you," Rebecca said. "Where did you find that dress you wore to Mrs. Woo's the first day? I haven't seen anything like it."

"Thank you. I made it."

"You made it?" Helen asked. "It must be wonderful to know how to sew. I'm stuck with going to a seamstress."

"It's hard to find a good one," I answered. "That's one of the reasons I decided to make my own things. Just after the fighting stopped and schools and stores opened, I bought some beautiful material. It was expensive, but I figured I could get a dress for both myself and my daughter out of it. I didn't have a sewing machine at that time, so I took it to a seamstress. She made me my dress, but when I returned, told me there was not enough for anything else. A week later, I saw her daughter in a dress out of the same material."

"You think she stole your material?" Joannie asked.

"I can't prove it, but it sure looked that way."

"I wonder," Rebecca said. "If I bring you some material, would you make me a dress like the one you wore? You don't have to," she quickly added. "And of course, I would pay you."

"I never thought about it," I answered. "Stand up a minute."

Rebecca stood up. She was about the same height and weight as me.

"That shouldn't be too difficult. Are you in a hurry?"

"You will do it then?"

"I'll give it a try."

"I'll bring the material to our next cooking class. How much do you need?"

Rebecca was overjoyed with her new dress. It turned out so well, and she bragged about it so much, that the following week Joannie and Helen brought me material and begged me to do the same for them.

Weeks later, when Mrs. Woo's class ended, many of the women were placing orders with me for blouses, skirts, dresses, or the new slacks that were becoming the latest rage. In order to get the work done more quickly, I hired Piah, an Indonesian clothes-mender who wasn't much older than myself, and who had done some mending for me in the past. Piah came to the house once a week. She had little experience on a sewing machine, but my patience was rewarded. In no time Piah could sew anything I cut and pinned for her.

The days sped by more quickly now, and it was only in the evening when I felt the loneliness. Then once again I worried about Mustapha wanting to live in Saudi Arabia; or worse, that he would not come home to me at all. I read his letters out loud to Nilofar, who sometimes listened, sometimes didn't.

Mustapha's letters were full of how charming everybody in Jeddah was, how it was an oasis in a hot merciless desert, how he had gotten a job at the international airport and was paid in gold.

"I wonder what your papa is going to do with all that gold,"

I said to Nilofar. "They'll only confiscate it if he tries to bring it into the country."

Nilofar looked up from the wooden pony she played with.

"Papa says he misses you and loves you."

"Where's Papa? When will he be back?" Nilofar asked, coming to my side and looking at the letter.

Word got around, and before I knew what happened, friends of friends were asking me to make them clothes. Piah went from coming one day a week, to two days, then three days a week. I created and cut new patterns, while Piah did all the tedious, time-consuming work.

It was the perfect business. I made good money, while still having time for Nilofar and to socialize. I tried to include Angelica in my new social life, but she refused. She was busy with Danielle, and now that Mother's baby was due any day, she frequently carried the burden of William and Walter.

Occasionally I felt a twinge of guilt for not helping my mother more and Angelica being so burdened, but Mother had the life she chose, and Angelica had hers. They couldn't deny me mine.

Mama, he's beautiful," Angelica said, looking down at Lex, the newest member to the family.

Mother and Rudolf beamed.

I had to admit he was a lovely baby. Fair-skinned like Rudolf, with big round eyes and a crop of black hair.

"Let me hold him." Angelica picked him up. "Babies are so soft and cuddly."

"I want to hold the baby," Nilofar put her arms up.

"No, no, he's still too little," Rudolf told her. "When he's a little bigger."

Pouting, Nilofar stood behind me. "I want to hold the baby," she cried.

I picked her up so that she could see the baby in Angelica's arms. "Not right now, sweetheart. He's so little. He might get hurt."

"I want to play with the baby," Nilofar whined.

"He can't play yet. All he can do is sleep and eat," I told her.

"Lex won't have to wait too long for a playmate his size," Angelica smiled.

We all turned to her.

Angelica's smile widened.

"You're pregnant?" I asked.

She nodded.

That evening, reading Mustapha's latest letter, I felt more miserable than ever. He wrote of entering the Holy Sanctuary through the *Bab Assalaam*, Gate of Peace. The sight of the Holy *Kaaba*, draped with a gold-inscribed black cloth, struck him with awe. I bit my lower lip. I saw Nilofar's face when she wanted to hold Lex, it struck me.

Mustapha wrote of how the pilgrims dressed alike in *ihram* clothes, signifying that they were all equal in the eyes of God. He had circled the Holy *Kaaba* seven times repeating that he was at God's service. He had walked back and forth seven times between the hills of Safa and Marwah, praying and examining his conscience. I put down the letter and prayed too. I prayed Mustapha would come home soon. That we would have a normal life. That we could have another child.

THIRTY-NINE
RETURN

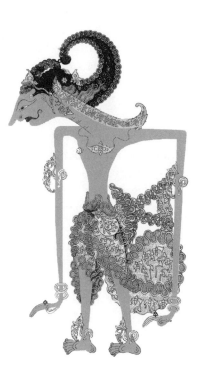

I hardly recognized Mustapha when Nilofar and I met him at the airport in Batavia. He had been gone for nearly four-and-a-half months, and sported a Saudi beard and mustache. He looked more handsome than I remembered and slightly more filled out.

"Look, there's Papa." I lifted Nilofar into my arms and waved.

Mustapha saw us immediately. With large strides he covered the distance between us and embraced both of us in a giant hug.

Nilofar recoiled and hid her face in my neck.

"It's Papa," I laughed. "It's Papa."

She raised her head with a quick jerk. Her dark eyes took him in critically. Slowly one little hand ventured out to touch his beard. She looked back at me, then giggled.

"Come on. Let Papa carry you. You're getting too heavy for Mama." He took Nilofar into his arms and gave her a kiss.

Nilofar put one arm around his neck, and with the other, continued to examine his beard.

"I missed you two," he said.

"And we missed you," I answered, searching his face. His dreamy eyes burned into mine. I could feel tears of joy threatening to spring from my eyes. He loved me. I could tell he was still mine.

Thunder rumbled and lightening flashed. "I have Lubna's car and driver," I said. "We better hurry."

We made it to the car just in time. "It's *Semar's* way of welcoming you home," I laughed, as we sat in the back seat of the Ford, and the rain poured down.

Mustapha rolled down the window to catch some rain drops. "Rain is truly a wonderful thing. We take water for granted."

I stared out the window with him. The rain tapered down, leaving the streets shiny with puddles. "Jiddah is very dry?"

"Very, and hot. I could never live in that dry heat."

"So you're convinced that this is the place for us?"

"My rash convinced me that Jiddah is not the place for us."

"Rash?"

Mustapha grimaced. "I got this horrible rash a couple of days after I got there, and it never left me. The thought of it makes me itch."

I smiled, but I was glad he had gotten the rash, glad he had come to his senses and come home.

Nilofar sat in his lap. *"Oma* and *Opa* have a new baby," she told him. "but he's too little for me to play with. And *Tante* Angelica's tummy is getting big because she has a baby inside. I have a new friend, and—" She jabbered on, until we reached Lubna and Ahmad's house. I was content to hold Mustapha's hand, feel his skin, smell his body.

Over supper Mustapha entertained us with stories of his trip, beaming with excitement like a young boy. He may have missed Nilofar and me, but he had thoroughly enjoyed his adventure.

"When Hagar, Abraham's Egyptian wife, was left in the desert with her son Ishmael," Mustapha explained, "her prayers and faith in *Allah* led her to a well, the well of Zamzam."

"What does the water taste like?" Ahmad wanted to know.

"It has an unusual taste."

"Sandy?" Lubna laughed.

"Not at all. It's refreshing, and quenches your thirst without giving that feeling of heaviness in your stomach. It is quite unusual."

Mustapha talked on of the beauty of the Grand Mosque, the overpowering feeling of God's presence when the *muezzin's* voice echoes through the valley in Mecca, and the extreme dedication of the pilgrims.

I sat close beside him, my hand still locked in his. I listened with fascination, but delighted when Mustapha finally begged to be excused. The journey home had been a long one and he was tired.

After looking in on Nilofar, who slept together with Lubna's daughter, I entered our room. It was dark, except for the moonlight that broke through the rain clouds and sent a shaft of light across the floor. Mustapha was already in bed. I could hear his breathing.

"Are you asleep?" I whispered.

"No."

Pierre-Jacques and Saitem seated in chairs at their daughter's wedding. Henriette is seated on the arm of Saitem's chair

Henriette's parents, Paul and Jeanne, on their wedding day.

Anglica, Henriette, and their parents. Father wears pajamas so many natives wore daily. A habit their mother hated.

Henriette with her sister and father in the back yard of their home in Oengaran.

Henriette standing beside her mother shortly after her mother learned how to drive and before the Japanese confiscated all cars.

Henriette and Angelica standing in the river that flowed behind their home in Oengaran. During the rainy season this river rose three times its present depth.

Mustapha as air
traffic controller
at Kamiran airport
in Batavia.

Mustapha and friend in front of
one of the many fighter planes
they helped to land.

In back, Rudof Cuenik, Jeanne, William,
and Walter. Henriette holds up little
Nilofar.

Nilofar with her paternal grandmother, Fatima.

Above: (Back far left) **Mustapha on his way to Mecca with friends to do the Hajj, hired himself out as deck-hand to get passage. The small ship was full to capacity with pilgrims.**
Below: **Pilgrim's camp**

Above: **The holy Kabba.**
Below: **Mustapha greeting Prince Feisal.**

Henriette wearing the latest women's rage, pants. Nilofar rid-
ding behind. The motorcycle was a model sold at Mustapha's
store.
Below: William, Walter, and Lex before leaving Indonesia for
Holland.

Henriette and Mustapha with Nilofar and Perihan.
The family portrait was taken the same day as their passport pictures. The family traveled on a Saudi Arabian
passport to America.

FORTY

GOOD-BYES

When the three of us returned to Ban-doeng a few days later, our euphoria was shattered by bad news. The Dutch had launched a new attack against the Indonesian Republic. They captured the Republic's capital and most of the major cities in Java. Sukarno, Hatta, and their cabinet were taken prisoner. "It seems things will never settle down," Mustapha said.

Even though he spoke with a quiet, dispassionate voice, I sensed his irritation. He, who had been my strength in getting through the war, who encouraged me that the next day would be better, seemed to be losing his patience.

"The United Nations Security Council has already called for the release of Sukarno," Bob told us. "I don't think we have much of a chance."

Mustapha and I exchanged looks, but Bob and Rudolf went on, thinking our beliefs were the same as theirs.

"I understand that the Indonesian guerrillas are as active as ever," Rudolf said. "Those Japs put all kinds of grandiose ideas into their heads."

"The world will not stand by and let the Dutch do this," Mustapha said cautiously.

"Can you believe it?" Bob said. "The United States has already threatened to use sanctions against the Netherlands and reduce its economic assistance."

"They'll never get away with it." Rudolf shook his head.

But as 1948 drew to a close, world pressure won, and the Dutch had to pull out.

I am taking Jeanne and the children to Holland," Rudolf told us.

"But why?" I asked. "Once Indonesia is established I'm sure there will be peace. You won't be in any danger."

"We have to go," Mother answered. "Those staying have to give up their Dutch citizenship. That would mean losing my widow's pension. That's all Rudolf and I have to live on."

"We're not leaving right away. I have to sell my real estate first," Rudolf added. "It will help us get a new start in Holland."

"You won't get full value on the places," Bob said. "Everything is worth half. The Indonesian government is keeping the other half. Borrowing it, they call it."

"I know we'll never see it," Rudolf said, shaking his head.

"You can bet on that," said Bob.

I didn't like the tone in Bob's voice. I wasn't sure why, but I felt defensive about Indonesia.

"What about you two?" Mustapha asked Bob and Angelica. "Are you leaving, as well?"

"Of course," Bob answered. "Eventually we'll go to Holland too, but we can't leave yet. The Police Department is involved with the transfer of power."

"I'm taking Indonesian citizenship," I said. "I'm not leaving. Now that Independence is accepted, it'll surely get better."

"Think it over carefully," Bob said, shaking his head, as if I made no sense at all.

"You may want to come to the Netherlands after all," Angelica said.

"No, not the Netherlands," Mustapha answered. "It's too cold there for me." He paused. "Maybe the United States. When I was young I used to dream about that country."

I rolled my eyes. "Come on. Stop dreaming. What would we do in the United States? We don't know a soul. We hardly speak the language and the way of life there is nothing like here."

"There's always the Middle East. We have family there. And remember, Ali extended an invitation to us."

"And what about your rash?" I raised my eyebrow.

"It doesn't hurt to have contingency plans, honey. There could be a problem with law and order when the Indonesians take over. It takes time to create an effective government."

Newspapers told of President Sukarno's arrival in Batavia. He had traveled from Djokjakarta with the Indonesian flag that was first raised at the proclamation of Independence on August 17, 1945. Now, this very same flag, the Indonesian red-and-white, was officially raised over the new country and the Dutch tricolor was lowered. I could hardly believe four years had passed since Independence had been proclaimed and nearly ten years since I was a little girl discussing the threat of Hitler and the possibility of war.

With the new government coming into power, many Dutch and Indo-Europeans, as well as Moluccans, who had loyally served the Royal Colonial Army, were in a panic to get out of the country. They hurriedly booked passage on outgoing ships, selling their possessions at ridiculously low prices.

In the midst of all this turmoil, Angelica gave birth to Richard. He was a beautiful baby, strong and healthy, with olive skin and amber-brown eyes. Little Danielle was just walking and could not be bothered by the new intruder into the family. But Nilofar wanted to hold Richard and to stop her crying, Angelica gently placed him in her lap for a minute or so.

"Mine," Nilofar said, when Bob picked up his son and she reached up her little hands to take him back.

"He's not our baby," I consoled her. "Come on, let's go into the backyard. We'll find one of your kitties."

Rudolf's real estate sold quickly, and within a few months he received their papers to board the *Willem Ruys,* an ocean liner bound for the Netherlands.

I could not remember the last time my mother and I had hugged each other so sincerely. A sudden child-like feeling passed over me, as I embraced her stout body.

"Henny, you're your father's child. Stubborn. But I've always loved you," Mother whispered. "Take care of yourself and your family. Come see us when you can."

"You take care too, Mama—I love you." I gave Rudolf a last hug, then kissed the boys.

"Come on, girls," Bob called to Angelica and me. "That was the 'all ashore who's going ashore,' call."

We followed Bob and Mustapha off the ship.

"Life really turned out different from what we thought as kids, didn't it?" I mused, as the ship blew its horn, and the steam fell like tears upon our cheeks.

Angelica sighed. "Who would have thought that the family would be broken up like this? That I would be going to live in the Netherlands. I always thought I would live and die here in Indonesia."

"It won't be easy in the Netherlands," I said. "Here we were the white elite in a dark world. In the Netherlands, you'll be the dark in a white world."

"I think Europeans are more intelligent than that."

"You think so?"

FORTY-ONE

TOLERANCE

September 1949

I'm sending Angelica and the children to Holland right away," Bob told Mustapha and me one evening.

"It's because of the *APRA* isn't it?" Mustapha said. We'd heard this group of Dutch sympathizers were kidnapping families of Dutch citizens who were reluctant to join their organization."

Bob didn't answer right away, but he paled slightly, and I sensed he was more involved than he wanted us to know.

"I can't do my work worrying about Angelica and the children. I've already booked passage for them."

"We leave as soon as there's space," Angelica said. "A month, maybe less." She paused. "I want the children out of here too."

"And what about you?" Mustapha asked Bob.

"I'll move into the police barracks for safety, and join the family in Holland as soon as I can get away."

I hated to have my sister leave so soon, but I was relieved that Bob would live in the police barracks. His possible involvement with *APRA* and close association with us, could put us in danger from the Indonesian rebels. Times were still confusing and hot heads from both sides lurked where you least expected.

I squeezed Angelica's hand. "The house will be so quiet without you. Nilofar won't have her cousins."

"*Allah* always provides," Mustapha said, putting his arm around my shoulders and giving a little squeeze. "I just got word my family is coming to Bandoeng. They can stay with us."

Had the Saudi sun damaged his brain? "I don't think so. That experience in Surabaya left things uncomfortable between us."

"If we don't take them in, we may have to take in strangers. Housing is still unstable. We will be forced to rent our rooms."

"He's right," Angelica said.

"Besides, my family is a forgiving one," Mustapha said, smiling wide.

"Forgiving? They will forgive me?" I didn't want to make a scene in front of Bob and Angelica, but the words hissed out.

Mustapha looked at me. I could see the surprise in his eyes. He had no idea why I was suddenly upset. What was he thinking? I had to do the forgiving? I wanted to scream, absolutely not, but my gold serpent caught my eye and I heard Saitem's voice, "You can never change people. You can only try to understand them, and hope they will try to understand you." I sucked my lips into a firm, determined line.

"It will be fine," Mustapha consoled me, when I didn't respond further. "I promise you. The house is a large one. Everyone can have his own space. And I swear to you, no more '*bagus putih*.'"

I cringed. I hated the phrase. It smacked of white supremacy. 'Beautiful white skin,' that was the bargaining power mothers used to offer their daughters as second wives. What did white have to do with anything anyway? I gave him a searching look. "Tolerance," I heard Saitem's voice again, "the Javanese have tolerance."

Angelica and her two children sailed for the Netherlands a week before Mustapha's family arrived. Although I spent sleepless nights worrying about their coming, their arrival was a pleasant one. Fatima and Mirna showered us with kisses, and brought good tidings from Halema and her husband, who had stayed in Surabaya. Ramzie and his wife Musna were delighted to find they could all remain together and no one spoke of the "misunderstanding" in Surabaya.

The family settled into the house, and Mustapha made sure I had my own section where I could cook and tend to things the way I saw fit, as well as run my growing sewing business. In a short time a comfortable routine emerged, whereby everyone seemed to accept the other. I had not believed it possible, but Mustapha kept true to his word and I was happier than I'd ever been. There were still differences of opinions but they only expanded my understanding of people and myself, and I could only hope that the others felt the same.

Mustapha gave Ramzie half his share in *Abuya's* store, and the two brothers joined Darsan in making the store more prosperous.

"Where did you get this?" I asked, when Mustapha rode up to the house on a new motorcycle and beeped as I tended a vine of jasmine along the front wall.

"It's a surprise," he answered, revving the motor. "We're carrying them at the store now. They arrived this morning. Motorcycles and scooters. We're importing them from Europe. Hop on. I'll give you a ride."

I climbed on behind him. Tucking my skirt under my hips, I sat with both legs to one side, holding tight to Mustapha's waist.

We took off down the street, the hem of my skirt fluttering as we picked up speed. Protected by Mustapha's back and the large shield that came up off the handle bars, I was able to look without squinting in the wind. The generously-padded seat was luxurious compared to the back of a bicycle and the way we leaned into curves was almost sensual.

"This is wonderful," I shouted.

"Want to learn?"

"Do you think I could?"

We got back to the house, and Mustapha and I switched places. I flung my leg over the seat like a man, tucking my dress in around me so I wasn't too unladylike.

"It's just like a bicycle, but with power. Here's how you give it more gas." He revved the engine. "Here are the brakes. And that's all there is to it. Ready?"

I nodded. It looked simple enough. I revved the engine as he had done.

He climbed on behind, putting both arms around my waist. "Push off slowly."

I gave it a little gas. We moved down the street. I felt unsteady at first, but as I relaxed the motorcycle moved more smoothly, and I allowed it to pick up speed.

Mustapha gave my waist a squeeze. "That's it! You're doing it."

We drove around the block, some people looking up at, no doubt, my unlady-like posture. I didn't care. Why should men have all the fun?

"*Ya Haram, ya haram,*" Fatima was yelling from the front veranda, when we came up our street. We stopped to see what was making her so excited.

With her sandals flopping and her sarong stretched tight, she rushed across the grass to the street. "Are you crazy?" She scolded. "Henriette is carrying your baby and you expose her to such danger?" She took off her scarf and beat Mustapha's shoulders with it, the soft puffs of silk landing like clouds.

"Mama, we weren't going fast," Mustapha said, not able to keep the smile off his face or the laughter from his voice.

"No matter." She replaced her scarf and took my hand. "Get off that thing. And look at you, sitting like a man. Get off!"

"The baby isn't due for months," I tried to console her, while stepping as gently as I could off the motorcycle.

"All the more reason to be careful. Come inside and rest."

FORTY-TWO

PERIHAN

As the child within me grew, I detected the symptoms of restlessness growing in Mustapha. The motorcycles, which at first had made him so happy, were no longer enough to keep him content. He let Ramzie and Darsan manage the store, while he became a silent partner, bored, until his interests were captured by the new flying school at the airport.

"Why do you have to keep your lessons a secret?" I asked.

"Because it will upset Mother."

"Everything upsets Mother. What are you going to do when you can fly, anyway?"

"I don't know yet. I've always wanted to learn how to fly. Now I'll be one of the first to get a private pilot's license in the new Republic."

"But then what?"

"We'll form a club. Do aerobatics."

"That will really upset your mother."

"She won't know."

"Your sister will tell her."

"My sister won't know either."

"I thought you didn't keep secrets from her."

Mustapha took a deep breath. "Let me handle it. Just don't you say anything."

I agreed. In a way it pleased me that I knew something his mother and sister didn't. It made me feel closer to him. I only wished I was close enough to help his restlessness. Perhaps all would change with our next child. Perhaps I would have a son. A son to do son things with his father.

Sit here," little Nilofar directed, pointing to a rattan lounge chair on the back patio. "I'll dance for you." She was a precocious little five-year-old.

"How can I refuse such a wonderful offer?" I kissed Nilofar's cheek. Secretly I wanted to rest. The baby was due any day now and the extra weight and the heat were causing my legs to swell. I had gone to the hospital early that morning, thinking the baby was coming, but the midwife sent me home. False alarm. I sat down in the cool shade. Enna, dear old Enna from before the war, had managed to find me and now slid into her old routine. She brought out a glass of cold tea.

"Thank you Enna. It's good to have you back."

Enna bowed. "Good to be back, *noni.*"

I smiled to think she still addressed me as if I were a child. She was a paid servant now, but I was sure her loyalties were the same.

"Watch, Mama," Nilofar shouted, as she twirled in her new dress.

The pressure in my lower back came and went in waves. "Bravo, bravo," I clapped.

My discomfort continued through dinner and into the evening, and so around eight o'clock I decided perhaps it would be best to go to the hospital for the night.

"Are you sure you want to do that?" Mustapha asked.

"It's probably nothing, and you can pick me up tomorrow morning, but I'd feel better if I didn't have to worry about having to go out in the middle of the night."

"The hospital's not far."

"I know, but the streets still aren't safe at night."

"There aren't any rebels in our area."

"Please, Mus, it would make me feel better."

Mustapha complied, and had the driver bring around the car. The house was in an immediate uproar, but I quieted them.

"Nothing yet. I just want to be on the safe side. I'll see you in the morning."

In no time at all we made it to the tiny hospital. Tucked into a residential area, the hospital was really no more than a large house, with four bedrooms set up to receive patients. Mustapha helped me into the building and relinquished me to the midwife.

"Do you want me to stay?" he asked.

"No, go home. Keep an eye on Nilofar."

He kissed me on the forehead. "I'll see you in the morning then."

I went with the midwife into a room, where I undressed and got into bed. She gave me an examination and we talked for a short while, until exhaustion overcame me, and I fell asleep.

Like spirits telling of the eleven o'clock hour, light rain tapping at the window awakened me. The pain in my back increased and my stomach tightened and became hard. I breathed deep. The pain subsided. I waited to see if the pain would come again. It did, and I knew I was in labor. I called out for the midwife, who in no time at all, stood beside me.

"Yes, it's almost time," she said after she'd examined me again. "Try to relax and breathe slowly." As she talked she gathered things from here and there in the room. Gently she positioned me for delivery, and with expert hands began massaging the area with soothing oils. "Slowly, slowly—you don't want to tear anything," she coached. Her fingers moved in slow rotations, my body relaxing without my telling it to.

I listened to the instructions the midwife gave, sometimes not feeling a part of this world. Minutes went by, hours. The sound of the rain added to the soothing ambiance of the dimly-lit room.

But eventually the need to push was strong.

"Harder, harder," the midwife said, her voice staying sweet and calm. "Push harder."

I pushed, I panted, I breathed. I pushed some more, harder and harder.

Shortly after 1:00 a.m. I heard the wail of a baby. My baby.

"What a beautiful daughter," the midwife said, as she held the baby up so I could see. "My goodness, look at this girl. She's nearly five kilos. And the hair. Look at all this hair."

I took the little bundle into my arms, examining all her finger and toes. Nilofar had a baby sister. A baby sister! I smiled, then drifted off to sleep.

The next morning I was already awake, when Mustapha arrived. I could hear him talking with the midwife in the hall.

"What are you doing here so early?" The midwife whispered.

"I'm picking up my wife."

"Your wife? For heaven's sake, she just had a baby! She won't be going home for four or five days."

"She did what?" There was a flurry of footsteps and then Mustapha peeked sheepishly around the door. "Hi," he whispered. "How do you feel?"

"Still a little tired, sore. Come look."

He stepped over and kissed my cheek, then with his long fingers he carefully picked up the thin blanket to uncover the bundle beside me.

"It's a girl," I said.

"She has hair," he laughed.

"And look how big she is." I held the blanket open wide.

Mustapha touched her little feet and hands, then curled a lock of her black hair around his finger.

"Yes, I think she's going to have curls from the beginning," I smiled. "Poor Nilofar. Remember how bald she was?"

Mustapha laughed. "She was even balder when you shaved her head."

"Well, that Chinese woman told me her hair would grow back in beautiful curls if I did," I defended. "And her hair did grow back beautiful."

"But there weren't any curls."

Mustapha leaned over and kissed me again. "Both our daughters are beautiful."

I pulled the little bundle closer to me. "Everyone was so sure we were going to have a boy. Mus, you aren't unhappy that it's another girl, are you?"

He shook his head. "The important thing is that you and the baby are well."

"All right, that's enough," the midwife interrupted. "You go home and come back later. Your wife needs her rest and it's a bit early for visitors."

"Think of a name," I whispered, as he left. "We need another beautiful name."

Five days later Mustapha brought me and little Perihan home.

"I want to see. I want to see," Nilofar begged.

Fatima lifted Nilofar up to see the bundle in my arms. With her little fingers she touched her sister's cheek. Perihan's head turned at the touch, opening her mouth like a baby bird.

"Can the baby play with me?" Nilofar asked.

"She can't really play yet," Mustapha told her. "She's still too small."

"Again? Why can't babies be made bigger?" Nilofar's lower lip protruded and tears began to form.

"She will get bigger and then you can play with her. Come on, sweet-heart." I took her hand. "You can help me by holding your little sister in your lap and singing a nice song to her."

Nilofar stretched out her tiny arms.

"No, sit down in the chair first. She's too heavy for you to hold."

Nilofar quickly jumped into a large heavily-cushioned chair.

I carefully placed Perihan in her arms.

Nilofar beamed, and Perihan seemed to look intently at the new person holding her. Quietly Nilofar began to sing, *"Slaap kindje slaap. Daar buiten loopt een schaap—"* It was an old Dutch lullaby I used to sing to Nilofar.

Preferring not to delegate servants to care for my children, I found that two were a handful. My only real quiet time came in the morning when Nilofar was in school. Then, while Perihan slept quietly in the shade of the overhanging wisteria vine, I worked with Piah on our sewing orders.

Our relationship had turned into one of friendship and the more I was tied to domestic work, the more Piah took on. She could now cut and pin any pattern we had done before, and I would often give her instructions while carrying Perihan.

When Nilofar returned home from school at noon, I fed her lunch and tried to get her down for a short nap, but more often than not Nilofar would have nothing to do with that. She wanted to play outside. She liked to roll in the grass, balance herself on the low border wall, put her cat in the stroller, or capture a chicken to bathe. Poor creatures. How they tolerated her, I'll never know.

By evening the exhausted five-year-old had no trouble falling into a deep sound sleep, and neither did the harried pets. With quiet settling on the house, Mustapha and I visited with the rest of the family on the veranda, drinking in the cool evening air. We sipped coffee and solved all the world's problems, while watching the stars. It was a happy relaxing time and reminded me of the pre-war days when I sat outside with my family. I allowed myself to daydream while I rocked Perihan in my arms.

"She's not asleep yet?" Mustapha asked.

"She's a little fussy tonight." I stood up and paced back and forth, patting her back.

"Just put her in bed. She'll cry herself to sleep," Fatima said.

"I don't like to hear a baby cry. And besides, she'll wake Nilofar. I'll walk around with her a bit." I took Perihan to the backyard where it was more quiet. "The rain leaves a fresh smell in the air, doesn't it, Perihan?" I spoke in a whisper. "And look at the sky. Isn't it beautiful the way the clouds are lit up by the moon?" A breeze blew, calling me to past times. I recalled a story Saitem had told me.

"Long long ago, there were seven sisters. They were the Nymphs of the Pleiades, who used to come down from the heavens and bathe naked in sacred pools. Their magical sarongs were the wings with which they transported themselves from the heavens to the earth." I looked to see if Perihan's eyes were closed yet.

"She looks like she's listening," Mustapha whispered.

"Where did you come from?"

"I followed you out. Go on with your story."

I took a moment to remember where I had left off. "Prince Raja Pala, who had gotten lost on a hunting expedition, came across the sacred pool of the seven bathing sisters. Spying Siti, the youngest of the nymphs, he became obsessed with her beauty. Quickly, he stole her sarong from the bank, so she could not fly back to the stars with her startled sisters."

I looked at Mustapha again and raised a questioning eyebrow.

"Still awake," Mustapha whispered, from the chair he had made himself comfortable in.

"The nymph begged Raja Pala to return her wings and let her join her sisters, but the prince insisted he would only return her wings if she first bore him a child, whose eyes would remind him of the world she came from. Siti agreed and months later bore him a beautiful child. This child was the first to be of both worlds—born of the earthly prince, and the sky goddess. Before Siti returned to the stars she told Raja Pala. 'You may have this child for his brief life on earth, but after that, remember, he returns to me.'"

"See, Perihan. See all those stars? They are the children returned home." Perihan seemed to stare skyward, but soon her long black lashes fluttered and fell shut.

FORTY-THREE

AMERICAN FRIENDS

"Henriette? Where are you?"

"Out here," I called. It was early afternoon and I didn't expect Mustapha home. Nilofar and I were working in our soon-to-be vegetable garden, while Perihan lay on a blanket in the shade.

"We have company," Mustapha called from the patio.

I put my tools in a basket and pulled off my gloves. "Come, let's see who's here."

Nilofar pulled herself out of the garden, clapping her muddy hands together and brushing at the knees of her overalls, while I picked Perihan up. Together we hurried to the patio, Nilofar skipping at my side.

I didn't recognize the couple standing with Mustapha, nor the little boy with them. "Please excuse my appearance." I ran a hand through my hair. "Mustapha didn't tell me."

Mustapha translated my words into English, which embarrassed me slightly, but made me more curious.

"I'm sorry we're barging in on you," the woman answered in slow deliberate English.

"This is Niazi and Aisha," Mustapha introduced them.

"And their little son Timur. Come, Nilofar, a new friend. Why don't you two play?"

Timur hid behind his mother, and Nilofar stubbornly looked at him, but made no attempt to play.

"In a while perhaps," Aisha smiled. She stroked her son's red curls. "He's only four. He's shy until he knows his way around."

"Yes, later perhaps," I said, demonstrating that I did know how to speak English.

"Nabeel left a message at the store this morning," Mustapha said, "telling me of a couple from the United States who were staying at the hotel. I guess since Nabeel knew I spoke English, he thought I might help."

It was clear now. Mustapha loved to meet people from foreign countries. I guess contact with them made him feel like he had been to that country. In his heart he was still a little boy looking for adventure

I motioned to the patio chairs, and called Enna to bring refreshments.

"You are American?"

"Of Turkish background," Niazi answered.

"Ahh," I nodded. "I thought your names were different."

"Niazi is doing research for a book," Mustapha said.

"What kind of book?" I asked.

"I'm still forming my ideas," Niazi answered. "I'm studying the political and cultural ties of Ottoman Turkey with the eighteenth-century Sultanates of Atjeh. One of Atjeh's princes married a lady of the Ottoman Royal Court, you know."

"I had no idea," Mustapha said.

Niazi continued, telling Mustapha some of his interesting findings. The two were like long-lost friends.

Bored with adult conversation, Nilofar wandered back into the yard and began chasing a chicken. Timur's shy eyes brightened. He stood slowly up, a big grin spreading across his face. He looked up at his mother, then bolted after Nilofar.

"Timur misses having a back yard to play in," Aisha said, watching her son run after Nilofar. "We're staying at the Homan Hotel. There is no play yard." She rubbed her swollen abdomen. "We hope to be a little more settled before this one comes."

"When is your baby due?" My English was slow and I had to think before speaking, but I managed simple sentences.

"Not for another three months," Aisha answered. She touched the tips of Perihan's toes. "I hope we have a pretty little girl."

"A hotel is no place for children. You should rent a house."

"We've looked all morning, but the housing situation in your country is very difficult."

"Yes, it is a problem. Perhaps we can help." I liked Aisha. The petite woman with large brown eyes, eccentrically-coifed hair, and bright red lips, was a refreshing change. She had graduated from the University of Peking, and spoke several languages: Turkish, Chinese, Russian and English; and was hoping I could teach her Indonesian. She was interested in tropical herbs and eager to learn about their medicinal uses. It pleased me to talk with her.

In the weeks that followed we became good friends with Aisha and Niazi. Nilofar and Timur had found a secret language they could communicate in, and Mustapha and Niazi seemed to have endless topics to discuss.

Mustapha felt sorry for them too—cooped up in their hotel. He agreed with me that a house would be much better for them, and began actively searched for available housing. With the help of a fellow member of the flying club, a banker, Mustapha succeeded in finding a newly-completed house only five short blocks from our own home.

Niazi and Aisha were beyond happy.

I further offered my assistance to Aisha by helping her find furniture and trustworthy servants. We had fun looking for good bargains. Many of the Chinese had bought furniture from the fleeing Dutch and it now stood in dimly lit stores waiting to be snatched up by those who had money. And I asked Enna's advice in finding servants Aisha could trust and be happy with.

"Mustapha, maybe you could help me with one other thing," Niazi said, after they had moved into their house and the four of us sat admiring how things had turned out. "I need a translator and someone who can teach me Indonesian."

Mustapha thought for a moment, but I could already see his mind working. "Would I be acceptable? I can do both."

I was not surprised. Perhaps this would be the distraction he needed to alleviate his boredom. The flying club, although a nice bunch of men, was not enough.

Niazi's blue eyes smiled out from his ruddy complexion. "I was hoping you'd say that. Of course I will compensate you for your time away from your business and all travel expenses will be paid for."

"Travel?" Had my English missed something?

"Some travel," Niazi said. "I'd need to visit Atjeh and some areas of Sumatra. I'd also like to see Djakarta and Djokjakarta."

He had the same look in his eyes as Mustapha did when he got excited; bright, alert, thoughtful. He talked fast, bouncing from one idea to the next, and in my minimal English I had difficulty understanding all he said.

It didn't seem to matter how I felt about it anyway. It was decided just like that. Not even Aisha seemed concerned that perhaps I might not be happy with my husband leaving for all parts without me.

"But we're not going anywhere until our car arrives. We're still waiting for it," Niazi went on, unaware of my concerns. "We had it shipped from the United States."

"It's not safe to travel in the countryside, you know," I said. "I hope you don't plan to drive outside the city."

"Of course we do. We can't be prisoners in this beautiful country." He spread his arm wide, as if to embrace Indonesia. "I'll make sure we have an oversized American flag on the car whenever we venture into the hinterlands." He winked at me.

I opened my mouth to protest, but Niazi laughed a great booming laugh.

"None of the guerrillas will dare to shoot at an American! Oh, that reminds me, we need to find a driver."

The weeks sped by and Mustapha and Niazi threw themselves into studying Islamic material and the Indonesian language. Aisha and I studied as well, but our studying took on a different format. We taught each other Indonesian and English as we shopped for groceries, took care of the children, and made meals. I told Aisha as much as I knew about Indonesian herbs, but the slow job of translating library books would come when Aisha understood the language better.

Foreign as it felt and at times uncomfortable, being with Aisha was an education for me in ways I had never imagined. She was outspoken, had her own ideas and didn't have a problem verbalizing them. She dressed differently, not caring that people were surprised at her bare shoulders or exposed legs. She adored her husband and made every effort to please him, but she was her own person.

At her home evenings were very different, probably American, but I enjoyed them.

"Help me with these appetizers, will you?" Aisha asked me one evening before her guests arrived. "The servants don't understand what I want."

"I'm not sure I do either." I laughed. "Indonesians don't serve appetizers."

"Americans serve them before dinner, with cocktails."

"We just eat dinner when it's ready. Most Indonesians don't drink alcohol, so cocktails would be wasted on them."

"Well, let me show you, because this is a different crowd."

Aisha explained about deviled eggs, bottled mustard, green olives stuffed with red pimentos, and caviar.

"Haven't you ever had caviar?" Aisha asked, as I examined the slimy black rounds.

I shook my head.

"They're fish eggs."

"Oh, I've had fish eggs before. We fry them."

Aisha made a face and clasped her arms over her chest, hiding the cleavage her strapless dress afforded. "This is different. A delicacy. They're divine. Let me show you how we eat them." She put a tiny spoonful onto a cracker. "In the United

States we usually spread a little sour cream on the cracker first, but we'll have to do without here." She popped the cracker and caviar into her mouth, then handed one to me.

I tried a small bite. "They're salty."

"A little. But they're wonderful with vodka." Aisha poured the clear liquid over ice cubes and handed the glass to me.

"No, thank you. I don't drink."

"Not even a little?"

I shook my head.

Aisha smiled. "No matter. I have some of that melon punch you showed me how to make. What about Mustapha?"

"He doesn't drink either. We're Muslim. We don't drink alcohol."

"We're Muslims too, but once in a while a sip is okay. Besides, I have to have something to serve these embassy people. Americans are used to having a good stiff drink." She took a sip of the iced vodka. "Ahh, it's awfully good. Sure you won't try some?"

I shook my head. Amused, I turned back to the appetizers. People's interpretation of religion was so interesting. "Shall I help you carry these out?"

"No, we'll let the servants do it. I just wanted to fix them."

Niazi and Aisha's guests were scholars, and U.S. Embassy people who traveled all over the world. Conversation ran from politics to religion, and the company remained mixed. None of that women and women's talk here, and men and men's talk there. The evening felt stimulating and enlightening. It was the way it should be. People discussing ideas. And if there was music and dancing, couples danced with each other. I couldn't imagine a party like this at our home. Fatima would surely have a heart attack.

FORTY-FOUR

TRAVELS

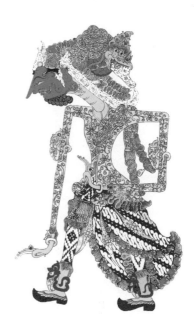

After their daughter Cihan was born, Niazi asked Mustapha to accompany him to Djakarta to register her with the U.S. Embassy.

"We're taking the car, but I promise we'll fly the U.S. flag," Niazi told me. "Look, I already have it mounted on the fender."

"And Rifai is a good driver," Mustapha added. He wore his little-boy look. I could tell he was excited. Not everyone got to ride in a big car with the American flag flying on its fender.

"It's a long drive to Batavia, I mean Djakarta." I still had trouble getting used to some of the name-changes that the Indonesians instituted. I had only just gotten used to Peltzer Lane becoming Imam Bandjol Street.

"We'll be gone overnight," Niazi said.

"Do you think you girls can manage?" Mustapha asked.

Aisha smiled, probably taking his question as concern. "Of course."

"We'll just be helpless without you," I said.

In the weeks that followed, Niazi and Mustapha took several short island hops. I slowly accepted the four-or-five-day trips and grew grateful that Mustapha had a job situation he liked. The store thrived under the care of Darsan and Ramzie, and neither one of them minded Mustapha's absence.

"These are American sewing patterns," Aisha told me one afternoon as we sat waiting for the men to return from one of their trips.

I read *Butterick* and *McCall's* on the large white envelope.

Aisha opened an envelope and pulled out its contents.

I spread out the patterns, examining them with a trained eye. "They tell you where to put the zippers, darts, and pleats? This is fantastic!" One by one I leafed through the pile of envelopes. I marveled at the dresses, blouses, shorts and slacks I could cut from the sophisticated patterns.

"They're for you," Aisha said. "I've used most of them, but you can use them again."

"For me?"

"I can get more anytime. Let me know if there's something special you want to make."

"I'll try these out as soon as I can." In the back of my mind was the knowledge that I could charge more for American styles. I would be at the forefront of Indonesian modern fashion.

We were still discussing the patterns when Niazi's car roared up the drive. It came to a screeching halt, the doors flew open and Mustapha, Niazi, and Rifai spilled out.

At first concerned that they were hurt, we rushed out, only to find them laughing hysterically.

"It's your fault," Mustapha was saying.

"But you didn't warn me," Niazi laughed back.

"The car would have been ruined if we had not closed the windows," Rifai apologized.

"What happened?" I asked. Then the overwhelming smell of *durian* assaulted us. "Oh, oh."

Niazi walked to the back of the car. "I couldn't resist." He opened the trunk to reveal at least ten ripe *durian* and some not-so-ripe ones.

"When it began to rain," Mustapha laughed, "we closed the windows."

"We forgot about the *durian*," Niazi said.

"The smell seeped into the car from the trunk."

"We thought we were going to die of *durian* toxicity," Niazi laughed. "I had no idea that fruit could be so potent."

"And they worry about us," Aisha said. "Rifai, take the fruit out and air the car. I think the smell will be gone by tomorrow."

"Next week at the earliest," I laughed. "You don't know *durian*.

Over dinner the laughter died down and I listened as Mustapha and Niazi discussed different governments. Aisha frequently gave her opinion, not only on politics but many other subjects that in my circle were not proper for women to discuss. It surprised me that Niazi accepted his wife's comments on 'manly' matters, and he even asked for her views.

"Not all Indonesians envisioned the same kind of country as Sukarno," Mustapha said. "There is the Darul Islam, a faction that opposed Sukarno, and there are rumors of communist interests as well."

"Islam is a growing faith," Niazi said.

"But will it succeed in government?" Mustapha asked.

"Not if it's run by radicals," Aisha answered.

"When we do the *Hajj*, we'll pray extra hard for Indonesia," Niazi said.

"You're going to do the *Hajj*?" I could feel my stomach begin to churn. Another five month trip? "When did you decide this?" I asked calmly.

"We'll only be gone for eighteen days. I didn't think you'd mind," Mustapha said. He maintained an air of nonchalance in front of our friends, and I had made it a habit not to make a scene at these more and more frequent surprises, but I could not stop my jaw from tightening.

Mustapha pleaded with his eyes. Eighteen days wasn't so long. I could deal with that, but I hated having to find out like this. Why couldn't he have told me, asked me, discussed it? I didn't say anything further and pretended the subject had never been mentioned. I made very little eye contact with Mustapha for the rest of the evening. He would know I was angry. But I also knew in the end, he would have his way.

When Mustapha and Niazi returned from the *Hajj,* Niazi was full of praise for the Middle East. "There is so much to write about. So much to see. Mustapha, we must go back. Make a more extensive trip. See more than just Saudi Arabia."

Mustapha was furiously agreeing, and Aisha did not seem to care that her husband wanted to take off again. She was enthusiastic about Niazi's ideas, and encouraged him to do what he thought was necessary. She had mastered enough of the Indonesian language that she was deep in the throes of her own research, as well as busy with her two children.

"Fine," I sighed, "if you're going to do this trip, then I would like to visit my family in Holland. Perihan is a year, and mother and Angelica haven't seen her."

Mustapha pulled at his lip. "I don't know if it's practical for you to travel by yourself with two little children. When I get back, maybe we can go together."

"Mustapha is right," Niazi agreed. "It's not safe for a woman to travel alone. We won't be gone long. Better wait for Mustapha to return."

"No." I was determined. "If I'm capable enough to stay here and take care of myself, I am capable of traveling. I can make arrangements for us, if you're too busy."

"What about your business?" Mustapha said. "You can't leave it like that."

"Piah can handle it." The business had slipped my mind, but I knew Piah was clever. She would manage. I would give her instructions and perhaps hire help for her before I left.

In February, two days before Mustapha and Niazi were to take off on their trip, I boarded a Dutch steamer with Nilofar and Perihan.

"You're sure you will be all right?" Mustapha asked, as he hugged me good-bye.

"Of course." I enjoyed the little bit of insecurity Mustapha was feeling. It counter balanced my own fears. I wanted to see my family, but five months was a long time to be away from Mustapha.

As the steamer sailed out of Djakarta, Perihan clung to my neck, and Nilofar stood holding tight to the rail. I had never traveled such a distance by myself. It had always been with my father. Thoughts of him now flooded me.

"I went to Holland with my Papa and Mama on a boat just like this," I told the children.

"Did it take a long time?" Nilofar asked.

"Many many days, with lots of stops."

Just like the trip I had taken with my father, the ship sailed to Singapore, Medan, and then to Sabang at the northern tip of Sumatra. There we stopped for charcoal and water. I smiled, remembering the stern look on my father's face when he discovered the children on board had put the loading time to good use. We had tied ropes to empty cans and flung them overboard to collect squirming jellyfish. Quietly we deposited several slimy creatures in almost every cabin bathtub. Oh, how the cabin boys had sworn at the extra work to undo the mischief. I decided not to tell Nilofar about it.

From Sabang we sailed to Colombo on the island of Ceylon and on through the rough Indian Ocean. My father and I had gripped the deck rail and watched the waves swell and dip as the wind whipped at the white foam, but now I kept my children safely inside the cabin. I was the parent, the only parent, and responsible for my babies.

The ship sailed into the Gulf of Aden, up to the calm, hot Red Sea, through the Suez Canal and into the Mediterranean. Eighteen years ago the light of the moon guided our ship through the Straits of Messina, past Mt. Etna, its awesome ooze glowing ominously before bubbling into the sea. Now there was nothing but darkness.

In Genoa, Italy, I took the children ashore for some sightseeing. Then we were back on board for the long leg of the journey through the Strait of Gibraltar and around Spain and Portugal to Southampton, England.

No dense fog hugged the English coast, as it had done in

1934, and there was no Queen Mary, which then was making her maiden voyage. We slipped quietly into port and then across the channel to Amsterdam.

It was April when we arrived, and there was still snow on the ground. Nilofar and Perihan were fascinated by the cold white blanket. They screamed and laughed and then needed to be bundled and warmed by *Oma's* potbelly stove.

"Your house turned out beautiful," I told Mother, while walking through the three-story home Rudolf had built for them.

"It's more costly than we thought," Mother answered. "We have to take in boarders to offset the cost."

How much life had changed and yet stayed the same, I thought. Here, in a different country, my mother, now a grandmother, took in borders, just as Saitem and Pierre-Jacques had done.

"Times are not easy here either," Rudolf said, lighting a fat cigar. "Holland is trying to recover from the war too. Jobs are scarce, housing impossible. People are forced to rent rooms."

"Doesn't sound much different than what you left," I said. "And the Dutch are probably not overjoyed to see the Colonists coming back."

"You're right," Angelica said sadly. "You knew it would be like this. I remember you telling me." She shifted her weight. She was pregnant again, and unusually large. The doctor said maybe she'd have twins.

"We manage, though," Rudolf said.

"But many of the Colonists have nothing. And the Dutch don't make it easier for them. We *Indos* are good enough to work for the Dutch, but they don't want us to live with them."

"Why don't you leave?" I asked.

"Where would we go? Bob has a good job with the police in Rotterdam. He wants to stay."

"Recovery takes time," Rudolf said.

FORTY-FIVE

IMMIGRATION

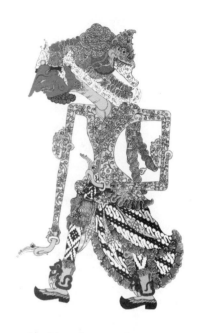

For the next three months I received letters and picture postcards from Pakistan, Iraq, Iran, Egypt, and finally Lebanon, where Mustapha discovered distant relatives. I missed him terribly, but knew if our marriage was to survive I had to have faith and trust in him, and he had to learn I was not a meek, everything's-okay housewife.

One day a postcard arrived from Turkey, and that very evening Mustapha was at my mother's front door.

"Surprise!" He walked into the house, looking better than ever. He kissed me, a quick peck on the mouth, when he knew no one was looking "I missed you. I had to come for a visit. Besides, I wasn't that far away."

He stayed a week, longer than he planned, but KLM had canceled many of their flights to Indonesia due Mossadegh taking over the oil fields in Persia.

"I've got to get home before *Ramadan,*" Mustapha said to me. "I can't wait for KLM."

"What are you going to do?"

"I booked a Pan American flight to the United States. I'll land in New York, then fly to Los Angeles and from there I'll fly to Djakarta."

It seemed like a ridiculous way to get home, but not for Mustapha. He was traveling the world, but he still needed excuses to do it.

Two months later, Mustapha waited at the dock in Djakarta when I disembarked with the children. He looked bright and happy.

"Papa!" Nilofar hugged him.

"So, did you two girls have a good time visiting your *Oma?*"

Nilofar nodded. "But I don't like it when it's cold. We had to wear heavy coats and you can't play in the rain."

Mustapha laughed.

"It was a good visit," I said, "but I'm tired of cobblestone streets with rows and rows of houses that all look the same, with their little lace curtains, tulip-potted windows and door fronts. I missed the rice paddies, the volcanoes, and the weather. I missed the people and our relaxed pace. And, I missed you."

Mustapha looked deep into my eyes. We could read each other's thoughts, even when we pretended we couldn't. A smile spread across his face. Mustapha took Perihan from my arms and directed us out of the crowd.

I sensed a difference about Mustapha, but I didn't know exactly what. There was excitement in his eyes, and something more. Perhaps he had a surprise for us. Then I worried he and Niazi were planning another trip. I prayed it was not too soon. I wanted to spend time together, just the two of us.

My wish came true. Mustapha was beside me day and night, playing with the children, telling me about his trip, complaining about the sniper fire that still continued in our country.

"While you were gone, Dutch rebels returned, shooting up the city," Mustapha told me. "It's still not safe here." And then he broke the news. It was what he had been keeping secret. The surprise I had suspected.

"What are you talking about?" The whole family was shocked. "You applied for immigration?"

"You'll love California." Mustapha talked fast. "I've never seen anything like it. The climate is gentle, the sky is deep blue, there are green rolling mountains and forests, and the Pacific Ocean roars along the coast, but people can swim in it."

Images of Mustapha's *National Geographic Magazines* floated before my eyes. He was acting out his boy-hood dreams and I didn't know if I wanted to be a part of the adventure.

"But your family is here," I said.

"They could leave too. I'm telling you, the United States is where we have to go."

"You'll be leaving paradise," Ramzie said. "I can't leave here. Not now. The business is doing so well."

"Indonesia is not perfect, but it's better than most places," Fatima said. "I know. I've lived in other places. Who put such nonsense into your head?"

"The economic and political situation is not getting any better," Mustapha answered. "In fact, with Communism gaining ground, it could get worse. I want better opportunities for my children."

"It won't be an easy life," Mirna said. "Everything will be different. It's not an Islamic country."

"You won't have any friends or family," Musna said.

"We'll manage," Mustapha answered. "It will be wonderful, don't you think?" He turned to me, but I was speechless. I stared in disbelief. He wanted to leave Indonesia? For good? I never believed he would do it, find the right place, follow his "dream". I consoled myself with the knowledge that he was at least taking me with him. Perhaps he was just over excited about his recent trip.

I managed a smile. "We'll see what happens."

I let Mustapha ramble on. Immigration laws were strict and it might be years before we got our visas. There was no sense in worrying now. By the time the visas came through, Indonesia would have recovered and Mustapha would change his mind.

August 1954 departure on the *M.S. Castleville* of the Klaveness Line. A Norwegian freighter that ultimately took the family to San Pedro, California. The voyage took more than 40 days.

FORTY-SIX

DEPARTURE

May 1953

Remember, if you decide to follow through with your immigration, we're happy to sponsor you," Niazi said, as they boarded the plane in Bandoeng.

I wished he would shutup. I was convinced that without Niazi and Aisha to remind Mustapha of how good the United States was supposed to be, he would forget all these childish dreams.

But four months after Niazi and Aisha returned to the United States, we received word from the U.S. Embassy.

"Look at this!" Mustapha shouted. "*Allah* is watching over us."

"What are you talking about?" I asked.

"It's from the U.S. Immigration," Mustapha read the letter. "They have established a new immigrant quota of one hundred people for each Asian country."

I felt light-headed. I knew what it meant but I didn't want to hear. I stared at Mustapha.

"Don't you understand? This means we're clear to depart in two weeks."

I sat down.

"It's a dream come true!" Mustapha smiled, then his face turned serious. "But we'll be traveling on Saudi Arabian passports, so we can't take any money out of the country. I need to quickly transfer everything we own and any money to Ramzie's name, or the government will take everything."

I began to cry. "How can you do this? How will we live?"

"Think of it," Mustapha put his arm around me. "We'll have a new and better life. We'll be safe from political unrest and sniper fire. Our children will have a better education and have opportunities we never had. They'll go to the University. They won't be like us."

"But how will we live? We'll have nothing."

"*Allah* will guide us."

Two weeks later, after many tearful good-byes, we boarded the small twelve-passenger freighter *M. S. Castleville,* of the Klaveness Line. From the deck I stared out at green coconut palms and blue volcanoes. Thunderclouds in shapes of dragons and snakes bid me farewell. A gush of cool air and a kiss graced my cheek.

"Papa, will you know where to find me?" I whispered. "Saitem, will I remember?"

Noor, the third and last daughter.
Born in California, September 1956

Glossary

Abuya   Father in Arabic.

Aleikum Assalaam   A response meaning peace be with you also.

Allah   God.

Aloon aloon   Central square.

APRA   Queen of Justice Armed Forces—Dutch rebels against Indonesians.

Arab Djin Djin   Derogatory description for an Arabic person.

Assalamu Aleikum   Greeting—peace be with you.

Bagus putih   Beautiful white.

Belanda   Dutch.

Belanda toto   Pure Dutch.

Beduk   Native drum.

Bhagavad Gita   Hindu Holy book.

Dalang   Puppeteer and storyteller.

Daging kambing   Goat meat.

Dalala   Matchmaker.

Dokkar   Horse-drawn cart.

Durian   A large fruit, that when ripe, has a very strong odor.

Eid   Muslim holiday at the end of the month of fasting.

Galabaya   A lose fitting tunic type piece of clothing, usually floor length.

Gambus   String instrument, more common in the Middle East.

Gamelan   Orchestra of percussion instruments.

Garuda   Giant mythical bird.

Goona goona   Island form of voodoo.

Grobak   A cart—pushed from behind.

Gudang   A storage space or shed in the back of the main house.

Gurkha   Indians fighting with the British.

Iklas   To quiet one's emotions and let go of a loved one.

Inlander   Referring to the natives before Independence.

Indo   Dutch and native mix.

Jepara   A type of wood.

Kaaba   Arabic, ("a square building") Islam's most sacred sanctuary and pilgrimage shrine, is located in the courtyard of the Great Mosque of Mecca.

Kampung   A section of town.

Kelepon   A jello-like dessert with a brown sugar filling.

Kempetai   Japanese secret police.

Kain   A more formal sarong—has pleats in front.

KNIL   Royal Colonial Army.

Kris   An Indonesian dagger.

Kraton   Palace.

Krupuk   Fried chips, often made from shrimp, but also vegetables.

Kueh mangkok   A type of pastry made with rice flour.

Lebaran   Muslim holiday, Indonesian word for the end of fasting month.

Lemper   Sticky rice stuffed with meat or vegetables.

Lereng   A batik pattern.

Malay   The language spoken by Europeans to communicate with natives.

Mahabharata   An ancient Indian epic.

Madbi   A way of cooking meat on a heated stone.

Nanka   A large fruit.

Nikah   An engagement ceremony—a marriage if consummated.

Non   Used by natives when addressing a young European lady.

Noni   Used by natives when addressing a young European lady (girl).

Nonna   Used by natives when addressing a young European lady.

Njonja   Used by natives when addressing a married European lady.

Oma   Grandmother.

Opa   Grandfather.

Oom   Uncle.

Oud   A sixteen string guitar type instrument.

Pelopors   Indonesian rebels.

Pofferjes   Tiny Dutch pancakes.

Pisang bol   Dessert made with bananas.

Rambutan   A fruit.

Rama   Hero of the Ramayana.

Ramadan   The month when Muslims fast.

Ramayana   An Indian epic adopted by the Indonesians.

Salak   A crispy fruit with snake-like skin.

Salam Aleikum   Arabic greeting.

Sambel   Spicy crushed red peppers.

Seik   Part of the Indian troops fighting with the British.

Selamat   Greeting.

Selamat pagi   Good morning.

Selamat malam   Good evening.

Selamat sore   Good afternoon.

Semar   The spirit guide of Java.

Slametan metik   Ceremony showing the ritualistic harvest of first fruits.

Sita   Heroine of the Ramayana.

Shahada   Muslim prayer.

Sociteit   A building used for dances and speeches.

Stroop soesoe   A sweet pink milk drink.

Taiso   Calisthenics imposed by the Japanese.

Tante   Aunt.

Tasbih beads   Muslim prayer beads.

Tempe   Blocks of soy beans.

Terima kasih   Thank you.

Tjikar   Cart with two large wheels usually drawn by oxen.

Tofu   Soy beans ground into a custard like consistence. Then cooked.

Tuan   Mr.

Warung   Small shop or eating stall.

Wayang   Shadow puppet.

Ya Haram   Arabic for, oh my goodness.